I0706014

UNION

White Rocket Books by Van Allen Plexico

Harper & Salsa
  Vegas Heist
  Miami Heist

Sentinels:
  The Grand Design Trilogy
    When Strikes the Warlord
    A Distant Star
    Apocalypse Rising
  The Rivals Trilogy
    The Shiva Advent
    Worldmind
    Stellarax
  The Earth – Kur-Bai War Trilogy
    Metalgod
    The Dark Crusade
    Vendetta
  Alternate Visions *

The Shattering:
  Lucian: Dark God's Homecoming
  Baranak: Storming the Gates
  Karilyne: Heart Cold as Ice
  Hawk: Hand of the Machine
  Legion I: Lords of Fire
  Legion II: Sons of Terra
  Legion III: Kings of Oblivion
  Cold Lightning

Other Fiction:
  Validus-V
  Alpha/Omega (Revised & Expanded) (forthcoming)
  MultiPlex (Collection)
  Gideon Cain: Demon Hunter (Revised & Expanded) *
  Blackthorn: Thunder on Mars *

Comics Commentary:
  Assembled! Five Decades of Earth's Mightiest *
  Assembled! 2 *
  Super-Comics Trivia *

**Editor*

UNION

A NOVEL OF INVASION
AND RESISTANCE

VAN ALLEN PLEXICO

WHITE ROCKET BOOKS

This story was inspired by the Valiant comics of the early 1990s, and is dedicated to Barry Windsor-Smith, for providing so much of that inspiration.

This is a work of fiction. All the characters and events portrayed in this book are either products of the author's imagination or are used fictitiously.

UNION: A Novel of Invasion and Resistance

Copyright ©2024 by Van Allen Plexico

Cover art by Chris Kohler and Daniel Jr.
Cover design by Van Allen Plexico for White Rocket Books.
Logo assist by Jeffery Hayes of Plasmafire Graphics.
Interior art by Chris Kohler.

All rights reserved, including the right to reproduce this book, or portions thereof, in any form, save for brief passages to be quoted in reviews.

A White Rocket Book
www.whiterocketbooks.com

ISBN-13: 978-1-962993-10-4

First printing: April 2024

0 9 8 7 6 5 4 3 2 1

DRAMATIS PERSONAE

John Smith, aka Legatus Constantine Vlahos, aka "The Man in Blue," a mysterious figure who has apparently lived through much of history.

Jack Gael, laborer.

Julian Alexius Lascaris, Roman centurion in the service of the exiled Emperor Justinian II.

Dr. Howard Torrens, human scientist serving the Union.

Xaveria Denali, human Sub-Administrator for the Union.

Dr. Erich Krenz, human scientist serving the Union.

Hoyt and Rodriguez, human police detectives serving the Union.

Administrator Filaree, alien member of the Union in North America.

Juvus Naxam, alien leader of the Time Commandos.

Justinian II, former Roman Emperor, exiled to the city of Cherson on the Crimean Peninsula.

Radolus, advisor to Justinian II.

Lhaza, girlfriend of Centurion Lascaris in Cherson.

Anna Joy, patron of the arenas.

PROLOGUE:

CHERSON, ON THE CRIMEAN PENINSULA. THE YEAR 701 AD.

The man in blue sat and stared at the silver ball.

The man was tall and slender, and he wore the blue robes of a chief advisor to the court of the exiled Roman emperor. A hood was pulled up over his dark hair, so that all that was visible among the shadows of his face was his sharp, angular nose.

The silver ball sat across the room from him. It was huge; nearly ten feet in diameter, smooth as glass and featureless. A mirrored sphere.

The man in blue wanted to open that ball. He wanted what was inside; wanted it desperately.

But there was no point in trying to open it. He was well aware that no force in existence, either now or in the far future, could crack that shell. Nothing could open it. Not until it was ready to open *itself*.

And so the man in blue simply stared at his own warped reflection on its surface, and he waited. As he did, he thought yet again about how he'd wound up in a plague-ridden backwater of a town on the shores of the Black Sea.

He'd come because he was fighting a war—a war for the survival of the Earth, and for what remained of humanity. A war taking place in the far future.

He needed weapons to fight that war, and he needed allies. He'd thought he could find both here. Instead he'd found betrayal.

A friend had come back with him, from the future. That friend had stolen a powerful weapon and then sealed himself away inside the ball. He'd thought to escape the man in blue by fleeing back to the future.

The fool. Did he truly not understand? All that would be required to catch him was *time*. And time was something the man in blue possessed in abundance.

Therefore he waited. He would continue to wait until the sphere opened of its own accord. And when that happened, he'd convince his former friend inside to listen to him. He'd trick the man into trusting him again.

And then he'd strike, and take the weapon back.

And then the work could begin again.

And maybe, just maybe, this time they would win the war.

So, yes, he'd wait. He'd wait as long as it took.

After all, it was all just a matter of *time*.

Nearly 1800 years later, the man in blue did exactly what he'd planned and promised himself he would do, all those many centuries earlier.

The sphere opened, and the man in blue was there, waiting.

He tricked his old friend that emerged from it.

He took the weapon he'd waited so long to acquire.

And then he set out, once again, to attempt to liberate the world.

How many times he'd tried before, he couldn't remember. But this time felt different, somehow. This time, he believed he might actually succeed.

It started for him again this time as it always did, with a visit to the mines.

And the choosing of a hero…

WINTER 2468

BOOK ONE:

THE GLADIATOR AND THE IMMORTAL

CHAPTER 1

PROTEST — THE INVADERS — INTO THE MINES — THE ARTIFACT

1:

Jack looked on in horror as the robot stood over the elderly worker and drove a shock stick down into his side again and again.

"You will comply," the robot squawked at the worker, over and over. *"You will comply."*

Electricity danced across the worker's back every time the robot stabbed at him with the shock stick. In response, the man—now huddled in a protective ball, though it was hardly doing much protecting—writhed and cried out in agony. Between jolts, he lay face-down, shaking all over.

"Comply," the robot continued to bark at him.

"See here now," Jack heard someone shout. "Leave the poor man alone! Can't you see he's not fit to stand up, much less to work?"

Where before a low buzz had marked the whispered comments of the human laborers all around, now silence descended. Someone had dared to speak up—to object to the treatment the robotic Kratons were giving their human thralls.

What a fool, Jack thought to himself. *What a fool to invite the attention of the Kratons.*

Indeed, the robotic overseer had ceased its methodic stabbing of the old man on the ground before it. Now, the mechanical nightmare–all silver and gray rods and cables and burning red eyes–was looking up from its victim. Looking up and directly at the person who had spoken.

Jack craned his neck around to see if he could find that person.

That was when he realized the robot, and every human in the area, was staring straight at *him*.

Frowning, confused, he rewound his memories of the last few moments within his mind: One of the older human laborers had fallen down and not immediately gotten back up, yes. He recalled that clearly. Then the nearest robot overseer had rushed forward, barking orders and jabbing the man viciously with a shock stick. Over and over the robot had done that, to the point the old man might never rise again. And then someone had shouted for the robot to leave the man alone. Someone…

With a sick, sinking feeling, Jack understood why everyone was staring at him.

He had been the person who had yelled at the robot.

Why? he asked himself. What had been the point of redirecting the robot's attention, and its anger, at himself? Why had he done such a stupid thing?

Before Jack could come to any conclusions on that score, the overseer casually knocked the previous target of its ire over onto the ground and advanced on him. The shock stick, pointed at his face, sparkled with electricity at one end.

"Out of compliance," the Kraton mechanoid stated as it bore down on him. *"Unacceptable."*

The shock stick came up and stabbed out. Jack attempted to twist out of the way. Sparks flew as the weapon's end made contact with his shoulder. Jack screamed and collapsed in a convulsing ball on the rough ground.

The Kraton turned back in the direction of the old man it had assaulted first. *"You will report to the mines for artifact search detail,"* the buzzing mechanical voice called out.

Another of the Kratons had moved in and was now bending down over the old man. It looked up and made a flatline motion with its right hand. *"Laborer 27J2327-M has terminated."*

Jack, lying on his side and fighting to regain his senses, took this in and suppressed a violent reaction. The old man had died. And he was dead because that stupid, sadistic robot had killed him.

Before he could think further on the matter, the first robot spun around and stood over him, its skull-face glaring. It raised one bony mechanical finger and pointed it down at him.

"You," it droned in that same flat mechanical voice. *"Laborer 39K40-C. You will take the place of Laborer 27J23-M in the relic mines."*

Jack opened his mouth and closed it again when nothing intelligible would come out. He knew he'd just been handed a death sentence.

"Get up," the robot commanded, the shock stick crackling. *"Report to the mines."*

2:

Jack shuffled along the trail leading down into the mine.

He was slender, almost rail-thin, with short, sandy blond hair. He wore a standard red jumpsuit with large, expanding pockets at the chest and hips. In place of a belt his jumpsuit had an elastic band at the waist that held the pants portion up.

The Kraton that had escorted him over had stopped at the entrance to the mine. It wasn't even bothering to make sure he descended all the way and got to work. So confident were the robots; so sure of themselves, and of the control they exerted over the remainder of the human race. Some of that control was based on fear. Some of it was due to other factors.

Jack made his way along the rough path, passing into and through the mouthlike opening that led down into the earth—or into the ruins of Mankind's past glories that had sunk so deeply into it. As he stumbled across the uneven ground, he allowed himself to bring his dangerous thoughts about those mechanical overlords to the surface of his thoughts, where he could metaphorically and mentally roll them across his tongue and taste them.

At times like this, he wished he was more like his friend, Raynor. Raynor was bigger, tougher, stronger, and far braver than Jack. Because of that, he wasn't one of the thousands condemned to the labor camps. No, he had been selected by the Kratons to serve as a gladiator in their monthly Games. Gladiators did not tend to live all that long, of course, but it was said that while they lived, they lived quite well. Jack laughed bitterly to himself. It wasn't like human laborers lived all that long, either. And at least the gladiators got to fight Kratons occasionally—when they weren't being forced to slaughter one another.

The emotions Jack felt were strong, and had only grown stronger in the past little while. Everyone he knew hated the Kratons, but no one would dare stand up to them, challenge them, or even think of opposing their collective will.

And the Kratons, for all their mechanical power, weren't even in charge. They performed their task of keeping the surviving human population in thrall, but they in turn served a mere handful of masters of their own. A cabal of alien beings of different races who, for the past two centuries or more, had dominated the planet.

No, fearsome as the robotic Kratons were, they were nothing compared to the Union.

Jack reached the end of the path, and now darkness surrounded him. He reached into one of the large pockets sewn into the shirt portion of his jumpsuit and fished around for a multi-tool. His fingers closed on the small rectangle and he drew it out, held it up and tapped on part of its surface. Even as he did so, he detected movement to his left. The multi-tool's light flared to life and, for an instant, he became aware of a figure passing by him on that side. He turned to look and thought he saw a man with black hair, wearing a dark blue jacket and matching pants. He started to call out to the person, meaning to ask about what lay in these particular depths, and what precautions he would be wise to take before completing his descent. But when he turned fully to face the man, he found there was no one there.

Jack stood there, staring into the suddenly illuminated space, surrounded both left and right by dirt and stone and the crushed remains of ancient machinery. Frowning, he shook his head wearily and continued on his way.

3:

The Union, Jack thought as he continued to descend. *Those alien bastards.*

Very little was known of them, even two centuries later. So many years since they'd arrived from the depths of space, commanding fleets of automated ships and armies of deadly robots. They'd made short work of the Earth's defenses. The Kratons wiped out humanity's armies and navies in a matter of days, before moving on to mass enslavement of what remained of the population. Ever since then, the handful of alien overlords known as the Union had run the planet their way, for their benefit. Humans had learned quickly to obey them—to do their bidding in all things, not least of which was participating in the systematic exploitation of the planet. Some went further and used the term looting; others simply called it rape. In any case, to do otherwise meant facing a fate too grisly to contemplate, at the segmented mechanical hands of the Kratons.

And that brought Jack's thoughts to the mines, such as the one he was venturing into now. In the last days of the invasion, the surviving human resistance had retreated to various underground shelters, from which to plan and launch their last-ditch efforts against the aliens. The most brilliant scientists and engineers humanity possessed were among their ranks, and the shelters had been stocked with the newest, most sophisticated and most powerful weapons and other machines the human mind had ever devised. Their efforts, however, had come to naught when the Kratons unleashed their ultimate weapon: Nanites. Microscopic machines that entered human bodies and made changes once in there. With the nanites, the last of the large-scale human resistance ended almost immediately.

Seeing their fellow defenders falling one by one under the mental sway of the invaders, the last few free humans had detonated explosives and sealed off the underground chambers. It meant the end for the scientists, and the end of any possible threat to the invaders.

The Union was not willing to simply give up on any potential new technologies and discoveries, however. Having beguiled themselves into believing the humans had developed some sorts of super-weapons in their last hours of life, the aliens ordered their Kraton servants to dig down into the buried facilities and salvage what they could. But those near-mindless automatons lacked the ability to judge and discern the items they found. They were as likely to bring back an old tricycle as a death-ray pistol. No, what was needed was an actual thinking, organic brain with the ability to discriminate and differentiate.

It couldn't be the aliens themselves who searched the ruins. In the first place, they were too few—a mere half-dozen, if that, the stories said. And in the second place, it was too hazardous down in the mines the robots had carved out. The ceilings were forever giving way and crashing down. Walls always collapsed. Pipes were constantly rupturing, flooding chambers with water or explosive gas. No, the mines were far too dangerous for one of the exalted Union to venture inside.

But a human? A human now firmly under the mental sway of the aliens?

By all means, the overlords had commanded. Send humans down into the mines. Have them search for anything interesting; maybe even as interesting as the big, silver sphere that had been found early on in the process. Or anything that might prove useful. Or deadly.

And so down climbed pale, slender, very human Jack, a pale and slender beam of light illuminating his way.

4:

The nanites infested Jack, of course, as they infested nearly every surviving human being. Jack knew this. The microscopic machines merely made it very difficult for him to try to do anything about it. They allowed him to think what he wanted, deep inside; they even permitted him, however occasionally, to speak out against the actions of his masters, as he had done with the robot that had murdered the old man. But they made him extremely susceptible to suggestion, at least when coming from the alien masters and their human lackeys. They also prevented him from taking any actions that might go against the wishes of the Union and their Kratons.

So when the robot had ordered him down into the mines, he'd mentally rebelled at the very suggestion of it, but at the same time his body had moved him there without hesitation.

Now he reached the point in this particular mine that required him to climb over piles of debris, probably left by workers sent there to do the same thing in times past. That being the case, Jack felt it highly unlikely that he would be discovering anything of value. Any artifacts worth digging out of here had surely been carted away years earlier.

And so it was that he blinked in surprise at the sight he beheld in the dim light of his multi-tool: There atop one of the piles of rubble and debris lay a shining silver object.

He hesitated at first. So out of place did the artifact appear to be, he wondered if he were only imagining it.

Carefully he took one step closer to it, then another. It was definitely new, or at least new to this area. Everything else around him was ancient and filthy and discolored, but this thing—whatever it was—had not even a layer of dust over it. No scratches, no smudges; nothing indicated it had been dredged up from the deep bowels of the old underground bunker.

It looked brand new, and it sparkled and gleamed silver in his beam of light.

Part of Jack's mind remained hesitant to approach it. He admitted to himself that he was somewhat afraid of it; afraid it might turn out to be a trap left to ensnare or eliminate the Union's workers. Another part of him, however, was already attempting to calculate how much this kind of artifact might be worth on the black market. That, of course, assumed he could somehow smuggle it out of the mine without the Kratons discovering it on him, and that was something he very much doubted he could do.

Caution aside, he had to know what it was. And then, "Where did it come from?" awaited its turn, along with a number of other follow-up questions.

He stepped closer, leaned over the object, stared down at it. Tried to figure out what it was.

It was a metallic silver strap, clean and polished and gleaming in the dim light. A bit over four feet long, it appeared to be made up of segmented squares, each about three inches across and half an inch deep.

Jack stared at the artifact for a long time, his eyes moving over its smooth surface. He found he couldn't look away. It was as if he'd been hypnotized by it.

A voice squawked from the multi-tool, startling him: *"Worker designated Jack Gael. Report."*

He didn't report. But he did come somewhat out of the hypnotic state he'd found himself sliding into. Blinking, he looked around to be sure he was still alone. Then he returned his attention to the object. This time, however, he didn't allow himself to be enthralled by it. This time he swallowed hard, reached out with both hands, and grabbed it.

He gasped as the artifact delivered a mild shock, but he didn't let it go, and the odd feeling passed. He lifted it and it sagged on either end, so that it hung from his hands like a limp strap, or a… a belt! Yes. That's what it was. A belt!

"Worker designated Jack Gael. Report."

The voice of the robot checking up on him hadn't varied a bit in tone from the first time it had sounded. The Kratons didn't tend to get annoyed or aggravated, at least not that you could tell from their voices. They simply dealt out punishment methodically and dispassionately, whenever they felt it necessary. Jack knew the one checking in on him now was likely concluding such punishment would be necessary upon his return to the surface.

Nevertheless, Jack continued to ignore the robot. All of his attention was focused on the belt. He knew he'd soon be handing it over to the same robot that was harassing him. But he was far too taken with it to just deliver it to his mechanical masters immediately. He wanted to examine it first. He felt strangely drawn to it.

He held it by one end and judged its length. It appeared to be a bit longer than something he would wear, his own physique being on the skinny side. Still, he couldn't resist trying it on.

As he brought it around from behind on both sides of his waist and touched the two ends together below his belly button, the entire belt shimmered and changed. Its length diminished as the ends retracted a bit into the central body of the belt. The two ends clicked together like magnets and now the belt was around his waist, fitting comfortably. He'd done nothing to accomplish this. The belt had fitted itself to him.

He had just enough time to wonder once more where it had come from and how it had gotten down here in the otherwise filthy mine before the belt itself spoke for the first time. In a soothing, perfectly clear and audible feminine voice, it said, *"Diagnostic mode operational."*

Jack frowned and looked down at it. Had it talked? Had he imagined it, or—?

"What did you say?" he asked, out loud.

For several seconds, nothing happened and no one said a word—not even the belt. But then, just as he was starting to think he'd imagined it, the belt spoke again: *"Foreign objects detected—potential hazard—initiating purge in three...two..."*

Purge? That didn't sound good. Jack grasped the belt where it was fastened together below his tummy and tried to figure out how to take it off.

"...one..."

There was no clasp that he could find. It wouldn't come off.

"Wait—!"

Electricity surged out and into Jack. Screaming, he tore at the belt for almost two full seconds before he collapsed unmoving onto the earthen floor.

He lay there in silence. A moment later, the belt spoke up again, though no one heard it:

"External dangers detected. Defensive field activated."

CHAPTER 2

DR. TORRENS – JOHN SMITH – THE EMPEROR
WITHOUT A NOSE – 701

1:

Dr. Howard Torrens regarded the wraithlike alien that stared back at him with utter contempt. He wasn't concerned about angering it; he knew it couldn't read human facial expressions with any degree of accuracy.

The tall, slender human woman in the skintight purple jumpsuit standing next to it, however—now, she was a different problem. She was Xaveria Denali, sub-administrator for this region of North America, and she wielded tremendous power in the name of her alien masters. Torrens reminded himself to be more cautious when she was around.

The strange, purple-robed alien emitted a string of sounds that resembled to Torrens' ears a series of gurgles and choking coughs. It sounded as if someone were drowning. It went on like this for several seconds before mercifully ceasing. The alien then looked at the woman, motioning to her with a flipper-like appendage.

"So, Dr. Torrens," Denali said, her tone arch and her posture arrogant. "Grand Overlord Gorvag would like to know of your progress. How go your efforts toward constructing the new weapons he has demanded?"

A gray-headed man in his late fifties, Torrens reached up and removed his pipe from his mouth. He set it on the counter of his workstation, smoothed his white lab coat, then looked back at the pink, fish-faced creature. He carefully ignored the woman who had translated.

"Some progress, Grand Overlord," he said. "Less than I would prefer."

The alien gibbered more sounds at him.

"That is unfortunate," the tall woman translated. As she spoke, the alien glided further into the laboratory, suspended on invisible waves of force. Its gaze swept here and there, looking over the banks of machinery and computers—some mechanical, some organic—and over the other handful of human laborers that had been assigned to serve as lab assistants. "The Grand Overlord had hoped your new assistants would speed things up," Denali added. "Are they not aiding you properly?"

Torrens started to comment on how little help they were, due to their general lack of scientific knowledge and lack of understanding of virtually anything he was doing there in the lab. They were, after all, merely laborers chosen from some factory or another in an apparently random fashion and sent to work for him. After so many years of ruling the planet, the aliens of the Union still seemed to have very little understanding of humans.

Torrens silently debated how much he should say with regard to his assistants, however. At least here, in his labs, they were treated somewhat decently and could be protected from the worst excesses of the Kraton guards. Who knew what fate might await them if he cast them back out? Then again, if they couldn't help him produce the items the administrator demanded, they might well be shortening his own lease on life. He opened his mouth to reply, but the being in purple spoke up again before he could say anything more.

"The Grand Overlord is concerned that these assistants might be proving to be more of a hindrance than a help."

As Denali spoke, the alien ruler floated over to Torrens' right, close to a young, female assistant with short, reddish hair and blue eyes. It reached out and its flipper unfolded to reveal six extremely long, bony fingers. Casually it stroked the assistant's chin. She flinched but didn't move away.

"Perhaps if a few of them were sent to the arena," Denali said. "I'm sure the gladiators would enjoy a few easy practice kills." She turned to look at him fully. "Or perhaps I could simply have the Kratons eliminate them here and now."

At her words, two of the tall, fearsome-looking, silvery-gray robots that had been standing like unmoving statues on either side of the doorway stepped forward, their gun-hands coming up, their blazing red eyes sweeping the room as they picked out targets.

Torrens understood the reaction the alien overlord and his sub-administrator expected to provoke here. He should feel afraid—terrified, even—for the potential fate of the humans who had been brought in to help him. Surely he would plead for their lives. Certainly he would make all sorts of extravagant promises in exchange for assurances of their safety.

Torrens was having none of it.

"They are, of course, yours to do with as you please," he replied to the sub-administrator. He'd caught the "I" in her suggested threat, and knew Denali had added the part about killing them herself, rather than translating it from something the alien overlord had said. Consequently, he addressed her directly for the first time.

"I would only point out that I have already invested substantial time and energy in training them to the staggering level of incompetence they are currently demonstrating," he said. "If you force me to start over with a new batch, there is no telling how long it could take just to get back to the level of inefficiency we have currently attained." He smiled flatly. "But, as I said, it is your decision." He paused before bowing slightly to the alien and adding, "And the Grand Overlord's, of course."

The willowy alien leader and the human sub-administrator both stared back at him, as if perhaps seeking to divine just how sincere this seemingly cold-blooded human really was. Several long seconds passed before the overlord spread his fanlike hands wide and nodded.

"The Grand Overlord accepts your reasoning, Doctor," Denali reported. She moved in closer to him. "Keep your assistants," she purred. "But know that I am watching you closely. And I expect to be able to report results to the Grand Overlord very soon."

Inwardly, Torrens laughed. *Fool.* All of the aliens were fools. But their willing human lackeys were even bigger ones.

"Of course," he said with another slight bow. "I am certain we will have new weapons for you very soon."

The alien turned and floated out of the laboratory. With a curt nod to Torrens, Denali followed.

Once they were gone, Torrens dropped back into his chair, realizing for the first time how much he was sweating.

"Dr. Torrens?" came the tremulous voice of one of the human assistants. She sounded utterly traumatized. "Do you really believe we'll have new weapons for them soon?"

Torrens picked up his pipe and started to light it, then scowled and slammed it back down on the console.

"I have no idea," he said.

2:

The man in blue had called himself Adrian Darke during the last cycle.

That name had seemed just interesting enough. Just mysterious enough. Just flamboyant enough.

But flamboyant hadn't done the trick. Not that any of the other identities he'd gone by during his many years on this Earth had seen much success, either.

So, this time around—this time, which he prayed would be the last time—he decided to adopt a much simpler name. The simplest one imaginable, in fact.

So it was that a human being calling himself John Smith stood hidden behind a pile of debris, high up on a hilltop and just next to the edge of a deep chasm, overlooking the entrance to the mines. From there he watched and waited for what he knew with absolute certainty was going to happen next.

But it did not. Instead, something entirely unexpected happened.

"Attention, human. What are you doing there?"

The Kraton had come upon him unawares, because it had never been there before. In all the times he'd done this, he'd never been accosted by one of the robots.

Turning around slowly, Smith kept his hands open, at waist level, as unthreatening as possible. He nodded once to the mechanical figure. It was at least two feet taller than him, and made all of silvery metal and wires and twinkling tiny lights. Its jagged, deadly claw hands clenched and unclenched.

"Well, hello there," he said to it. "This is unexpected." He grinned. "And a little awkward."

The robot's skull-face stared back at him uncomprehendingly. Its left arm, which Smith knew housed an energy blaster weapon, was not aimed directly at him—not yet—but it was pointed just close enough to him to cause him a great deal of concern.

And concern was something Smith definitely felt. Concern that something, somehow, had gone terribly wrong.

Up until this point, everything had proceeded precisely as anticipated. Smith had known where to go and what to do to avoid the Union aliens, their mechanical Kraton minions and their human agents. As part of that effort, he'd kept away from North America entirely for as long as he could, these past few years, knowing it was the central focus of the alien presence on Earth. But now he'd had no choice but to come. It was time.

His flyer, parked and camouflaged nearby, had easily gotten past all the security measures—another advantage of having done all of this so many times before and knowing what to expect, what to prepare for. Everything, in fact, had gone perfectly.

Until this very moment. And this random Kraton, who had no business whatsoever being here, in this place, in this time.

The robot leaned in closer to him, trapping him between itself and the cliff edge, hemming him in. He could smell the hot metal and lubricants; he could hear the low hum of its internal motors and servos. The Kraton hadn't made an overtly hostile move—not yet. But it was clearly considering doing so, and putting itself in a position of advantage for it.

"You are under arrest," the robot intoned in its dry, mechanical voice. *"You will come with me."*

Smith shot a look down toward the mouth of the cave. Still no sight of the person he'd come to meet. They'd passed each other earlier, when Smith was coming back out of the mine and the guy had been descending into it. But there'd been no sign of him since then. What was taking him so long?

"You will come with me," the robot repeated, its dry tone somehow more strident. It reached for him with its right hand.

Smith moved instinctively, relying on the knowledge he'd gained over so many lifetimes and so many repetitions of dealing with the Kratons. He sidestepped the mechanical right hand even as he reached out and grasped the left—the one containing the energy weapon. It took a great deal of his strength, but he managed to direct that gun away from him before it could fire.

The Kraton drew back its right hand and then came at him a second time with it. Again Smith was ready. He seized that hand and twisted it around and down.

The robot, as surprised as a machine could ever be, proceeded to demonstrate its awful strength, waving both of its arms in an effort to shake the human loose. In response, Smith released the right hand while performing the first in a series of judo moves that led to the robot—despite its much greater strength—being forced down onto its knees. Keeping its hands occupied, he lashed out with a couple of kicks to the face and torso that caused the Kraton to draw back in surprise. By the hardest, the robot regained its feet. Then, having taken their measures of one another, the two antagonists squared off again.

The Kraton seemed to conclude that simply grasping this human with its mechanical claw of a hand was not as effective as it always had been when apprehending humans in the past. Instead, it must have decided Smith needed a bit of tenderizing first. It charged at him, like a linebacker coming on an inside blitz, and only Smith's carefully-honed reflexes and surprising speed allowed him to sidestep and not be bowled over and crushed. Instead, the Kraton stumbled forward and landed face-first on the rough ground.

Smith understood the one thing he had to do was to never let up. A single moment of hesitation and the Kraton would have him. He therefore executed another series of martial arts moves he'd studied extensively during his many journeys through history.

Still struggling to rise, the robot squealed in anger and frustration—and maybe pain? He could hope!—before it was finally able to surge back up onto its feet, looming over him.

Ah well, Smith thought to himself. *I thought I had him there, but he's too tough for me. I suppose I'll file this little encounter away and prepare better for it next time through. If there is a next time through...*

He couldn't help but wonder why it had happened at all, though. Why history was suddenly playing him for a fool.

Just as the Kraton seized him with its right hand and brought up its left arm, preparing to thoroughly ventilate him, a sound came to his ears and the robot's sound receptors: *Humming.*

Someone was humming? Here? At the entrance to the mines?

Curiosity getting the better of him, even though he knew he was about to die, Smith twisted around just enough to see who was making all the noise.

A big, heavy-set Black man strolled along the path toward the mine entrance. He looked familiar. Smith tried his best to remember the guy's name, and what he was doing here—how he fit into things.

Smith wasn't entirely certain of the name, but he thought it was… "Bennie."

That, too, was new. He had never encountered Bennie at the mine entrance.

All of this worried Smith tremendously. Why was history suddenly deviating from the norm in such small ways, and in such dramatic ones? Just how much could he trust his hard-won knowledge of the future now? Would he be better off to just let this homicidal machine kill him, and hope he'd return to try it all again—and this time, just maybe, without so many surprises?

The mechanical man, however, was distracted by the newcomer as well. For the briefest of moments, it appeared to have forgotten Smith entirely. Its death-grip on his forearm loosened as it craned its metal head around to peer down at the singing man.

Smith knew this might well be the only opening he would ever get.

In a well-practiced move, he wrenched his arm free while dropping to one knee. Then, in a single smooth motion, and before the Kraton could process what was happening, he spun around and kicked backwards with all of his might. His booted feet struck the Kraton squarely in its chest, propelling it backwards.

The big robot skidded, stumbled, almost righted itself—and then tumbled over the cliff's edge.

Smith approached the edge as carefully as possible and peered down. As he looked, he wondered if this particular Kraton was equipped with flight jets.

The metal figure struck the rocks far below and broke in half, then exploded.

Well. Clearly not.

Smith grinned to himself. Maybe his luck was finally changing. He'd never actually beaten a Kraton one-on-one before, though he had to acknowledge that, this time, he'd had gravity and terrain on his side, plus a distraction.

He hurried back over to where he could see the mine entrance. Bennie was there. He had stopped his humming and walking and was looking around. He'd probably heard the explosion. After a few seconds the man shrugged and picked back up on his tune, right where he'd left off.

Meanwhile, there was still no sign of the person Smith was looking for.

Sighing heavily, he sat back on the one patch of grass atop the hill. He continued to watch and wait.

3:

The Roman soldier drew his gladius from its scabbard and in one quick motion severed the man's head from its shoulders and sent it tumbling down the path.

Most of the peasants could not help but follow the grisly orb with their eyes as it bounced away down the hill. No sooner had it disappeared over the cliff's edge and plummeted toward the sea than they all turned back to stare in open-mouthed astonishment at the man responsible. Clad in leather and bronze armor, that figure still held his short, broad and bloody sword out, glaring down at the now-headless body at his feet.

The soldier's name was Julian Alexius Lascaris and he had once been a centurion of the Imperial Palatinae—the highest-ranked troops under the command of the emperor Justinian II. Now, because he'd refused to sever his pledge of loyalty, he was merely a bodyguard for a deposed and exiled has-been. The ex-emperor had informed Lascaris that the man now issuing torrents of blood onto the dusty soil was very likely an assassin sent by the current emperor. Whether Lascaris believed his boss's paranoid ramblings didn't matter; he obeyed.

Ignoring the stares of the rabble, Lascaris wiped his blade on his victim's clothing and sheathed it. He took another quick look around, making sure no other would-be assassins lurked nearby. The townspeople, mostly farmers and the like, gawked in astonishment and terror at him before fleeing. No one stood out as exceptional or particularly dangerous. Satisfied that he'd killed the only assassin extant, he strode confidently back along the path toward the city of Cherson.

City, he thought with a bitter laugh. *It's a pigsty.* Its only grace was its location hard on the Black Sea, along the Crimean coast. The new emperor had not banished his defeated predecessor there, after all, as some kind of reward. Still, for all its shortcomings, exile beat the new emperor putting them all to death—which very well could have happened.

"You killed him?" came a particularly whiny voice from just ahead. "He's dead?"

Lascaris looked up and saw the emperor—or, rather, the former emperor—running toward him, a few more bodyguards in tow. Younger than Lascaris, he was at least a foot shorter and a hundred pounds lighter than the muscled frame of the former centurion. His hair was dark and his eyes blue, both like that of Lascaris. Where the exiled emperor differed the most from his bodyguard, however—and from most everyone else around—was in the fact that Justinian lacked a nose. It had been hacked off by the usurper, Leontius, just after the coup and just before they'd been sent into exile in the East. Now the young has-been's scarred face made for a macabre mask, reflecting and emphasizing his mercurial nature and his paranoid mentality.

To be fair, Lascaris thought, *I suppose if someone had chopped off my nose when I was twenty-three, I might be a little paranoid myself.*

The big soldier bowed respectfully. Straightening, he said, "The man is quite dead, great Caesar."

Still wild-eyed, Justinian nodded. Then, as an afterthought, he reached up and patted Lascaris on the shoulder like a faithful hound.

"Well done, Centurion," he muttered, before turning and scurrying back toward the village.

Lascaris sighed heavily and followed him.

4:

Lascaris had a woman among the local tribespeople; a golden-haired young beauty named Lhaza. Lhaza didn't speak much Latin or Greek at first, but the two of them found ways to communicate with one another well enough. At one point, after they'd been together a few months and had gotten better at each other's languages—and were lying together in bed, as usual—Lhaza had managed to ask Lascaris a question that had puzzled her. Why, she wondered, had he stuck with that "hideous little man" and accompanied him into exile if he hadn't had to—if he had, indeed, been offered a prominent role in the military forces of the new ruler?

"There are several reasons, my love," the big Roman had replied, running a hand back through his wavy, close-cropped, dark-brown hair. "For one thing, the new emperor would never trust me. Not completely. Not coming over from his enemy's camp like that. And that being the case, all it would've taken was a single bad word about me in Leontius's ear, and…" He'd drawn a finger across his own throat.

Lhaza grimaced at that, her eyes wide as she listened and parsed out what he was saying.

"That aside," Lascaris went on, as he snuggled the blonde closer, "I honestly felt my chances of advancement are better with Justinian than they would be otherwise."

The girl frowned at this. "Here? In Cherson? Amid the tribes and the horse-people? How can that be?"

The Roman smiled and shrugged. "As I said, I believe any tenure with the new man would be brief and end badly for me. But Justinian here, he knows my worth. He sees it daily. He sees my loyalty, and it is unquestionable. He would amply reward me, and I would not live under a constant threat of death."

Lhaza met his eyes. "Do you think it possible he could retake the throne someday?"

Lascaris shrugged. "It is possible. For any obvious faults, he is still a young man, and ambitious. And driven by hatred toward those who took his throne and disfigured him." He smiled flatly. "Such things can be powerful motivators."

She stared back at him, and he felt then as if she were seeing directly through him.

"What is it?" he asked.

"You see yourself on the throne someday."

Lascaris snorted a laugh. "Please."

Her expression did not change. "You do. I can tell."

"You can *tell*? How can you tell such things?"

"I just can. Call it my tribal magic or something."

"Tribal mumbo-jumbo," he said with a grin.

She waved this away. "You think you could one day be emperor. But how could that ever be?"

Lascaris began to dismiss her statements again, but then he realized he could not. This woman would know if he was lying to her. He wasn't sure how that was so, but he was becoming convinced it was true. Was she some sort of witch? Did he even mind it if she was?

So, instead of deflecting, he sat back and ran a hand over his stubble-covered chin and said, "It is possible."

"How?"

"Because our beloved emperor-in-exile is as reckless and emotional as he is driven. As I said, those qualities make it more likely he will reclaim his throne. They also, in my view, make it more likely he will not keep it for long—again."

"Someone would overthrow him again," she said. "And kill him, this time."

"Very probably."

"And you would be there, at his side, to pick up the crown when he falls."

"We don't have crowns. That's for you tribal people."

She ignored him and continued. "What if you—no, no, I dare not say it aloud."

"Say what, love?"

She considered a moment, then leaned in closer to him and whispered, "What if you—if *you*—were to…" She leaned back and mimicked his motion of cutting his throat. "…to *him*?"

Lascaris stared at her blankly.

"You—you mean if *I* were to…" He searched for a word he was comfortable with, but could find none. "If I were to do that to *my own emperor*?"

Her eyes sparkled as she gazed back at him and shrugged. "Why not?" she asked.

He sputtered before managing to reply, "Because I have sworn my loyalty to him. Because it is a matter of honor."

"Ah," she said. "So you would never…"

"Never!" he shot back angrily. His face was now bright red.

"Calm yourself, my love," she said, patting him on one muscular arm. "I am but a simple farm girl. I did not understand before, but you have made it more than clear."

"You are nothing like a 'simple farm girl,' Lhaza," he said, his eyes still flaring. He looked at her a few seconds longer, as if considering getting up and leaving. She continued to stroke his arm. At last he appeared to be calming down. She pulled him close.

"So," she went on, as if nothing had happened. "You said that perhaps your emperor might regain the throne? When could this happen?"

He snorted a laugh. "It may never happen, love. Probably it won't."

She nodded slowly, gazing off into the distance. Then her eyes met his, and they were as fiery as he'd ever seen them.

"When that happens," she said—and he noted that she'd said *when*, not *if*—"promise me you will take me with you."

He stared back at her for a moment, then grinned and crushed her in his embrace.

"Of course I will, my dear."

Her own smile lit up her heart-shaped face.

"After all," he added, "your political ties with the barbarian kingdoms would be invaluable."

The smile soured and she punched him in the chest.

He laughed, then kissed her. A moment later he rolled over on top of her.

Outside, a cold moon rose over the Crimea.

It was the year 701 AD.

CHAPTER 3

CLARITY – THE BUBBLE – THE TRUEST THING – FREEDOM

1:

Jack Gael slowly came back to reality.

His memories were fuzzy. He recalled being sent down into the "mines"—the bunkers where humans had retreated during the invasion, centuries earlier—to look for valuable high-tech weapons and artifacts.

Something about that nagged at him, he realized. Something he'd never thought about before. But he could worry about it later. He forced his brain, which was at last coming back to full consciousness, to focus on his current situation.

He remembered something had shocked him. Not shocked like a surprise, but shocked as in an electrical current. And it had knocked him out.

What had done it? What had it been?

He struggled to think back, and the memories gradually grew more distinct.

A belt. He'd found a silvery belt, somewhere down there in the mines. He'd picked it up. He'd... put it on? Yes, yes, he had. It had clasped together, all on its own. And then it had talked to him. It had said something he didn't fully understand.

And then it had shocked the bejeezus out of him, and knocked him out cold.

Looking around now as best he could, still on his back, he discovered he was lying on a folded blanket that in turn lay on the hard ground. His head still spinning, he managed to sit up.

"Jack! You're awake. I was beginning to worry."

He turned in the direction of the voice and beheld one of his friends: Bennie Williams. Bennie was squatted down next to him, and reached out to help him sit up, but then pulled his hand back before Jack could clasp it.

Jack barely noticed, so disoriented was he. "Bennie," he said, "what are you doing here? Don't you have factory duty today?"

Bennie was looking at him funny, but now he grinned. "Man, you have been out a long time. I got off work two hours ago. As soon as I got home, I got a message from the supervisors saying you were hurt, and to get over here as quick as possible."

"Oh. Well, I appreciate you coming to check up on me. But I think I'm okay now." Jack frowned. "What time is it, anyway?"

Bennie checked his old, dinged-up wristwatch and answered. "Seven."

Jack took this in with some degree of surprise. He'd been out at least five hours. Another surprise was that, now that he'd woken up, his faculties were returning swiftly. In fact, he felt good—better than he had in a long time. Now that the cobwebs were clearing away, his head felt clear—clear for the first time since he'd been a kid. He hadn't been aware of it at the time but, looking back now, he could see that his brain had essentially been swimming through quicksand for years. He'd been sluggish, dull-witted. Not bright.

Something occurred to him then: the nanites. Could they have been the problem? And—were they no longer doing their job on him? If not, why not? Could that possibly be it? The Union had always spoken of the nanites as an aide to workers in getting their jobs done—providing more focus, more alertness, and so forth. Like a constant shot of caffeine. Jack had never heard them described as making people… duller. More controllable. Could that be the case? Somehow, he suspected it might.

His newly-nimble mind now alive with thoughts that would've seemed radical mere hours earlier, he brought himself back to reality and looked past Bennie to his surroundings. He saw that he was on the ground just outside the entrance to the mine. He shook his head. "I see they didn't bother to take me to the hospital or anything," he said.

"Well, now, Jack," Bennie began, his face creasing into a frown, "there's a reason for that."

"Oh yeah?"

"Same reason I couldn't help you sit up just now," Bennie added.

Now Jack was frowning, too. "Bennie," he said, "what in the world are you talking about?"

Bennie scrunched up his dark face, thinking. Then he appeared to hit upon an idea. He reached out his right hand toward Jack, holding it palm-out toward his friend, as if he were telling him to "Stop!"

"Lean against my hand," he said.

Jack's frown had grown to epic proportions. "Do *what* now?"

"Just lean forward. Rest your chest against my hand," he explained. "If you can."

"If I *can*?" Half-convinced that maybe it had been Bennie who had undergone unscheduled shock treatment instead of himself, Jack nonetheless complied. He was already sitting up on the blanket. Now he allowed himself to sag forward, expecting his momentum to carry him into Bennie's waiting hand and stop him before he face-planted into the ground.

He stopped, alright. But Bennie's hand was still at least six inches away from his chest.

He tried to figure out what was happening. His muscles were relaxed—by rights, he should be smacking the ground with his nose right now—but, somehow, he was being held up by an invisible... *what*?

"I don't understand what's happening," Jack told his friend.

"Sit back up," Bennie said. "Now—shake my hand."

Jack didn't ask questions this time. He did as he was asked. It didn't work at all. As he reached out to his friend, Bennie's hand simply slid away from Jack's.

"Stop moving away," Jack said.

"I'm not doing it on purpose," Bennie replied.

They did it a couple more times to the same effect. It reminded Jack of something—of trying to push two magnets together when the poles were the same. Doing so created the sense of an invisible bubble of force that kept them apart and couldn't be overcome, no matter how hard one pushed against it.

But that begged the question: Why were his and Bennie's hands acting like magnets of the same polarity?

He looked at Bennie, very confused now.

The other man shrugged. "It's your entire body," he added helpfully.

2:

Jack was struggling to come to grips with two entirely different but possibly related situations at the same time.

One, his mind felt freshly cleaned and pressed. It was as if, to mix metaphors, the oil had been changed in his brain. A bunch of old, gunked-up stuff had been dumped out and replaced by the newest synthetic blend. He could think so much clearer and more quickly than ever before.

And two, it seemed his entire body was surrounded by an invisible bubble that, so far, could only be penetrated by air and visible light.

How could this be? What to make of it?

The obvious answer was the belt. All of this had begun the moment he'd put the belt on.

So—should he take it off?

Why should he?

The part of him that was used to the life of a menial laborer, subservient to his alien overlords, urged him to take the belt off immediately and to present it to said aliens. Surely he would be rewarded for bringing them such a remarkable artifact—possibly the greatest one ever found in the mines.

The rest of him—and it was nearly all of him, now—wanted to keep the belt. He'd found it; why give it away? Keep it, and find out just what it was, and what it could do.

So, yes, air and light could get through the bubble. That much was obvious, since he wasn't currently suffocating inside a pitch-dark space. But what about food? Could it get through? Would he slowly starve to death, trapped inside this invisible sphere? Exactly what control did he have over it all? And how did he go about controlling it—if it could indeed be controlled?

He needed to understand more about it. And about the belt that clearly was generating it. For that matter, what else could the belt do?

"Jack? Are you okay?"

Bennie's voice brought him back from his musings.

"Ah, yeah. Sorry. Just thinking."

Bennie nodded, his expression still wide-eyed as it had been when he'd woken up.

"Do me a favor," Jack said, pulling himself to his feet. He looked around and spotted an idle excavating machine parked nearby. He walked over to it and turned back to his friend. "Do you have any food on you?"

"Food?" Bennie looked confused.

"Yeah. I haven't eaten in a while."

"Oh. Yeah!" Bennie patted himself down, appeared to find something, and reached into one of the big pockets on the chest of his jumpsuit. He drew from it a sandwich in a plastic bag. "Here you go," he said, holding it out. Then he hesitated and looked confused again. "But—how are you gonna—?"

"Just set it down on there," Jack said, pointing at the top of the excavating machine's track treads, which were at about waist level.

Bennie nodded and put the sandwich on the treads.

"Take it out of the bag first," Jack added.

"Huh?" Bennie looked even more confused.

"I don't want the plastic bag interfering with this experiment," he said.

"It's an experiment?" Bennie said. "Oh, okay." He slid the zipper open and withdrew the sandwich, then placed the bag on the tread, with the sandwich on top of it, so that it would remain clean.

"Thanks," Jack said. He stepped forward, reached out his right hand, and the sandwich moved away from him momentarily, pushed by the invisible bubble. Then suddenly it was in his grasp.

"You got it," Bennie exclaimed.

Jack nodded and took a bite. "There was a little resistance at first," he noted, "but then, yeah, it came right through." He took another bite and chewed it. "Thanks for the sandwich," he added.

Bennie nodded. "So I can touch you now, then?" He reached out, but again was turned away by the invisible bubble around his friend. "Oh!" He looked down at his fingers. "How does it work?" he asked. "Why did it let the sandwich through, but not my hand?"

"I don't know," Jack said. "Maybe…" He reached out himself, and this time his fingers met those of Bennie. He grasped the hand and shook it firmly. Then, in response to Bennie's clear but unspoken question, "I think maybe it's as simple as, I *wanted* to touch you—or the sandwich—and so I could."

Before the experiments could proceed any further, the sound of activity behind them caused both men to turn away from the excavator machine. They beheld a party of four Kratons approaching along the path. Their mechanical legs worked like pistons as the stalked toward the mine entrance, and their blazing red eyes looked this way and that, always scanning for trouble.

The trouble is right here, Jack found himself thinking. That was followed by him wondering why he'd thought such a thing—and then by him knowing exactly why. He brought a hand up to his head, feeling it ache again. It was as if two different versions of himself were fighting it out for control—the version from before he'd put on the belt, and the version after.

"You'd better make yourself scarce, Bennie," Jack said to his friend.

Bennie reluctantly nodded and then hurried along the path. When the advancing Kratons passed him, paying him no mind whatsoever, he stopped and turned back to see what happened next.

"*Laborer 39K4041-C,*" barked the Kraton at the front of the procession, as it stopped just in front of Jack. "*You appear to have recovered from your injury. You will return to the mines.*"

Jack felt the slightest hint of desire to obey. It vanished quickly. What was left was nothing but raw defiance. *Resistance.*

Before he could say anything back, the robot's glowing red eyes locked onto the belt at his waist. "*You have found an artifact,*" it exclaimed in its harsh mechanical voice. It moved closer to him, its claw-like metal hand coming up at him. "*You will hand it over immediately!*"

3:

"I think not," Jack replied to the robot that confronted him. He made no moves whatsoever. He simply stood there. That still-conditioned and frightened part of his mind cried out that this was insane. The rest of his persona—his new, strong, confident persona—told that other part to shut up and stuff it.

The Kraton's hand moved in, met the invisible bubble, and deflected away, causing the robot to make an involuntary quarter-turn to its left. Taken aback, the automaton righted itself and came at him again, moving faster. This time it was deflected to the right, and the force of its lunge caused it to stumble and fall on its face.

Jack stepped past it and confronted the other three robots. He patted the silver belt at his waist. "Who else wants to try to take it from me?" he asked.

The other three moved in unison, as if they'd long practiced the maneuver. They rushed forward, and then two angled around to come at him from both sides while the third attacked head-on.

Of course, all three of them bounced harmlessly away and fell to the ground.

By this point, the first robot had regained its feet and now it came at him from behind. It bounced away before Jack even knew it was there. Turning around just in time to see it stumbling back down onto the ground, he nodded in satisfaction. That was good—it meant the bubble around him kept things out, even when he didn't know they were coming.

"Holy cow, Jack!" cried Bennie from up along the path. He was jumping up and down, waving. "You showed those guys!"

Jack waved back and motioned for his friend to settle down. He was still coming to grips with what was happening and wasn't looking to needlessly provoke the robots. Besides, it wasn't like they'd been destroyed. They'd just made themselves fall down.

He waited as all four of the Kratons climbed back to their feet. The robots huddled up, uncertain of how to proceed. Finally the one that acted as the leader stepped forward again. It motioned toward Bennie as it spoke to Jack.

"You will hand over the artifact or we will terminate Laborer 38L2322-J."

Jack blinked at this. "What?"

Before he'd gotten the word out, one of the other three Kratons had raced up the pathway and grasped Bennie's arm. It dragged him, kicking and screaming, back toward the mine entrance.

"You have five seconds to consider your plight and comply," the first Kraton stated flatly.

Fury engulfed Jack. He rushed forward and swung his fist, not even considering the potential consequences—for himself, his hand, or the human race in general.

His fist, of course, never contacted the Kraton. He never felt the metal yielding, bending, warping, tearing—even as it happened. All he knew was that he wanted to knock the red-eyed machine out, and he swung a roundhouse blow that the robot probably could have dodged if it had even dreamed such a thing might ever happen.

Instead, the leading edge of the bubble surrounding Jack's fist smashed into the robot's jaw and shattered it, spraying sparks and bits of metal out in its wake. What was left of the robot's head spun around backward, just before the Kraton dropped to its knees, sparking, and then pitched forward onto the ground.

The other three robots merely gawked. Nothing they had experienced in all the years since they'd landed on this planet had prepared them for what had just happened. They stood frozen, in a mechanical form of shock.

Jack advanced on the nearest one. He didn't think through what he was going to do—he just acted on instinct. He swung his fist out in a backhand motion and clobbered that robot, then punched the next one as it attempted to charge at him. His fist was pulverizing that one's head even before the body of the previous one hit the ground, its cranium split apart and shooting out cascades of sparks.

Now three of the Kratons were down, and looking unlikely to be getting back up. The fourth stood in place, arms out and hands up in a defensive posture. What was it going to do? Jack watched it closely, ready to defend himself.

Instead of moving in on its opponent, the Kraton silently extended a little antenna up from its shoulder. Jack saw the movement of the slender metal filament and knew what that meant: It was calling for reinforcements.

An idea came to him then, and he instantly put it into effect. He stepped toward the last of the robots, reaching out with his right hand for its head. These Kratons were about the same height as Jack, so he didn't have to reach up very far. As he did so, he thought about wanting to touch the robot's head the same way he'd wanted to touch the sandwich. Sure enough, the silvery metal head passed easily through the bubble and Jack's hand closed around its face. The robot squawked and started to bring its hands up to defend itself. Jack had not willed for them to be allowed inside the bubble, however, so the metal hands bounced off and then clawed at the invisible barrier.

Now the robot was struggling, wriggling around, its head trapped firmly inside the bubble with Jack but the rest of it still outside.

"Send this word back to your masters," Jack hissed then.

The Kraton stopped thrashing and its blazing red eyes locked in on his. Perhaps it knew its time was nearing an end. It was listening.

Jack wasn't sure why he said what he said next, except that it just felt right. He doubted it was really true, but maybe—just *maybe*—they would believe him.

"Tell them they can't control me anymore. And if they don't leave me alone, I'm coming for them. For *all* of them."

Jack waited a couple more seconds, until he felt sure that if the message were going to be relayed, it had been. Then he willed the bubble around him to re-solidify. Everywhere. Including around his arm.

With a squeal of metal, the robot's head separated from its neck and remained in Jack's hand, like a palmed basketball. The body, meanwhile, dropped to the ground with a thud. Sparks flew from it and strange fluids drained out of its neck.

Grimacing, Jack willed the bubble to open again, then let go of the Kraton's head. It dropped to the ground and rolled to one side. The red lights had gone out from the eye sockets.

Bennie walked up to Jack, still in a daze. He looked upon his friend in an entirely new way—as if he were somehow unrecognizable.

"What have you done, Jack?" he asked.

A number of comebacks occurred to him, but finally Jack shrugged. "I don't know," he said. "But I suppose we'll find out soon."

4:

The thrill of victory—of soundly defeating four Kratons—quickly gave way to the dawning realization that life as Jack had known it up until then was over.

Whether that was a good thing or a bad thing, he wasn't yet sure.

"But you destroyed the last of the robots before it could report on you, didn't you?" Bennie was asking. "So now you can just go home and pretend you don't know anything about this." There was a pleading tone in his voice. It was clear that Bennie had not yet thought through all that had happened this day. Perhaps he was incapable of it, due to his still hosting a swarm of nanites—the microscopic machines that kept him and most other surviving humans docile and under control.

While he considered that situation, Jack responded to what his friend had said.

"They know, Bennie. I made sure they know."

Bennie gawked at him.

"Why, Jack? Why would you do that?"

"Because I don't think it would have mattered either way." Jack shrugged. "I don't know for sure that they hadn't already turned in my name or number or picture or something," he said. "And even if they didn't know I did it, they know I was assigned here today. They'd have come and arrested me just to ask questions. From there, who knows where it could lead?" He shook his head. "No, I'm not going to hide from them. I'm not going to back down. I'm not afraid of them anymore."

Bennie looked puzzled. "What are you going to do, Jack?"

Jack shook his head. "I don't know yet." He reached down and patted the silver belt he wore. "But I have options now. And not many humans have been able to say that in a long time."

Bennie frowned at this, as if the merest notion of freedom disturbed him. Jack understood why. He motioned for his friend to come over.

"I'd like to try something, Bennie," he told the other man. "It could be painful—it might even knock you out, like it did me. But afterward, if it works, you could be a new man. A better man." He paused, considering, and restated, "You could be yourself again. Or maybe for the first time."

Bennie looked at him warily. "What are you talking about, Jack?"

"The Kratons and their masters put something in our bodies when we were kids," he explained. "Little mechanical creatures."

"You mean like tiny Kratons?" Bennie exclaimed, his eyes wide.

"Pretty much, yeah," Jack said. "This belt—" and he pointed to his shiny new possession— "I think it killed them, or maybe just removed them from my body. I'd like to see if it can do the same for you."

Bennie absently began to chew on a fingernail. "Gosh—I don't know, Jack," he began.

"And for other people, too."

"For other people?" Bennie was blinking now. "So—you could help other people?"

"If it works, yes," Jack said. "But, one way or another, I plan to help people. A lot of people."

Reluctantly at first but with growing certainty, Bennie nodded. "Then let's give it a try," he said, offering his friend a smile.

Jack nodded back. "Let's try it," he agreed. And meanwhile, silently, he said to himself, *"Please let this work—and don't fry his brain."*

Unsure of exactly how to go about it, Jack reached out with both hands and willed the force field that surrounded him to allow Bennie's head inside. As the bubble expanded past him, the other man gasped and staggered but remained upright.

"You okay?"

"I…think so," he said. "I felt something kind of…ticklish…in my head for a second. But now it's gone."

Jack thought about that. He released Bennie and looked down at his belt. What had it said before? He'd forgotten at the time, but now it was coming back to him.

"Diag…diagnostic mode—?" he tried.

The belt spoke up for the first time since it had knocked him out.

"Diagnostic mode operational."

He reached out with his right hand and cupped the side of Bennie's head.

"Foreign objects detected—potential hazard—initiating purge in three...two..."

Bennie's eyebrows creased. "Jack, I—"

"One."

A jolt ran through his arm and hand and into Bennie's head. His friend spasmed and his knees buckled. Jack kept his right hand in place while he reached out with his left and caught Bennie, easing him down gently to the ground. Meanwhile, the sense of energy coursing through his arm ended as abruptly as it had begun.

"Purge complete," the belt said.

Bennie lay still for a few seconds, then groaned and opened his eyes. He started to try to get up, but Jack knelt beside him and motioned him down.

"Just take it easy for a minute, okay?"

Bennie nodded. He was blinking his eyes rapidly and groaning.

"Nice work," came a voice from nearby, in the opposite direction from the mine entrance.

Jack stood up quickly, on the defensive. He looked in the direction the voice had come from and saw a man walking towards him.

Three different enemies made up the Union threat on Earth. One enemy was the cabal of alien overlords, who were supposedly small in number and bizarre in appearance. They were rarely seen out in the open. Much more common were the robotic Kratons, with whom Jack interacted every day.

The ones Jack had always considered the worst of them all, however, were the collaborators. The human beings who, for whatever reason, sided with the Union against their fellow men and women. Jack hated such people passionately—and even more now, he realized, now that his mind was free of any malevolent influences.

Surely this newcomer was one of the collaborators. The man looked healthy—way too healthy to have spent much time laboring in the fields or the mines. In Jack's experience, the collaborators always looked healthy and fit, due to their access to the best food and drink, the most advanced healthcare, and the easiest work.

And now this newcomer was simply strolling up to him, as casual as could be, no robotic handlers in sight.

Jack balled up his fists and kept them at the ready.

The man appeared to be in his thirties, with wavy, shoulder-length dark hair. His features were angular, though not so severe as Jack's own. And he wore dark blue, including a heavy jacket and matching pants of that color, over dark boots. He nodded to Jack and then to Bennie, who was just now managing to get back up on his feet.

"I wanted to give you the chance to take care of—Bennie, isn't it?"

"Bennie, yes, that's me," the other man said, his voice already sounding different. "How did you know?"

"Not important," the man in blue said. He looked back at Jack. "I just knew it's always important to *you*."

Jack was puzzled by this statement but refrained from remarking on it.

"You're looking better already, Bennie," the man in blue said. "But then, you always manage to recover so much more quickly. You have a stronger constitution than Jack does."

The two looked at one another and then eyed the stranger with puzzled expressions.

"But now," the man went on, "we need to get you two idiots out of here. Before company arrives." He winked. "Unwanted company."

"Hold on a second," Jack said, frowning and raising one hand. "Just who are you supposed to be?"

The man in blue smiled back at both of them. "Ah, yeah—you don't know me yet, do you?" He laughed. "Call me John Smith," he said. Then he added, "This time around."

Jack started to say something, but Bennie surprisingly beat him to the punch.

"You're with the Union, aren't you?" he asked.

"A collaborator? With those nitwits?" The man scoffed. "Hardly. Quite the opposite, in fact."

"What's that supposed to mean?" asked Jack.

The man spread his hands and his smile widened.

"It means I'm going to help you overthrow the Union, the Kratons, the collaborators—the whole disgusting lot of them."

Jack just stared back at him.

Smith snorted and shook his head. "Sorry—that was probably a bit much to throw out there so soon. I always seem to overdo it, the first time we meet."

Jack continued to stare at him uncomprehendingly.

The corner of Smith's mouth turned upward in a wry smile. He waved dismissively, as if trying to make the whole line of discussion go away.

"It's fine—I know you need some time to work all this stuff out. I learned very quickly before not to try to rush you into anything." He raised both hands as if in surrender. "Go home. Rest up. Process it all. Take as long as you need. When you're ready to talk to me, come to the Blue Dolphin Bar on Fifteenth Street in the Down Town. If you don't see me, tell the bartender, and he'll know how to contact me." Smith grinned. "Got it?"

Jack shook his head. Nothing the man in blue was saying made the slightest bit of sense to him. He turned to Bennie and saw that his friend was running his eyes like he'd just woken up. He said, "You feeling okay, pal?"

"I'm feeling really good, actually, Jack," the other man replied. His voice sounded different. More mature. Less awkward, somehow.

"Good." Jack waved in the direction of the city. "Let's get out of here."

"You got it," Bennie said.

Jack cast one quick look back at the man in blue, who was still standing there, hands on hips, watching them go.

"Take your time," Smith called out as the two crested the hill and started down the other side, away from the mines. "Have fun in the arena. Soon enough, you'll come and talk to me. And then we'll take it to them."

Under his breath as he turned away, he added, "And this time we'll make it stick!"

CHAPTER 4

ARENA — PAY ATTENTION — ASSASSINS — AT THE BLUE DOLPHIN

1:

Jack couldn't help but wince when he heard the announcement over the loudspeaker: "Ladies and gentlemen, our next brave volunteer—Jack Gael!"

He'd thought about using an alias, but had decided there was no point. His identity would only matter to the Kratons, and they had any number of ways of determining who he really was.

And maybe his message to them would actually dissuade them from messing with him. Though he suspected what he was about to do might change that. But he was willing to take the chance.

He'd gained power. Shockingly, totally unexpectedly, he'd gained power. He'd thought long and hard about what he should *do* with it. And he'd decided the answer was, *Make life better for myself.*

Perhaps that wasn't the noblest answer he could have come up with. But, virtually since birth, he'd lived a life of near-misery in the labor pits, barely daring to dream of anything better. One could understand his first impulse was not toward self-sacrifice, but self-aggrandizement.

He had no real family left, to speak of. Few friends; none very close, other than Bennie—whom he'd helped already. No wife or steady girlfriend. Just that daily drudgery in the labor pits and the fields and the mines.

All he wanted was a better life. A life of hope.

The thought that he might use his newfound power to provide that hope to the dwindling remnants of humanity that also survived—that hadn't fully sunk into his mind. At least, not yet.

No, his ambitions at this point weren't particularly noble. But they were most definitely *human*.

He wanted a better life. He wanted respect.

He wanted to be a *winner*.

So here he was, about to attempt to become just that.

He could have worn a head covering; some fighters preferred to dress like the famous masked luchador wrestlers of Mexico, from back in the Before Times. There was little point, though. If the Kratons or their human servants had ordered him to remove it, and he'd refused, they would have likely tried to remove it themselves. And they wouldn't have been able to. And that would have given away things he didn't want given away–at least, not quite yet. So he'd abandoned any sense of anonymity and privacy and stood before the global audience as Jack Gael, a supposedly lowly and random laborer from the mines. He even wore his standard laborer's faded red jumpsuit. The silver belt still encircled his waist, of course–he'd yet to take it off, or even discover how to– but he had it mostly covered up by a broader leather belt.

How the world saw him a little while later would depend on how things went in the next few minutes.

"Our volunteer only has to survive one minute in the arena with the defending champion to win a thousand credits and two days off from labor detail!"

The crowd cheered, though not very enthusiastically. They knew nobody ever lasted a minute against one of the arena's champions.

The rusty metal fence in front of Jack rattled open and he walked slowly out of the holding pen and into the arena. He blinked at the sudden change in lighting and brought one hand up to his brow, shielding his eyes from the sun that shone down bright and hot into the open circle. Walls a dozen feet high surrounded the entire tableau, creating a dirt-floored arena some thirty yards across. Now he could see the raucous crowd of humans filling the seats above, yelling and waving their arms. This was one of the small, local arenas. Win a few times here, and he'd qualify for the larger ones, where the rewards were vastly better.

Few volunteers survived even their first matches at this level, though. Fewer still actually *won*.

Jack's eyes moved from the arena to his opponent, and he felt his stomach sink. From the opposite side of the arena, and to the lusty cheers of the crowd, came a monstrous gladiator who stopped short and leered down at him. The sun surrounded him in a bright halo, giving him the air of some ancient god.

The gladiator looked him up and down and sneered. "You think you can last a whole minute with me?" he rumbled.

Jack shrugged. He was surprised the big man had bothered to speak to him at all.

The gladiator chuckled. "First time fighting, little man?"

Jack nodded once.

"It'll also be your last," the gladiator said.

Jack swallowed dryly. He felt confident enough, at least in theory, but natural levels of fear and doubt nagged at him anyway. He took an involuntary step back and looked to his left and right.

Maybe this wasn't such a good idea after all, he thought.

It was not lost on him that the man in blue—Smith, he seemed to recall the guy's name was—had said something about this place. Predicting he would go there. And wishing him… *fun*?

But that wasn't what had spurred Jack to actually do it.

No, he'd decided entirely on his own that the arena was his best option. He could learn more about the abilities of the belt, even as he won some cash and some vacation time from the pits and maybe even started to work his way up the ranks.

The fact that he just might impress his buddy, Raynor, didn't hurt either.

So here he was, in the gladiator arena.

He'd gotten there by showing up hours early and standing in the line of volunteers wanting to compete. Yes, quite a few humans—most all of them idiots, in Jack's estimation—were willing to volunteer to go into the arena and take on whatever opponent the local Union overlord chose, in an effort to win money, easier work details, and the like. Sometimes they were made to face a wild animal native to Earth. Sometimes it was the equivalent creature, but obviously from some other world. And sometimes it was another human.

Jack had drawn another human as his opponent. But that human was not some random volunteer. He was a monster, and in more ways than one.

Jack couldn't at first remember his name, but his appearance was terrifying.

At least seven feet tall, the gladiator appeared to be made of muscle. Beneath his shaved head and massive Fu Manchu mustache, he wore an outfit consisting almost entirely of leather straps and metal rings, making him look something like a butcher—which was apt—or a blacksmith—which fit with the treatment he usually administered his opponents, before he finished them off.

He was a professional fighter. A professional killer.

He was a gladiator for the Union. In the employ of the Earth's alien overlords.

Now, being a gladiator didn't necessarily make him bad. Not at all. After all, Jack's friend Raynor was a gladiator. Jack had always been jealous of the relative money and fame that being a gladiator brought his friend, as well as how it allowed him to avoid work details.

But this man—this *creature*—confronting him now? He was an entirely different story. Jack recognized him. He'd seen the broadcasts.

This man-mountain was no part-time fighter. He reveled in combat with other humans. He *loved* it. And he loved killing them most of all.

No, he was no sporting gladiator. He was something much worse.

He was a collaborator. He worked *with* the aliens, not *for* them.

And he had no trouble whatsoever in carrying out their orders.

At that moment, the monstrous gladiator bellowed an animal scream and flexed his massive hands. Each looked capable of crushing a man's skull, with room to spare.

Jack found himself backing away.

"There's nowhere to run, little man," the gladiator said as he closed the distance between them again. "You're mine now."

"Looks like our latest contestant may die of fright before we even sound the horn to begin," came the voice of the announcer over loudspeakers arrayed around the arena. "Or before the Mangler even lays a hand on him!"

The Mangler. Well. At least now Jack knew the name of the horrifying individual he was facing. Memories came back, then. The Mangler had been fighting as a gladiator for the Union for many years, and in his time he'd sent quite a few humans to the hospital, and even more to the morgue. He was a bad man, yes—but he was also a terrible human being. If he even qualified as one of those anymore.

Jack had backed as far away from his foe as he could manage. Now he had no choice but to turn and face his opponent.

The Mangler appeared to understand the situation very well. Surely in his years of fighting in this arena and other, similar ones, he'd dispatched dozens if not hundreds of outclassed and mismatched opponents. For him, this would be just one more mercy killing.

"I have to make it look good for the cameras," he hissed at Jack as he closed in again, "but I'll try to keep your suffering to a minimum."

"Thanks," Jack said casually. He stood absolutely still and awaited the inevitable attack.

The horn sounded, loud and long. The clock started. The attack came.

Quick as a cat and belying his massive bulk, the Mangler surged forward, intending to crush him in the vice grip of his massive hands.

What happened next surprised the Mangler, everyone watching in the arena, and those viewing the broadcast at home or in bars. It even surprised Jack himself, on a purely emotional level. The one person it didn't surprise was the figure in dark blue that watched from the back of the crowd to Jack's right. As the rest of the audience gasped in shock, that man simply nodded at what he saw.

And what he saw was this: The Mangler leapt at Jack. Jack didn't move. The Mangler appeared to crash into Jack with all of his massive bulk.

And he *bounced off.*

Or, rather, he appeared to impact Jack, only to glance off to the right like a huge, ricocheting bullet and crash headlong into the wall.

Jack stood exactly where he'd stood a moment earlier, not having moved a muscle or a millimeter.

The Mangler lay in a dazed heap, shaking his head to clear it.

The crowd gasped in shock, then stared in silence at what they'd just seen.

The Mangler climbed back to his feet, his face now a scowl of anger. Lowering his head, he charged again, clearly intending to drive Jack into the wall, or into the ground.

Again he impacted Jack—or, rather, the invisible shield around Jack—and again he deflected away, sliding off him like Jack was covered in ice. The Mangler wound up once again lying in a heap at the base of the surrounding wall.

Jack had never moved a muscle or lifted a finger.

The Mangler rolled over on all fours and was back on his feet a second later. His face now blood-red, more from shame than from exertion, he swung a fist at Jack's jaw.

Jack decided to try something. He mentally told the belt to allow the fist into the bubble—but only part of the way.

The fist struck something, though not Jack's face. It was still two inches away from that.

The Mangler tried to push it forward, but it wouldn't go. Then he tried to draw the fist back, to take another swing.

The fist stuck, unmoving, seemingly hovering in midair, two inches from the bridge of Jack's nose.

The Mangler's expression morphed from rage to incredulity. He tried again to draw his hand back and found he couldn't. It was as if it had become stuck in molasses, or wedged into a crack in invisible stone.

Jack smiled as he swung his own punch at the Mangler's face, at the same instant willing the bubble to expand rapidly outward from his fist. The resulting blow knocked the bald gladiator's head back in whiplashing fashion. Jack did it three more times—it was the outside of the shield impacting the Mangler, not his own hand—then had the shield release the Mangler's hand.

The big man teetered, then dropped to the ground like a felled oak.

The crowd remained deathly silent as Jack made a quick hand-wiping gesture over his opponent.

The Mangler groaned and forced himself up again, but this time he didn't attack. He simply stood there, hands on hips, staring. The furious glare was gone from his face, replaced now by utter befuddlement.

Jack looked at him, then turned his back on him and faced the crowd.

The horn sounded again. The required one minute was up.

Grinning, Jack took a bow.

The crowd erupted.

2:

The tall, sleek human woman swept into Torrens' laboratory like she owned the place. Behind her, two Kraton guards hurried to keep up, their servos whining in protest.

Torrens looked up from his lab equipment and frowned at the sight.

Xaveria Denali. Again, so soon. Well, well.

The two big robots took up guard position behind her. There were very few humans who could command the Kratons. She was a rare one, indeed.

"Ah–Dr. Torrens," the dark-haired woman called out as she spotted him and headed over. "I was hoping to catch you here."

"Catch me you have, Sub-Administrator," Torrens said, doing his best to disguise the contempt he felt for her. He wanted to believe it was because she was an even bigger collaborator with the invaders than he was. Part of him suspected, however, that it was mostly because she was much more successful at it. And truly seemed to enjoy it.

She stood over six feet tall, with narrow features and eyes dark as her hair. Today her jumpsuit was a shimmering dark blue, and it fitted her like a second skin.

She glided up to him and, hands on hips, looked him over like a lab specimen.

"Still nothing, then?" she asked. "No weapons for the Grand Overlord?"

"Progress continues," Torrens replied, barely sparing her a glance.

Her small mouth twisted downward.

"Does it, though?" she said. "I wonder."

Torrens chose to ignore that comment. Instead he asked, in a voice dripping with impatience and bother, "What can I do for you, Sub-Administrator?"

She leaned in closer and her voice dropped to a conspiratorial whisper. "Do you follow the gladiatorial contests, Doctor?"

Torrens frowned at this. He wasn't sure why she would be asking him such a thing. "Not as a rule, no," he replied. "I've never seen the point. I have too many other things that hold my interest."

"Perhaps you should," the woman replied. "There is someone taking part in them who might well hold your interest."

Now Torrens was intrigued. What could this woman possibly be talking about? A gladiator in the silly arena contests? Why would that interest him at all?

Xaveria Denali motioned toward one of the nearby display screens and barked an order at the nearest Kraton. The robot hurried to obey. It didn't do anything overt, but it must have connected wirelessly with the monitor, because the screen suddenly flared to life. An image of a combat arena appeared, two men circling one another at its center.

"Sub-Administrator, I don't know what this is all about," Torrens began impatiently, "but—"

The tall woman silenced him with a sharp gesture of one hand and motioned toward the screen with the other. "Pay attention, Torrens," she hissed.

Reddening, wanting to strangle this person but knowing the Kratons would murder him before his hands could close around her throat, he instead forced himself to focus on the contest being displayed.

At first he didn't understand what was supposed to be of such great interest. One of the combatants was a huge hulk of a man, dressed in almost Medieval fashion, clad all in leather and metal— obviously a pro at the gladiatorial games. The other figure was a much more normal person; one who had no business in the ring with such a monster.

As the bigger figure advanced on the smaller one, Torrens braced himself to witness a slaughter.

What happened next was anything but what he expected to see.

Several seconds into it, and with his brows knitted in surprise and confoundment, he glanced over at Denali.

She was leering back at him.

"You see why I thought you would find it interesting," she said.

On the screen—somehow; impossibly—the slender, apparently normal man was beating the massive, professional gladiator to a pulp.

"How is that possible?" Torrens asked, once the fight was over and they'd carried what remained of the big man out on a stretcher.

Denali met his gaze with her own. "That is what the Union expects you to find out, Doctor," she said. "And soon."

3:

Three times in as many weeks, assassins had come for Jack.

He'd had to move to a different apartment, of course. By making such a public splash, and doing so while using his own name, he'd guaranteed he'd have no more privacy. No, people surrounded his building and shouted his name—and their many requests—all day and all night. It was as if he'd become some new god, and a cult had developed around him almost overnight, filled with parishioners hopeful that he could solve their particular problems for them.

In response to this, he'd found a new place to live, and registered for it under an assumed name. The Kratons knew what he'd done, of course, and didn't object—at least, not yet. They, or perhaps their alien masters, were happy enough that a new and exciting gladiator had entered the lists. They apparently had not yet figured out exactly *how* he'd survived the Mangler, though he assumed they were breaking down the video of the match frame by frame even at this very moment. The next time he fought, if he did fight again, the robots would likely bring all sorts of sensor equipment to try to analyze and study what was giving him such a remarkable advantage. He was certain from the beginning that, sooner or later, they'd work it out, and either find a way to counter his belt and nullify the shield or simply send someone to take it from him.

Four days later, he wanted to kick himself for not guessing they'd simply try to kill him and then analyze his technology after they took it from his corpse.

The first assassin to visit him could have been anybody, sent by anyone. The man had possessed no special weapons and carried no sophisticated defenses or camouflage. He'd simply crept into Jack's apartment through an unsecured third-floor window and come at him with a short, straight knife.

What probably saved Jack was the fact that he still had no idea whatsoever how to control the belt. From the moment he'd put it around his waist and it had fastened itself onto him, the shield bubble had been there, surrounding him. He could control its distance from his body, as well as its permeability, with simple thoughts. But he had yet to figure out how to turn it off completely.

And, to be honest with himself, he was afraid to.

Once surrounded by that miraculous wall of invisible protection, the idea of doing without it for any length of time scared him to death. He found himself wondering how he'd lived as long as he had without it.

He did worry that he might be overusing it—that its unknown power supply might run down, being used so steadily. Or that some sort of unpleasant side effects might occur if he left it on all the time. Those considerations, however, paled in comparison to the sense of security he enjoyed simply by wearing the belt and having it in operation.

So it was that he'd been lying there in bed, well after midnight, trying to get to sleep and still surrounded in an invisible, seemingly-undetectable force field, when a man dressed entirely in black leapt on top of him and drove a knife toward his chest.

The blade, of course, slid off like a spoon hitting a block of ice. The would-be assassin, who must not have watched the video of Jack's battle with the Mangler very closely—or at least not fully comprehended what he'd seen—stared in shock and confusion at his blade. Then he raised it over his head, in order to bring it down and strike at Jack with even more force.

By this time, Jack was coming fully awake and blinking his eyes, trying to figure out what was going on.

"Lights," he shouted, and the resulting glare revealed the man in black straddling him, the knife poised up high.

Jack instinctively brought his right hand up, between himself and the knife. At the same time he mentally ordered the shield to expand from close to his skin, where it had been while he was asleep, to about three inches away in every direction.

The blade came down hard and struck something invisible, three inches out from the palm of his hand. Again it was deflected, and the assassin's momentum carried him forward.

As the bubble around Jack had expanded, it had lifted him those three inches above his bed. This in turn caused the lunging assassin to further lose his balance and tumble head over heels to the floor.

The assassin was clumsy and uninformed but he wasn't entirely stupid, as he proved a moment later by giving up entirely and scampering back in the direction he'd come from. By the time Jack got out of bed and ran after him, he'd jumped back out the open window and disappeared into the shadows of the nighttime streets.

Jack returned to his bedroom but was too wound up now to sleep. He paced around the little room, thinking.

Until that moment, he'd been uncertain if the shield remained in place while he was asleep, and thus when he was not consciously desiring it to be there. Now he knew it was. As far as he now could tell, it had never gone away; not since the moment he'd first accidentally activated it. The mere possibility of such a thing had been a tiny, nagging worry all along. Now it blossomed into a full-blown concern. A whole-body force field could be a wonderful thing, obviously, at the right time and in the right place. But having it there all the time, day and night, and with no way to get rid of it—that seemed a little much to Jack.

His opinion on that matter didn't change a lot after the second assassin came for him, a week later. That one brought improved weapons, but fared no better, and barely escaped. By that point, Jack had appeared in the gladiator arena a second time and then a third, easily defeating human opponents each time. Those last two occasions, instead of merely surviving for a full minute, Jack had been required to actually defeat his opponents. He'd done so–in less than thirty seconds each.

It had seemed everything was going well. And then someone had started trying to kill him.

Frustrated, Jack visited his friend Raynor, the longtime gladiator. Raynor embraced him and shook his hand, congratulating him on his victories. Then he leaned in closer and said, "I'm not surprised they're trying to kill you. You're bad for business."

Jack frowned at this. "Bad for business? What business?"

"Show business, of course," Raynor replied.

"I don't understand."

Raynor laughed, rubbed his chin for a moment, and then tried to explain.

"Jack, I don't know how you're doing this—all this winning—and not getting beat up or killed. But clearly you've got something going for you. A gimmick. And that's fine," he added, raising a mollifying hand. "Good for you. But I have to warn you—your wins are coming too easily."

Jack was taken aback. "Too easily? Should I try to *lose*?"

Raynor grinned at him, his face friendly despite his broken nose and bruises on forehead and cheeks. "No, you shouldn't try to lose, you idiot. But you should at least make the fights more interesting. More entertaining. More sporting, yeah? Remember–you're doing this mainly to provide diversion for the laborers out there. Following your exploits in the arena–and mine–takes their minds off their crappy existences as slaves to our alien and robot overlords for a little while. So you need to give them something. If you keep knocking off the champions every week, and in record time, you're going to ruin their show."

Jack thought about this for a few seconds.

"Wait–you mean, you think it's the people that run the arena that are trying to kill me?"

"Probably," Raynor replied. "And people is right–it's got to be humans doing it. Running it on behalf of the Union. Because if it was our dear alien masters who were trying to kill you, they'd have sent a battalion of Kratons over and you'd just be a greasy spot on your apartment floor now."

"Maybe; maybe not," Jack replied idly–to which his friend merely stared back at him with an astonished look on his face.

Jack blew this off and continued.

"So you think the humans running the arena want more bang for their buck, so to speak?" he asked.

"Yeah. Good way to put it," Raynor said. "Let the viewers and the fans wonder a little bit—will he survive this time? Is this the moment he gets his comeuppance?"

Jack nodded slowly, absorbing this.

"If you just keep thrashing all your opponents," Raynor continued, "the Kratons will take more notice, and they might conclude you're doing more harm than good to their little racket here."

Jack chewed on a fingernail, deep in thought.

"Oh," Raynor added. "Expect more assassins, too."

4:

The third assassin visited a couple of days later.

After surviving that attack, and then moving to yet another new apartment under a different name, Jack went on to make a number of other decisions he'd put off until then.

He decided he needed to understand the belt better, and he needed to be able to control it. He couldn't simply keep crossing his fingers and hoping it would work every time he needed it to. He needed answers: Would it run out of power? Were there other things it could do?

Another question, "Where did it come from?" could wait. That was an admittedly excellent one, and one he was quite curious about. But it was not an immediate, practical question, and could be dealt with later—or perhaps not at all.

He decided he needed to talk to that man—the man in blue, who'd been there when he'd come out of the mines. The guy who'd been saying all the really cryptic things; things that had done nothing at the time but give Jack an even worse headache.

For all his vagueness and his odd pronouncements, the man in blue had sounded like he knew things nobody else knew, or should have known. Having no other leads on finding out more about the belt, Jack figured he might as well talk to the guy.

So Jack used one of his bonus days off and some of his prize money, both won in the arena, to pay for a private lift out of the labor zone where he lived, and into Down Town.

That area was dangerous. Down Town was the portion of the New City that had been built directly on top of part of Old New York, or Ony. Jack had to remind himself he didn't have much to fear there anymore, thanks to the belt. But it still made him nervous to be there.

Eventually he located the Blue Dolphin Bar, and went inside. The man he was looking for wasn't there, so he dutifully inquired of the bartender: "Dark-haired guy; blue jacket; blue pants?"

"Yeah?"

"He wanted me to meet him here?"

The bartender took a step back, sizing him up. When he spoke, it was in a low tone. "You're the *Gladiator*, aren't you?"

Jack felt himself grow embarrassed. This was all still too new for him to be used to thinking of himself that way. Then again, he liked the sound of that name. He could just *hear* the capital letter at the start of it. *The Gladiator*. He nodded once.

"Yeah. Thought I recognized you. Say—how'd you beat the Mangler like that? I still can't quite believe it."

Jack spread his hands wide. "Trade secret," he said with a smile.

The bartender stared back at him for a few seconds, and then his face split in a wide grin. "Yeah. Yeah, sure," he said, nodding. "I can understand that." He gestured toward the row of booths along the wall to his left. "Okay. Have a seat. He'll be along shortly."

Jack thanked the man, paid for a beer and then seated himself in one of those very booths.

Twenty minutes later, a very recognizable figure entered the bar. He wore the same dark blue pants and jacket.

Jack struggled to remember his name. It had been something very simple; very basic. Was he Jack too? *No... but...*

The man in blue walked past Jack's booth without looking up at him. He continued until he reached a small door just to the right of the bar. Then he stopped and looked back at Jack.

"This way," he said.

Puzzled, Jack hopped down from his stool and followed the man through the doorway and into a dimly-lit hall.

Jack... John... John? John.

John *what?*

Surely not...

"John Smith," the man said as he reached another doorway in the back and turned around to face Jack. "Glad you decided to come." He grinned. "I'd shake your hand, but I know that's not exactly easy for you yet."

This remark puzzled Jack—not because it was untrue, but because the man seemed to know it and take it for granted. He let it slide by with just a nod.

Smith led Jack into a small storeroom with only a single light fixture above a table with four chairs. He motioned for Jack to take a seat, then shut the door and sat down himself. He leaned back, smiled, and regarded Jack as one might a close relative over for a visit. But he said nothing.

After several seconds of this, Jack grew impatient. He leaned forward. "How do you know so much about me, and about what I'm dealing with, Mr. Smith?"

Smith spread his hands wide. "You've been the focus of my attention for a very long time, Jack."

Jack blinked. "What? Why?" Involuntarily he looked down at the silver belt around his waist, then back up at Smith.

"The belt, yes," Smith said, "but long before that. In fact, I made sure you were the one who found it."

Jack started to react dismissively to this, but then he remembered seeing a figure in blue, out of the corner of his eye, passing him on the way out of the mine as he'd entered it. He'd found the belt soon after, and right out in the open.

"You're saying *you* put it there? You left it for me?"

Smith nodded.

"But—why?"

Smith shrugged. "I've found it works better to allow you to find it and experiment with it on your own first, before I get involved." He chuckled as if to some private joke. "And a couple of times you wouldn't have found it at all if I hadn't left it right out in the open for you." He smiled at Jack. "But I decided that now is the time you were set on the right path."

Jack stared back at the man, then slowly shook his head. "You're not making any sense."

"I'm making perfect sense," Smith replied. "It's just that sometimes it's hard for me to remember to think—and speak—in a fully linear fashion."

"That didn't help," Jack said.

Smith held up both hands. "Fair enough," he said. "I also get impatient to move things along, after doing them over and over, so many times. But that isn't fair to you. For you, every time is your first time through. So I will endeavor to communicate with you in as linear a fashion as possible."

Jack's head was spinning. "This is a waste of time," he said. "I have better things to do." He stood up and started toward the door.

"Yes," Smith said. "You've become quite the successful gladiator—thanks to that belt I left for you. And you've also attracted the attention of the Kratons and the Union administrators." He smiled a crooked smile at Jack. "How many assassination attempts have you survived so far? Two?"

Jack froze and stared down at the other man. "What do you know about that?"

"It's what they always do, because you always end up drawing attention to yourself too soon. That's okay, though—we need the publicity for other reasons, so I've learned to let you go with it."

Jack was still standing there, wavering between leaving and sitting back down.

Smith held up a hand. "There I go again," he said. "Let me start over," he added, gesturing toward the chair, "from the beginning."

"That would be a novel approach," Jack said, but he did move back around the table and sat back down. No matter how insane this man might be, or at least come across, he knew far too many things to be a complete crackpot.

"The problem with beginnings," Smith said, "is that it's hard to find them when you're dealing with a loop. It's like finding the start to a roll of tape that's stuck down—you know? You can just go round and round, forever."

Jack was just staring back at him dully, so he motioned it away.

"I'll warn you up front that there are some things I simply can't tell you," he noted. "Things that it would be counterproductive for you to know, at least so early in the cycle. You'll just have to trust me on that." He looked away for a moment. "This must be the seventh or eighth time we've had this conversation, yet I never get any better at it."

"Just get on with it," Jack growled.

"Yes. Very well." Smith cleared his throat and began.

"Long ago, I chose you to lead the uprising against the alien domination of this world," he said. "And now I simply have to help you stop being so incredibly incompetent at it."

CHAPTER 5

THE PROBLEM — RESPONSIBILITY — SURVEILLANCE — FANS

1:

"You see the problem, then, Dr. Torrens?"

Howard Torrens stared with fascination at the monitor, and at what was playing back on it.

The tall, blond, scrawny man, wearing only a laborer's red jumpsuit, was standing up to powerful blows from three other gladiators, all at the same time, and all without seemingly taking a bit of damage or injury. Over and over the three adversaries—brutal monsters, each of them—came at him, striking him with furious blows. They hit him with clubs, with blades, with cudgels. Each time, it was as if the weapons didn't quite touch him. Oh, at first glance they appeared to. But when Torrens looked closely, he could tell that something—*something*—was coming between the weapons and the man's flesh, deflecting them away.

Whatever it might be, however, it was effectively invisible.

"Do you see, Dr. Torrens?" Xaveria Denali repeated.

I don't see anything at all, he started to say. *It's invisible. And that's the problem. And perhaps the promise—?*

Instead, "Oh yes," he answered her. "I see very well."

Denali nodded. "And what do you make of it?"

Torrens continued to stare at the screen. The blond man had gone over to the offensive at last. A swing of his bony fist and the closest of the three gladiators crumpled to the ground, as if hit by a piledriver.

Fascinating.

"And this isn't staged?" Torrens asked, his eyes never leaving the tableau that was playing out. "They're not faking this, for the sake of entertainment?"

"They are not," the woman replied. "I have questioned the organizers thoroughly and at great pains." She gestured toward the man in the jumpsuit. "This laborer showed up just over two weeks ago, volunteering for the arena. They lumped him in with all the other self-destructive types that are willing to gamble their lives for an extra day off of their work and a few paltry credits in their pocket. But this one was different. He beat one of their best on day one, and has continued to wreak havoc with their top talent during his every appearance since." Denali clasped her long fingers behind her back and stalked back and forth across the smooth tile floor of the lab. "They dare not ban him—he's become too popular with the masses, and their vid ratings are through the roof. But he's decimated their ranks of gladiators. Few remain to challenge him, and fewer still are willing, now that his... *abilities*... have become widely known. In fact, I believe the organizers have tried to have him killed, away from the arena, at least twice. They hoped if it looked like an accident, their ratings wouldn't suffer and their viewers wouldn't riot." She shook her head. "As you can see, they failed. Apparently he defeats hired killers as easily as he defeats gladiators."

Torrens absorbed this information in wide-eyed astonishment.

"Ah, one other thing," Denali noted. "We found a record from some weeks ago. It had been overlooked or simply discarded as unimportant at the time. A Kraton near one of the mines reported being attacked by a human matching his description. He made a couple of threats before apparently destroying the Kraton. No one took it seriously at the time."

"Why would they?" Torrens asked. "It must have come across as a silly prank."

"Yes. And when the Kraton failed to report in, no one considered that a simple human laborer could have done any harm to it."

Torrens nodded.

"Now, however…" Denali gestured toward the screen, where the blond man was finishing off his adversaries. "I suspect that message may have been recorded just after he first acquired this ability. So…"

"Something from the mines," Torrens said.

"Yes."

"Some kind of defensive field."

She nodded.

"He can't be hurt," Torrens went on. "But he's certainly able to hurt others."

"Precisely so," Denali said. "And I want to know how, and why."

So do I, Torrens thought.

"What would you like me to do?" he asked.

"Go and see him. Talk to him. You're not threatening—he won't kill you. See if you can figure out what he's doing."

Torrens let the slight go past him. He'd heard far worse from Denali over the past few years.

"I will go and visit him tonight," Torrens replied. He found he had no need to generate false enthusiasm in order to impress the woman. He felt plenty of enthusiasm from watching the video. "Oh—what's his name?"

She checked something on her data link. "Jack Gael. But he's currently living under an assumed name, in a brand-new location. I'm forwarding it to you."

"Got it." Torrens smiled. "I'll find out what this guy has going for him."

And how to get it for myself, he added silently.

2:

Jack, as he had done so many times in previous cycles, had stormed out of the storeroom and the Blue Dolphin after a very abbreviated conversation with John Smith.

Smith had expected it. Sometimes Jack stayed a little longer, but he never made it all the way to the end of Smith's spiel, no matter how much Smith abridged it and edited it to try to hold his interest.

That wasn't really accurate, though, Smith admitted to himself. The problem wasn't Jack's interest—it was his own credibility. The claims Smith was making were extraordinary, and they therefore required extraordinary proof. That was hard to provide in a brief conversation with a stranger. Smith was still working out the best way to handle it all. More often than not, however, this approach did tend to result in Jack coming back later, wanting to know more, after he'd processed what he'd already been told.

Smith had sweetened the pot by making a bold prediction as Jack was leaving:

"Another assassin will visit you tonight," he'd said. "This one will be much harder to deal with. Be ready."

And then, to Jack's back as the man had exited the room, "I'll see you here tomorrow."

And indeed Jack did return the next day. Smith was waiting for him in the same spot as the day before.

"How did you know?" Jack demanded, standing in the doorway. "Did you *send* him?"

"Of course I didn't send him," Smith replied. "I don't want you dead. I want to make you a hero—no matter how hard you resist it." He motioned for Jack to take his seat, and the blond man did so, reluctantly.

"As for how I knew? I knew because you tell me," Smith explained. "You always tell me." He grinned. "Was it hypersonics again? They're pretty sure by now that you have some kind of invisible shield, and they figure a sound-based weapon might penetrate it."

Jack looked surprised. "No. It was some kind of laser gun, I think."

Smith raised an eyebrow. "Hard light? So soon?" He brought a hand to his chin. "That's different."

"So you don't know everything."

"Never claimed to," Smith said. "Little things change every time. Big things, not as often. Still, it's to be expected." Even so, he was frowning, troubled. He rubbed absently at his jaw.

Jack studied him for a moment. "All right," he said. "We have to have this conversation, so let's proceed here as if I'm buying what you're saying."

"Let's," Smith replied with a smile.

"You told me yesterday that you've lived through this part of history over and over."

Smith's face took on a look of disgust. "That is all too correct. Over and over."

"But you won't tell me how or why."

"No, sorry—I have to keep that information private, at least for now."

"But it's decades, every time. Right?"

Smith grimaced and nodded. "*Interminable* decades, yes."

Jack grunted something that seemed to indicate acceptance if not agreement. "And you said that you've approached a number of different people about leading an uprising against the aliens, but you have decided I'm the best choice."

Jack nodded. "The last few times, yes."

Jack shook his head. "There you go again," he said.

"Whoops—yep, sorry. I'm trying not to do that—trying to stay linear for you—but it's not easy."

Jack waved it aside impatiently. "Why me?" he asked.

"Well, now I have to do it again—go all non-linear—to answer that," Smith said with a little shrug.

Jack sighed. "Go on, then."

"Because the plan has come the closest to succeeding when you and I work together."

"But we haven't actually succeeded before, right? Because, if we had, none of this would still be going on—?"

"That is true. Absolutely true. You see? You get it."

Jack ignored this. "And what, if I may ask, is the *plan* you're referring to?"

"Simple," Smith replied. "We make a popular hero out of you, fighting in the arena, and then parlay that into you calling for the formation of a Resistance—a rebellion against the Union. Oh—and then you lead it to victory."

"I do?"

"Well…" Smith pursed his lips. "We haven't gotten quite that far yet. But I have confidence that you will. We just have to see that everything works out this time."

Jack stared back at him. "You do understand, right? That this is a lot to take in."

"Of course," Smith replied. "But so is the world being conquered and ruled by a tiny cabal of aliens and their robot servants. And yet…" He spread his hands wide, to encompass the world.

"Fair enough," Jack said. "So I'm giving you the benefit of considerable doubt. For now." He thought for a moment. "You said every time you fail to change history, you get thrown back in time again. How far?"

"It varies. Usually about fifty years. Long enough for me to get my feet back under me and start working on the plan again."

"If it's happened a bunch of times before, why haven't you died of old age? How are you still—what? Thirty?"

"Something like that." He shrugged. "I don't know. But I've been stuck at this age ever since it all started."

"You're saying you don't age at all." Jack stared back at him, incredulous.

"Not recently, no." Smith snorted. "I guess it's a side effect of this time loop I seem to be stuck in. And it might sound great at first, but believe me—it gets quite tedious after a while."

Jack ignored this and kept pushing along. "In fifty years, over and over, the best you could come up with for a hero is *me*?"

"Ah! Don't sell yourself short, Gael," Smith said. "You've come the closest." He grinned. "I figure I'll give you a few more chances to succeed before I move on to other candidates."

"Thanks," Jack said sardonically.

"It hasn't always been fifty years, though," Smith noted. "At least once, it was a lot further back." He spread his hands. "It all kind of runs together for me, but, yeah, the first time, for sure—the very first time it happened—I went back centuries."

"Centuries?" Jack stared at him.

"Back to the Dark Ages, I suppose you'd say. To around 700 AD." He shook his head. "And let me just tell you right now, that was no picnic. I mean, sure—no big silver robots stomping around, threatening to kill you. No alien overlords. But the fleas, the lice, the healthcare in general…" He made a face. "And don't even get me started on the dentistry."

Jack waited patiently through this, then asked, "And you lived all that time over again, right up to the present day?"

"Well beyond the present day, actually. All the way up until my plan failed for the first time. Not," he added, "that I had *much* of a plan that first time."

Jack was chewing on this.

"So, you lived through all this history again, knowing what was coming. Why didn't you…" He trailed off.

"Why didn't I what?"

"I don't know—why didn't you *do* something? To stop the Union from conquering us in the first place."

"*Do* something?" Smith stared back at the other man, his eyes wide. "What a brilliant idea!"

Smith got to his feet and paced the short distance from one side of the room to the other and back.

"Why didn't I just *do* something?" He shook his head and laughed. "Are you *kidding* me?"

"Well?" Jack asked, not moving. "Why didn't you?"

Smith had grown agitated; even angry. Now he visibly forced himself to settle down. "You absolute twit," he muttered. "You're always able to get me going. Part of me hopes I *will* have to give up on you, and move on to a different potential hero soon."

"No—tell me the answer, if it's such a ridiculous thing for me to ask," Jack persisted. "Why didn't you try to change things?"

Smith stopped pacing and looked at Jack. "What makes you think I *didn't*?"

Jack spread his arms wide to encompass the world. "Well, I'm sorry," he said, "But—just look around. If you tried something, it didn't work!"

Smith regarded him balefully from under hooded eyes. "No," he said, "it didn't."

The two of them stared hard at one another for several seconds. Then Smith sat back down in his chair, inhaled deeply, and looked at the other man again.

"Way back in the Dark Ages, I didn't dare say anything. They weren't ready to hear what I had to say. How would they have reacted? I'd have been burned at the stake or something.

"Honestly, by not speaking about it for so long—just centuries and centuries—I almost started to believe it was all a fantasy, and that maybe I had dreamed it all up. Of course, the fact that I wasn't aging, wasn't dying, occasionally served to remind me it was true. Even so, it just didn't seem possible. Despite the fact that I'd lived through it, so much time had passed, and it was all just so fantastic. And that had been ages earlier. In another life. In another world. So I kept my mouth shut, moved around a lot, took advantage of my future knowledge to scratch out a good living here and there, and otherwise bided my time. I served as an advisor to William the Conqueror, George Washington and the Duke of Wellington, as well as to Churchill and Corrigan. I amassed a personal fortune and kept safely anonymous behind the scenes, while moving the pieces of history around the board the way I knew they needed to be moved." He looked down at the floor, composing his thoughts. "But, even so, with centuries and centuries passing by since I'd arrived in the past, I began to doubt I'd ever actually lived in the future. I decided I'd dreamed it all.

"But when the Twentieth Century rolled around, and I started seeing science fiction books and then movies and television shows, it started to seem quite plausible indeed. It hit home with me that the aliens would be arriving pretty soon, and that all of my success would be taken away when that happened." He motioned around airily with one hand. "Oh—and of course most of the world would be destroyed, too, yeah." He sat back and continued. "I understood then that I'd wasted a lot of time. So I started saying and doing what I could. Here and there, quietly at first. Discreetly." He raised his hands in the air in a gesture of futility. "And nobody listened to me. Not that it would've mattered. They didn't have the weapons to fight back, if they'd wanted to. Not yet.

"By the Twenty-first Century, I was raising the alarm full-throat that aliens were coming, and were going to take over the world; that they were going to kill most of the human race, and enslave the few survivors. I told people in positions of authority that, over and over. And you know what it got me? A movie deal! And when I pressed on with them that I was serious, not just trying to sell a story to Hollywood, it got me something else: A one-way ticket to the psycho ward! The rubber room!"

Jack took this in and nodded reluctantly. "That makes sense, I guess," he said. "How could you prove anything? It had to sound insane to people back then."

"Yes. Exactly. So, finally, I got released and there were still a few years to spare before the Union arrived and started raining killer robots on us. Not a lot of time, but maybe enough, I thought.

"Eventually people in a few countries started to listen to me. I was able to produce some super-futuristic tech that helped convince them that maybe I wasn't entirely nuts. So I came up with the idea of helping them develop futuristic weapons. Cutting edge technology—the best that could be made at that time. Would it be enough to stop the Union? I didn't know, and suspected not—but what else could I do? I encouraged those countries and organizations to keep the weapons and other tech hidden away in underground bunkers, so the Union wouldn't find it and destroy it from orbit." He laughed bitterly. "And then almost none of it got used when they arrived. They blitzed us. And it all got lost. Buried."

Jack considered this. His eyes widened as he understood what it meant. "The mines," he said. "You were responsible for the mines existing."

"Exactly." He met the eyes of the other man. "And now, every time I cycle back around to that same point in time where I've been starting over, about fifty years ago, I hope things have played out differently—that I, or someone else, has managed to convince the world to arm for war. But, every single time, they're all still in the experimenting-in-the-lab phase. And then their bunkers get bombed and all the fancy tech they dreamed up gets covered over with rubble. And later on, your mines get created."

Jack stared back at Smith, astonished.

"I know," Smith said. "It's a lot to absorb. Like I said, there were entire centuries where I was sure I'd imagined it all—dreamed it up myself. But it's true. It's all true."

"How can you prove it, though?" Jack asked.

"Besides the fact that I knew you were going to say that?" Smith smiled and pointed at the silver belt Jack wore. "That right there. The belt I found, and passed on to you."

"*You* found it?"

"Quite a few cycles ago, the first time, yes. Maybe twenty. It's all gotten to be a blur in some places, for the most part."

"And you always give it to me?"

"Of course not. Am I an idiot? I wanted it for myself, obviously." Smith shook his head. "I couldn't get it to work right, though. It was a pain. I wasted five cycles that way—trying to make it protect me. But it would switch off in the middle of a firefight, or..." He pantomimed getting shot in the stomach, then shrugged. "For some reason it works much better for some people than for others. Maybe it's a DNA thing—it recognizes the same family as that of the inventor who created it? I don't know. But it works for you. It works *very well* for you."

Jack sat back in his chair and ran his hands over his face, thinking. For nearly a minute he didn't speak. At last he met Smith's eyes and said, "You think I can lead an uprising against the Union."

"I think you could, yes."

"And you think it could succeed. You think we could drive the invaders away, never to return."

"Possibly," Smith answered. "We came very close the third time you and I tried together. That's why I've kept coming back to you, these last few attempts. My plans enjoyed their greatest success so far with you. And I'm never going to stop, until I stop coming back. If it turns out that our near-success that one time was a fluke, and we don't get any closer to succeeding, then I'll move on to someone else. I wouldn't know what else to do."

Jack mulled this over, then stood up from the table. "Mr. Smith, you tell a fascinating story. I can see how you got those movie deals, as you said. And it's almost—almost—believable." He chuckled. "But I'm going to pass. Life is going too well for me right now. Why should I give all that away? Especially just to go out and maybe get myself and a whole lot of other people killed, in some futile rebellion?"

Smith stared back at him. "I don't know—maybe for *freedom*?"

"Freedom doesn't pay the bills," Jack said flatly. "Freedom doesn't put food on the table. Fighting in the arena does." He glanced at his chrono. "And I have a match coming up in a few minutes, so I have to go." He looked at Smith and laughed. "They're calling me Gladiator now. As in, *The* Gladiator."

"That's new," Smith noted, frowning. He shook his head. "But how will you keep on being a gladiator–excuse me, *The* Gladiator–without the *belt*?"

Jack's eyebrows knitted. "Without the belt?"

"Well, certainly," Smith replied. "Leading a rebellion is the specific reason I gave you the belt. If you're not going to *do* that, I'll need it back." He looked away, thinking. "There's just enough time left, I think, to train up someone new with it."

Jack was staring at him. "I'm not giving it to you," he said.

"Of course you are. It doesn't belong to you. It belongs to *me*. I told you–*I* left it for you in the mines."

"All I know is that I *found* it. I don't really know how it *got* there. But I found it, and it's *mine*." He grinned at the other man. "If you want to try to take it away from me, go right ahead."

Smith simply looked back at him.

"That's what I thought." Jack turned and headed for the door. Just before he opened it, he looked back at Smith, a gleam in his eye. "Say–how many times have I done *this* before? Just up and left, at the end of your spiel?"

Smith's eyes were cold and black. "This is the first time," he said. "Congratulations on achieving peak a-hole-ness, this time around, Jack."

Jack laughed.

"Here," Smith said. He held out a card.

Jack looked at him a moment, then came back over and took it. It passed smoothly through something invisible. "What's this?"

"How to contact me."

"I won't need it."

"We'll see."

Jack eyed him once more, shook his head, then opened the door and stepped through it. When it closed, Smith's stare could have burned a hole through the wood.

Smith bent forward and banged his head gently on the desk.

"Dammit," he whispered.

3:

Detectives Hoyt and Rodriguez watched from the relative comfort of their patrol hovercar as Jack Gael exited the Blue Dolphin and made his way along the street to his own vehicle: a late-model sports car parked along the opposite curb. Rodriguez stared at the sleek, teardrop-shaped construction of aluminum and plastic as he absently stroked his long, curving black mustache.

"Wonder how much he dropped on that?" he asked his partner.

Hoyt, a lanky man in his thirties with sandy blond hair and a ruddy complexion, stifled a yawn. He wasn't particularly interested.

"Who knows? I'm sure he could afford it. He's making a fortune in the arena."

"And he will, right up until they kill him," Rodriguez noted. "Which could be any day now."

"I'm not so sure about that," Hoyt said as he started up the hovercar and followed along after Jack, keeping a discreet distance between them. On the street beneath them passed all manner of conveyances, from beaten-up, gas-driven cars and trucks to horse-drawn carriages. And mixed in all among them, what remained of humanity, shuffling home or to work, most of them probably in between shifts in the labor pits or the mines.

"I think if he were that easy to kill," Hoyt added, "they'd have done it already. Days ago."

Rodriguez considered that and nodded slowly. "Maybe so."

"I'm more bothered," Hoyt went on, "by the fact that we couldn't hear anything from inside there." He patted the bulky mechanical device that rested on the console between them. A slender arm extended from it and aimed out the car window. He brought it in and folded it away. "The laser-mic has always worked before."

"You should have let me plant bugs inside the building, after we found out he went there yesterday," Rodriguez said.

"Yeah, probably," Hoyt said. "But I wasn't sure he'd go back any time soon. And who'd have guessed a low-class dive like the Blue Dolphin would have some kind of shielding against comm lasers?"

Rodriguez said nothing. Hoyt continued to maneuver the hovercar so that they kept Jack's vehicle in sight as they traveled above the winding and ancient streets of Down Town, but weren't too obvious about following him.

After a few moments of silence, Rodriguez looked over at his partner again. "You don't really think this Gael guy is a higher-up in the rebellion, do you?"

Hoyt glanced at him but didn't answer.

"I mean," Rodriguez continued, "he just doesn't seem bright enough for it, honestly. Seems more like he's just got himself some kind of fighting gimmick and is milking it for all it's worth on the arena circuit."

"Nobody's been able to lay a hand on him," Hoyt said. "It's a hell of a gimmick."

"Yeah, sure—I'll give you that," the other man replied. "But, even so, how great can it really be? Some piece of ancient tech? Sooner or later, somebody's gonna get him. Whether it's in the arena, or one of these assassins the organizers keep sending after him, or the Union itself, or—"

"We have a job to do," Hoyt interrupted. "We watch him. We listen to what he says, and what is said to him. And we report in. That's it."

"For now, anyway," Rodriguez said.

"For now, yeah."

The comm system built into the dashboard beeped and a red light flashed on it. Hoyt reached out and tapped it. A female voice filled the cabin.

"Unit 279. Control here. Report."

Hoyt glanced at his partner and cleared his throat. "This is Unit 279. We are currently tailing the person of interest. It appears he is headed to Newport Arena. We believe he has a match scheduled there."

"What has he been doing over the last hour?"

A chill descended within the cabin. Rodriguez looked at Hoyt. Hoyt blinked, then swallowed. "We, ah, we are not entirely certain, Control."

"Why not?"

"He went into a bar in Down Town. The Blue Dolphin. Something there blocked our audio snooper. Then he exited the establishment before we could take further action to surveil him."

There was a pause, and then a different female voice came on the line. They both recognized it immediately, and they both blanched.

"Officers, your job was to find out where Jack Gael was going, with whom he was meeting and what was said there."

Rodriguez had begun to sweat. Hoyt swallowed nervously and replied, "Understood, ma'am. We have him in our sights now. We won't lose him again."

"See that you do not." A pause, then, "If you are incapable of doing your job, you will be replaced. With extreme prejudice."

"Understood," Hoyt repeated, and the line went dead. He switched it off and turned to his partner. For the first time since they'd gone on shift that morning, he looked afraid.

"That was Denali, wasn't it?" Rodriguez said. "Xaveria Denali?"

"Pretty sure it was," Hoyt said. He blinked his eyes, then turned back and focused his vision tightly on the rear end of Jack Gael's vehicle, a short distance ahead.

"Rod," he said after a minute, his voice thin and shaky, "what the hell have we gotten ourselves into?"

4:

Jack parked his vehicle in the VIP lot next to the Newport Arena and climbed out. He could hear the sound of the crowd even through the walls of the massive edifice. A guard standing next to a door saw him, recognized him instantly and motioned for him to come inside.

As Jack entered the huge, indoor arena, he thought again about how quickly his life had changed in recent weeks. From a laborer barely getting by, he'd moved up to small-time arena fighter and now to celebrity combatant in the major leagues, insanely quickly. His time fighting in the crude outdoor facilities hadn't lasted two weeks. Once he'd bested all of their champions, the league had promoted him up to the big-time: the indoor halls like this one, where he would go up against the best fighters in North America.

He was late for the start of the event, but not for his match, which was scheduled for near the end. He was to fight three of the most dominant gladiators in the area—all at once. Of course, they were gladiators—but *he* was *The* Gladiator. Everyone called him that now. As if he were the only one, and everyone else was a pretender.

So far, it had worked out that way. No one had so much as laid a hand on him. Nobody could figure out exactly how he was doing it—how blows and blades and blasts from his opponents never seemed to touch him, or how he inflicted such devastating damage to them with mere punches and kicks and chops. Nor would they. He kept the belt covered up by his clothing and its existence a semi-secret. They all suspected he was using some kind of lost or forbidden technology, of course, but no one could prove it. And none of the scans they'd attempted had penetrated the invisible bubble that surrounded him constantly.

And he had become such a sensation, such a ratings draw, that they didn't dare ban him from competition. No, instead they kept up a steady stream of scary-looking opponents for him to destroy.

He knew the novelty would wear off soon, the ratings would drop, and the fame and money would surely end. But he intended to milk it for all it was worth, while the opportunity was there. He'd come from nothing, and to nothing he'd surely return. But he planned to enjoy the ride.

Clearly, someone else had decided he'd already outlived his welcome. He had no doubt the assassins who had visited him in his homes had been sent by the higher-ups in the arena league organization. If it had been the Union that wanted him eliminated, they probably would have simply sent a battalion of Kratons after him.

He idly wondered how he would fare against that kind of opposition. He hoped he would never have to find out. After all, he still had no real idea as to the upper limits of his protective bubble.

Mere minutes later, he would discover his hopes to be entirely in vain.

For now, however, he emerged from the dressing room and made his way up a long tunnel, emerging into the arena itself. The crowd took note of him as he walked up the ramp toward the combat area, and the building shook even harder as they unleashed cheers and boos in roughly equal measure upon him.

Jack idly raised one hand and waved, acknowledging them.

A league official saw him approaching and motioned for him to come over to a saved seat. He dropped heavily into it and gazed around, seeing the rows and rows of thousands of spectators surrounding the open, circular area more than fifty yards in diameter.

In the arena below them, two men in banded metal and leather armor were circling one another. Both were breathing heavily. They had suffered wounds and were bleeding profusely. Both held short, broad-bladed swords. As they moved, one and then the other would feint or lunge, only to be parried. It was clear neither of them relished the idea of going on the attack. Jack began to wonder if either had volunteered for the arena, or if both of them had been pressed into service, perhaps as punishment for crimes.

After more than a minute of this, the crowd grew impatient and more and more of them began to express that frustration in the form of a cascade of boos.

At that moment, a door slid open on the far side of the arena and a massive figure emerged.

Bald he was, and as he turned his gaze left and right, Jack could see the many rough scars on his face and around the back of his head. He wore only a sort of leather loincloth; the rest of his body was a mass of muscle covered in a thin layer of coarse, dark hair. He carried a sword the size of an ironing board in his right hand and a sort of mace in the other. His tiny eyes blazed with fire and fury.

With a guttural roar, the newcomer charged at the other two combatants, who appeared to have been caught completely by surprise.

A wrinkled, older man to Jack's right leaned over and said in low, excited tones that were barely audible over the noise of the crowd, "Skullcrusher will handle this right smartly!"

Jack ignored him. He looked on with mounting interest as the massive warrior slashed out with his sword, just missing the neck of the nearest man. The other leaped back before the blade could come his way, but Skullcrusher countered by bringing the mace down, right in his path. Only by the barest of margins did it miss, before crashing heavily into the ground.

Jack shook his head in disgust. "This isn't sporting," he said. "It's going to be a slaughter."

The old man to his right didn't reply. He only grinned his teeth wide at Jack before turning back to leer at the spectacle.

Jack got up and made his way in the direction of the dressing room, to get something to drink.

When he reemerged a few seconds later, a quick glance at the screens suspended around the building showed that the two challengers were still alive–though one of them had a couple of bleeding gashes in his side and neither looked particularly healthy. The fact that they'd managed to stay alive this long surprised Jack.

"You're going to fight *that* guy?"

Jack heard the child's voice asking him the question and he looked down and saw a little boy of about six standing next to him. He was holding a small sign with a crude drawing of a man in red, and the word GLADIATOR scrawled above it. Jack smiled at this.

"I'm gonna do my best," he said.

"Can you sign this?" the kid asked. He offered Jack a pen.

"Sure." Jack took the sign and the pen and quickly scratched out his new "celebrity autograph" he'd been working on lately.

"Why can't they hit you?" the kid asked as he did it.

Jack handed the items back over and looked at the kid. The young man didn't seem star-struck at all. One would think he chatted with his celebrity heroes every day.

"I've watched your last three matches, since they started showing you on the Big Show channel," the boy said, "and nobody ever hits you. They never lay a hand on you."

"Not if I can help it."

"But—*how?* Why *can't* they?"

"That's my secret," Jack replied with a wink.

"But—"

"If I tell you how the magic works, it might stop working!"

"Oh." The kid frowned deeply and looked away, then slowly nodded. "I guess I understand that," he said. "Okay. I wouldn't want your magic to go away."

"Me either," Jack said.

"Me either," said a woman's voice to his right.

Jack glanced up from the kid, who was already drifting away, having become fascinated by some other shiny object. Now Jack was looking at a tall, slender, redheaded woman in a short, purple dress. She flashed a bright smile at him. "Anna Joy," she said, offering a hand.

Jack took it, shook it, and held onto it for a moment longer. She reddened a bit more and smiled. Jack started to say something to her, but then realized he had no idea what to say. Being a celebrity was new to him. Having fans was new. A few weeks earlier, this woman never would've looked twice at him. It all seemed so bizarre.

He tried to come up with some clever or charming witticism, but before he could, the woman noticed something and pointed over his head. "Hey! It's us!"

Jack looked up at the nearest of the monitor screens hanging all around the perimeter of the arena. On it was his face. Not the bodies of the three fighters currently engaging in combat on the arena floor. *His* face.

Seeing this, the crowd woke up and started cheering and booing again.

"There he is," bellowed the voice of the announcer over the loudspeakers. "The Gladiator!"

The cheers and boos grew louder.

"The Gladiator is scheduled to take on the surviv–the *winner*–of this match. But I think we all know who that's going to be. So I'll tell ya what, folks–"

By this point, even the combatants had ceased their struggle and all three were listening with interest.

"—Why don't we just skip over the rest of this battle, and have the Gladiator go on out there and face *all three* of them at once?"

The crowd's noise amplified to a whole new level. No boos–not anymore. Now it was nothing but cheers. Apparently the announcer had hit upon something that appealed to nearly everyone present.

Nearly, but not all.

Jack cursed. He hadn't wanted to have to fight the other two guys. They would bring nothing to the contest, in terms of tactics or interest for the audience. And meanwhile he'd probably have to kill them, or at least severely disable them, in order to satisfy the terms of his financial arrangement with the arena owners. He'd been hoping ol' Skullcrusher would do them substantial but non-fatal damage, enough to prevent them from continuing on, and him from having to be involved with them at all.

"Sounds like they want you out there right now," the redhead said.

"Yeah," Jack said absently. Frowning, he looked toward the open arena, where the three fighters were still standing motionless, their own battle now forgotten. They were all staring up at the screen. Staring at Jack's face. And waiting.

Waiting for *him*.

CHAPTER 6

POPCORN — SKULLCRUSHER — ROBOTS — JOY

1:

Rodriguez spilled some of his popcorn as he pushed through the crowd and sidled up next to Hoyt. Cursing, he grabbed for it, but could only watch as a substantial portion of his snack fell on the floor.

Hoyt reached up and took the bag containing what was left from him. "Thanks," he said.

Frowning, Rodriguez leaned against the railing. He gazed out over the heads of all the people in the bowl of seats surrounding the arena floor. He and his partner had only been able to secure standing room tickets for tonight's event.

"There he is," the dark-haired cop said. He nodded at Jack, who was emerging from the tunnel and onto the arena floor. He was clad as always in his red laborer's jumpsuit. No armor, no weapons, nothing.

Hoyt watched him enter; watched as the other three men—all of them fearsome warriors, and one of them terrifying—backed slowly away.

"How can that scrawny guy be so dangerous?" he asked. "What's his deal?"

Rodriguez said nothing in response. The two officers continued to watch as the tableau unfolded.

2:

Jack suppressed a laugh.

In his first three or four bouts, his opponents—each of them far larger, more muscular, and better armed than him—had charged right at him, like lions spotting a lone gazelle on the plain. It had gotten each of them a resounding, painful defeat.

Now, at last, the opponents seemed to have learned.

Without a spoken word among them, the three warriors spread out, surrounding Jack. He let them. In other circumstances, a gladiator might be seriously concerned that his opponents had outflanked him. Given *his* circumstances, Jack was not concerned.

One of the two smaller fighters rushed him, coming from Jack's right. Jack dropped, spun around, and chopped out with a karate move he'd been practicing. The edge of his hand—or, rather, the invisible and utterly undetectable field of force surrounding it at a distance of mere millimeters—impacted the man in the chest and sent him stumbling backwards, all of his momentum gone in an instant. The guy choked and coughed, struggling to catch his breath.

There came a smattering of cheers and applause from the audience.

Barely had that clash resolved than the other of the two "slightly larger than normal" guys came at him. This one took a boxer's stance and jabbed with compact, tight punches. By the time the fifth one made impact, the man's brow was furrowed and his knuckles were bleeding. Jack stepped forward and backhanded him, hurling him through the air and bringing him to a crashing halt against the far wall.

The crowd erupted at this. Most of it came in the form of cheers, but a noticeable proportion of the sound was booing. Jack had noticed in the last week or so that he had accumulated a sizable fan base, but quite a few people at every match also very clearly wanted him to *lose*. And not just to lose but to get beaten down.

He'd decided that many of the devotees of arena combat enjoyed the idea of a world where everything was black or white, good guy and bad guy, and where most disagreements could be settled by a good fist fight. It made the world a simpler place, and they liked it, as long as it was their guy giving out the butt-kickings. Many of the attendees and probably many more watching at home desperately wanted Jack to receive one of those butt-kickings. It frustrated them no end that he kept winning—and winning almost effortlessly.

Jack surveyed the damage he'd done so far, and only then did the sounds around him reach his ears and his brain. The crowd had elevated itself to another level and was now howling with glee; the announcer was calling out fanciful descriptions of the moves Jack had used.

Jack turned to face the monstrous third figure.

"Okay, Mr. Skullcrusher. Or can I call you 'Skull'?" He smiled. "Ready to take your beating, too?"

The huge gladiator growled in his throat; the sound resembled a bulldozer or steam shovel firing up. His big fingers loosened and tightened on the hilts of his weapons, over and over. And then he started forward. The monstrous figure seemed as inevitable and unstoppable as a tsunami rolling in. Jack mused that nearly anyone else would be terrified to be in his shoes at that moment.

Jack was not terrified. He sighed and almost reluctantly raised his hands in a fighting stance. Around him, the crowd was buzzing. Everyone knew he had easily defeated other gladiators, but Skullcrusher was in a class by himself. At that moment, Jack remembered the admonition given to him by John Smith. He didn't recall the exact words—the guy had talked and talked forever—but it was something like, *"Don't make it look too easy."*

Whatever nonsense Smith had been going on about otherwise, from time travel to immortality to who knew what, Jack understood he'd probably been right about *that*. It made sense. If he just took down this bruiser with a couple of punches, the crowd would feel let down and maybe cheated. And in that situation, the arena managers would probably determine Jack was cheating, even if they couldn't say how. That being the case, they might be reluctant to keep bringing him back. And paying him.

And so, with all of this in mind, Jack changed his tactics from offensive to defensive. He lowered his hands and allowed Skullcrusher to charge into him. The two of them collided with massive force, tumbled head over heels and rolled across the dirt and sand enclosure until they both smacked into the far wall.

Jack managed to extricate himself from the other man and stood, waiting for him to get up.

Instead of rising, however, Skullcrusher suddenly unleashed his massive sword, swinging it out in a broad arc that culminated in Jack's left side, just below his armpit. There it struck; it *lodged*.

The crowd gasped. This was new. Never before had a blow from an opponent done anything other than bounce cleanly off of Jack.

For a long moment the two of them engaged in a bizarre tug-of-war. Jack tried to pull away from the sword even as Skullcrusher gripped it with both hands. Finally Jack twisted to his left and the sword was wrenched from the larger man's grasp.

Skullcrusher scrambled to his feet as quickly as he was able. He stared in naked astonishment at the sword—the one the size of an ironing board—for, at first glance, it looked to be lodged deep between Jack's ribs. He waited for the smaller man to fall, for surely this was a killing blow that he had struck.

But Jack didn't fall. He just stood there, the sword projecting out from his side.

The crowd's excited noises became a puzzled hum. For now, on the video replay boards, they could see that the sword hadn't actually pierced Jack's skin at all. The blade was trapped a mere half-inch from his side, and it literally hovered in midair, moving as he moved. It was as if Jack wore an invisible coat and the sword had become stuck in it.

Puzzled by the sounds coming from the audience, as well as by the facial expression of his opponent, Jack looked down at the sword—becoming aware of it stuck there for possibly the first time. His eyes widened, and then he motioned with one hand. The big blade fell to the ground as if he'd been holding it in his grasp and had then let go.

Skullcrusher continued to stare back at him, mouth agape.

Jack motioned to the sword. "Sorry," he said, "that was an accident." And then, when the dumbfounded big man didn't respond, "You can go ahead and pick it up."

The mystified, musclebound monster had just bent over to pick up his weapon when the ceiling collapsed and the army of killer robots rained down on them.

3:

For a moment the crowd must have assumed it was all part of the show.

An explosion shattered a large section of the roof high above the arena, showering the audience as well as the gladiators with chunks of debris.

Automatically Jack dropped into a crouch, reacting to the unexpected shock. Skullcrusher backed away toward the edge of the arena floor, just as more jagged pieces of masonry smashed down. The other two gladiators, still struggling to rise after Jack's previous actions, were caught flat-footed. Without thinking, Jack caused the shield around him to extend out and over the nearest of the two, saving the man from a particularly big and jagged chunk of concrete that surely would have smashed his skull to jelly. As the piece of concrete struck something unseen a mere foot above his head and then bounced harmlessly away, the man blinked and looked around, uncertain as to what had happened.

Unfortunately, Jack was not in time to save the other gladiator, as an even larger piece of debris struck just beside him, knocking him down, and then another couple of pieces smashed into his chest and face. Blood splattered across the sandy ground.

After only a few seconds of cheers and applause, the crowd came to realize that this was no act. At that, their whoops changed to screams. The ones not killed or badly injured by the initial attack began to trample one another in an effort to escape the building. Shouts of terror competed with the crashing sounds of falling concrete and metal, only to both be drowned out by the roar of rocket engines as the first wave of Kratons descended through the hole they'd blasted in the ceiling.

Jack looked up just in time to see a pair of the killer robots zooming directly towards him. In the back of his mind he registered that these particular Kratons were gleaming gold from head to toe, meaning the elite units. They had stronger than normal armor and equipped with bigger and more powerful weapons. Jack saw that they would reach him well before he could make it to the tunnel, so he turned and put his back to the arena wall. There he assumed a fighting stance.

The nearest Kraton directed its right arm at him and fired a blindingly bright red beam: coherent light. Perhaps this approach might have worked if Jack had not seen it coming, though he wasn't at all certain. Perhaps the shield around him would have perceived the beam as only visible light and permitted it to pass through and inside, there to strike him. Jack's reaction, however—knowing it was beyond deadly to him—could have caused the shield to alter its properties enough to deflect that particular wavelength harmlessly away. Whatever the case, the beam did not penetrate the shield and did not strike him.

Before the other two Kratons could attack, Jack raced forward and swung a roundhouse punch at the one that had fired at him. His encased fist caught the Kraton in its metallic jaw and separated its head from its shoulders. The head spun through the air, hit the ground and rolled to a stop in front of one of the video cameras broadcasting the events to the public. The camera zoomed in momentarily on the golden Kraton head, its formerly blood-red eyes now dark—"The Gladiator has decapitated an Elite Unit," screamed the TV announcer—before returning to the battle happening in the center of the arena.

The other two Kratons had landed and were facing Jack, even as more Kratons dropped down through the new hole in the roof. Jack raced toward the nearest one and tried another move he'd been practicing: he dropped low and swept his right leg at his opponent. His foot came up short by at least a… *foot*… but it didn't matter; the invisible aura surrounding it clipped the Kraton's golden legs and chopped them off at the knees. Squawking in rage, the robot tumbled to the ground and lay face-down, sparks shooting from its stumps.

Out of the corner of his eye, Jack saw his former opponent, Skullcrusher, squaring off with the third Kraton. He started to intervene, then thought better of it. Instead he allowed the monstrous human to get in a couple of licks, enough to maintain his honor and dignity. But when the robot knocked the man back and then leveled a particle beam cannon at him, Jack reached out with his right hand and, across a distance of some twenty feet, crushed the automaton's skull.

The three initial attackers having been defeated, Jack at last allowed himself to look out at the scene all around. It was worse than he had feared.

Throughout the ring of seats, dozens of spectators had been badly injured or killed by falling debris. Most of the survivors had fled, but the second wave of Kratons was arriving and, with it, more panic among those still in the arena. At that moment Jack saw the redheaded woman in purple he'd been speaking with earlier. She was standing there, seemingly frozen in place, staring at something in front of her, and looking as if she wanted to scream, but couldn't remember how. Meanwhile, another trio of Kratons was closing in on her area of the stands.

Jack made it there in only a few seconds. He placed himself between the woman and the advancing robots, ready to defend her. And then he saw what she'd been looking at. What was so horrifying to her.

It was the little boy. The one who'd had the homemade sign of him. The one who wanted his autograph.

The little boy was dead. Apparently crushed by falling debris.

Jack's vision blurred. He saw red. Blood red. And he saw something else: the three alien robots. Robots that very likely had brought the roof down in the first place.

At that moment in time, all Jack cared about was revenge. All he wanted to do was destroy those robots.

He sprinted towards them, catching them by surprise. In all the time the Kratons had been on Earth, no human had ever done that.

Before any of the three could level its weapons at him, he was in their midst, punching and kicking and chopping with every move he'd managed to learn during his brief career as a gladiator. He felt no need to be sporting about it this time. No need to make anything look competitive for the cameras. He wasn't even sure if the cameras were still on, or still working. No, now he felt absolutely free to deal with these particular robots in as quick and harsh a manner as he could.

The three Kratons never knew what hit them. He punched and chopped and kicked and slashed. Approximately ten seconds later, all three of them lay in sparking, smoking ruins.

Looking up from his handiwork, he became aware of another wave of robots descending through the hole in the roof. This time it was a mixture of the golden elites and the silver rank-and-file units. It appeared the Union was sending their entire local complement of robot warriors on this mission—whatever it was.

Just as he started to brace himself to take them all on, he realized the redheaded woman was shouting from behind him. He turned around and saw that she was confronted by two more of the robots, their clawlike metallic talons extended out and flexing as they closed in on her. He started to charge at them. Then he realized that, by the time he did, the massive wave now descending would reach him, and possibly bury him under its mass. He still wasn't entirely sure what his full capabilities were, and he worried the Kratons might decide to form an unbreakable weight on top of him, and simply never move until he died of thirst or starvation, or perhaps suffocation.

He had only an instant to act. He hesitated for just a fraction of that instant, because to do what he had to do, he would be violating one of his primary rules; one of the first promises he'd made to himself.

The Kratons charged at the redhead. She closed her eyes and screamed.

4:

Anna Joy closed her eyes and waited. She wasn't aware she was screaming until a few seconds later. A few seconds after she should most assuredly be dead.

Abruptly she stopped screaming and opened her eyes.

The Gladiator had his back to her. He was in a crouch, positioned between herself and a half-dozen more robots, fighting them. Winning.

She looked around. The two that had just attacked her lay shattered in pieces, their insides and outsides strewn across the walkway.

They had charged at her but they had never struck her.

Somehow, they had been deflected away at the very last instant. They had bounced off of her.

But how could that be?

She understood it then: That was the same thing that happened to the robots that attacked the Gladiator.

Somehow he had shared that ability, that protection, with her.

She wrinkled her brow. Had he left it in place? Was it still there now? Or had he taken it back once she was safe from that attack?

She watched him fighting the Kratons for a few seconds and paid particular attention to how his hands struck at them but never seemed to actually touch them.

Then she squatted down next to the remains of one of the Kratons and swung her fist at a metal skull. Before she could touch it, the skull went flying away, as if she'd hit it with a baseball bat.

She raised her hand up before her and studied it carefully.

Nothing.

There was nothing there to indicate she was currently surrounded by some sort of force field.

And yet she knew it to be true.

Gladiator had given a portion of his power to her, or was at least extending whatever was around himself to also cover her.

She considered this and smiled.

Then she waited patiently while he finished off the last of the Kratons.

When he was done, and the pile of deactivated and half-trashed robots stood some fifteen feet tall, Anna Joy rushed over to him and embraced him. He was caught by surprise to such a degree he offered no resistance when she followed that by leaning in and kissing him.

CHAPTER 7

SURVIVORS — INSIDE — OFF THE GRID — GO HOME

1:

Hoyt and Rodriguez barely made it out of the arena alive, but they did survive the Kraton attack. Somehow.

The two men sat in their police cruiser, bruised and bloodied, their uniforms torn and singed. A fire had broken out in the office area of the massive arena building, toward the end of the conflict, and they'd done their part to contain it until the firefighters arrived. At that point, they'd exited the building, counting their lucky stars that they'd survived at all.

Now Hoyt was yelling into the radio: "No, captain—*I'm* telling *you*, it was a disaster! The Union dropped a whole crap-ton of Kratons on the arena! They nearly killed everybody!"

"They just attacked?" The captain's voice was strained and frantic over the line. "They weren't provoked somehow? They didn't think something was going on—some kind of insurgency—that demanded they sort it out?"

"Provoked?" Hoyt was incredulous. "They weren't even *there* until they suddenly came blasting down through the roof! And we were there, watching everything. It was business as usual—until it wasn't."

Silence on the other end for a few seconds, then, "Alright," the captain replied. "I'm sure the Union had their reasons for it, and it's not my job to second-guess our benevolent leaders. I'll look into it, of course, but you two are not to say anything else about it. Understood?"

Hoyt glanced at Rodriguez, who simply stared back at him, open-mouthed, eyes wide. "You've got to be kidding," the other officer whispered.

Hoyt straightened up again and said into the radio, "We understand. But—Captain—should we—"

He was interrupted as a harsh female voice came on the line.

"Do you have eyes on the Gladiator at this moment?"

Hoyt swallowed hard. He looked at his partner again; the man's expression had only grown more pronounced.

"We do not," he managed to say.

"Why not? You were to monitor him. Watch his every move. And report back."

Hoyt mouthed the name "Denali" at Rodriguez. The other man nodded slowly, and added a silent expletive.

"With all due respect, ma'am—we nearly got killed just now! The Kratons—"

"The Kratons do not concern me," Denali broke in. "You are to locate the Gladiator—Jack Gael—and keep him under tight surveillance until you receive further instructions. Do you understand?"

"I—um—yes, ma'am," Hoyt replied.

"Are you certain that you do?"

"I am, ma'am. Yes." Sweat was running down his face. "It will be as you say."

Denali cut the connection from her end and the radio went silent.

"Good lord," Rodriguez muttered. "She's really interested in Gael."

"You saw why," Hoyt snapped back at him. "We all did—before the attack. He's got some kind of gimmick, and Her Majesty wants it. Bad."

Rodriguez nodded at this before turning to gaze out the window of the cruiser at the dark alleyway where they'd parked.

"Now what are we gonna do?" he asked a few seconds later.

Hoyt appeared to have come to a decision. "We find Gael," he said.

Rodriguez groaned. "I'm not sure which would be worse—disappointing the sub-administrator again, or trying to take the Gladiator into custody."

"The worst Gael can do is kick our tails," Hoyt replied as he lit a cigarette. "Denali, though? Honest to God, I don't want to find out."

Rodriguez offered a reluctant nod of agreement.

Hoyt fired up the engine and the cruiser came to life. It zipped out onto the street, its red and blue lights flaring in the darkness.

2:

Jack led the redheaded woman along shadowy alleyways until they reached the back door of his new home.

He'd insisted on hanging around the arena, helping as many trapped and injured people as he could. By the time the last of the Kratons had been destroyed, however, his vehicle also had been ruined. It was just one more casualty of the battle that had raged inside and outside of the building.

For his part, Skullcrusher had survived as well, and he'd walked away in the opposite direction, though not before sharing his contact information with Jack. As it turned out, the monstrous fighter was more intelligent and more intelligible than Jack had expected. He also seemed to have developed a healthy respect for Jack's combat prowess, and vowed to fight alongside him, one day in the future, if the opportunity arose.

"And it will," Skullcrusher had said, clasping Jack's hand—or at least clasping the space about two millimeters around it—in his giant mitts. "I can feel it. Something's coming. It's gonna swallow you and me up. Maybe we'll both come out the other side. Maybe we'll be the survivors. The winners." He'd flashed Jack a toothy grin. "Or maybe not."

Jack had taken this in and nodded. "I think you're right, that something is coming," he'd said. "And I'd rather have you with me than against me."

Skullcrusher had grinned at that, smacked Jack on the back in a friendly gesture that would've paralyzed anyone not currently protected by an invisible, impervious shield, and then walked away, disappearing into the night.

Now Jack opened the door to his small house and ushered the woman inside. He offered her a drink—"Afraid all I have is beer and Fizzbo"— and she accepted a beer. As he handed it over, he noted, "We haven't been formally introduced. I'm Jack. Jack Gael."

"Anna Joy," she said with a smile, as if anticipating some sort of half-clever remark or observation; as if used to such reactions. She seemed taken aback when his only response was to clasp her hand, shake it, and say, "Good to know you, Anna."

They were finishing their second beers when Jack realized the woman was still inside the bubble with him. He'd mentally caused it to expand around her during the attack, and apparently it had continued to cover her the entire time since. After all, he'd never mentally canceled the command. For perhaps the twentieth time since he'd first put on the silver belt, he found himself wondering what exactly its limits truly were.

She'd sat beside him on his new, red and gold sofa and was sliding closer. His immediate instinct was to retract the force bubble so that she was no longer inside it. She was, after all, the very first person he'd allowed inside there with him for more than a split-second. Of course, it was entirely likely she didn't even know she was inside a bubble.

As he considered these thoughts, she scrunched up tightly to him and turned her head slightly, so that she was gazing up into his eyes. At that point, all thoughts of pushing her to the other side of an impenetrable wall vanished from his mind. He'd been alone for so long. In that moment, he would have moved heaven and earth for her—for a woman he scarcely even knew. He leaned his head down and kissed her, and she kissed back. From there, things got rather intense.

Eventually they both fell asleep, on top of the covers, only a thin blanket over them both. Jack slept more deeply than he had in ages. Likely he would have slept clean through till morning, but he was awoken abruptly while it was still dark outside by something tugging very gently at him. He opened one eye and saw a mass of red hair at the level of his chest. Anna Joy was her name, he remembered. What was she doing?

The belt, he realized with a start. She was trying to unhook the belt from his waist. He was still wearing it, mainly because he had yet to figure out how to take it off. Of course, given the number of would-be assassins that had visited him of late, he wasn't particularly unhappy to have it on all the time. He knew that he might have taken it off with Anna, but he didn't know how, so he'd left it—and it alone—on his person. Which had looked odd, but she hadn't seemed to mind at the time. In fact, he realized now, she'd almost studiously avoided giving the impression she was even aware it was there. As if she didn't want him to think she was thinking about it.

Now she was most *definitely* thinking about it. She was, in fact, trying her best to *remove* it.

He sat up suddenly and she scrambled back away from him on the bed, making him acutely, distractedly aware that she was wearing only her undergarments. The distraction disappeared as soon as he met her flashing green eyes and saw a murderous intensity in them.

"What are you doing?" he asked, though he knew the answer.

She reached into her purple dress where it lay in a pile to one side. When she brought the hand back out, it held a knife with a very thin but very dangerous-looking blade. She brandished it at him.

"It's the belt, isn't it?" She smiled. "That's what's creating this… this wall around us." She reached out with her free hand and tapped at what looked like thin air. There was no sound, but her hand was definitely coming into contact with an invisible barrier.

Wrestling with sadness, disappointment and anger, Jack simply glared back at her.

"Just give me the belt and I'll be gone," she said. "Nobody has to get hurt."

Too late, Jack thought. But, "I really liked you," he said out loud.

"Well, I really like your little device," Anna said. "So hand it over, and I'll leave you alone."

"I'm not giving you my belt," Jack said. "I couldn't if I wanted to—not that I want to. I don't know how to take it off."

She blinked and frowned at him. "Seriously?" she said.

Jack nodded. "It didn't come with instructions."

Anna's eyes flicked rapidly from one spot in the bedroom to another as her mind raced. At last she announced, "I'm sorry, Jack, but I don't have much of a choice in this. I suppose in that case I'll have to cut if off of you."

She leapt at him, knife first. Before Jack could react, the blade was plunged into his side.

Jack screamed. Everything that happened after that, happened instinctively for him.

In one motion and with barely a half-conscious thought, he shoved Anna away from him. He ordered the protective bubble to allow her out, even as he drew it in tighter around himself.

A split-second later, however—and purely as a defensive reflex—he willed it to be even more solid; impenetrable. This instantaneously increased its solidity from that of air to that of diamond.

Stumbling backwards from Jack's push, the woman had passed about halfway through the contracting bubble wall when it hardened, cutting her in half.

Jack saw what had happened to her, saw all the blood from his own wound mingling with the blood from Anna, threw up, and passed out.

3:

The man who called himself John Smith had also been in the arena when the Kratons attacked. He'd barely escaped intact, and was furious; he'd come to hate it when completely new things popped up that hadn't happened to him before.

He'd seen Jack leave with the redhead in the purple dress, and he hadn't quite been sure what to make of that. But then again, he was working entirely without a net now. In no previous trip through the timeline had Jack still been working as a gladiator this far into things. In no previous timeline had he rejected—utterly dismissed—Smith's appeal in the first place. Having no idea what was going to happen next, he had decided to sit back and simply observe, for now.

That had changed when the man named Bennie had frantically called him a few hours after the disastrous events at the arena. Bennie was Jack's friend, and he'd gone over to Jack's new house to ask him about all the crazy things that had happened, only to find him passed out on the floor, mostly naked, with a knife in his side—and two halves of an also-mostly-naked woman on the floor. Understandably horrified, Bennie hadn't at first known what to do. Then he'd found Smith's card on Jack's kitchen table and remembered him from earlier, and had called him.

The main thing Smith had done after using Bennie's hasty directions to come over—after putting a blanket over the dead woman—was to try to remove the knife from Jack's side and dress the wound. Of course this was impossible, because of the shield bubble. Only Jack could give orders to the belt, and Jack was unconscious and going down fast.

This was all incredibly frustrating to Smith, because currently there were several metaphorical clocks ticking, the time on all of them growing short, and Jack's remaining lifespan was only one of them.

After much effort and calling out by both Bennie and Smith, Jack had awakened long enough to become aware of his predicament. Delirious, barely lucid, he'd strung together in his mind a very weak sense of his plight, and the belt had apparently understood. It had responded by contracting tight to Jack's skin, surrounding the knife and leveraging it out.

The bleeding increased.

Smith shouted to Jack to wake up and turn off the bubble. Jack drifted in and out of consciousness for a time. Smith had begun to fear the bubble might be protecting a corpse for who-knew-how-many years to come. Finally, Jack drifted back to his senses and ordered the belt to stop the bleeding. Smith wasn't sure how this was accomplished, but something the belt did—constricting around and into the wound, perhaps?—had managed the feat.

Smith was intrigued. In all the years he'd passed the belt over to variations of Jack, and to years before that when he'd given it to other people, he'd never seen it actively try to save its owner's life in that way. It made him wonder what else the belt could do, that neither he nor the other owners had ever made it do.

The bleeding having stopped, Jack simply lay there, unconscious, in a slowly-drying pool of blood. Smith reached down to touch him and found the bubble around him had everywhere retracted to only a few millimeters from the surface of his skin. It was as if Jack had been covered in a few thick coats of very clear lacquer.

Smith considered this, then looked at Bennie. The larger man was seemingly distraught at the plight of his friend.

"Do you want to help Jack?" he asked.

"Sure I do," Bennie replied.

"The Union knows where he lives," Smith said. "They had to be behind what happened earlier tonight, because they control the Kratons. I have no doubts they will try to kill him again. And they will keep on doing it until they figure out a way to get to him."

"They can't hurt him," Bennie protested. "Nobody can."

In response to this, Smith simply pointed down to Jack's prone, unconscious body, and all the blood pooled beneath it.

"Yeah, okay, you're right," Bennie muttered. He looked up at Smith. "So we need to take him someplace safe, where he can recover."

Smith started to say something in reply, but then Bennie squatted down, attempting to lift Jack. It didn't work; the shield made the unconscious body feel like it was covered in oil. Giving up at last, Bennie stood and shrugged.

"Okay, Mr. Smith," he said. "What do we do?"

Smith frowned at this. He leaned in and studied Jack's condition one more time. The blond man was pale but didn't appear dead quite yet.

Sorry I got you into this, Jack, he thought to himself. He looked again at all the blood. *And sorry this happened. But we* need *you.*

At that moment, a queasy feeling washed over Smith. The room shifted, as though an earthquake were happening, but he was the only one experiencing it. Light flared all around him. He stumbled back a step, feeling an overwhelming sense of danger. His every sense suddenly screamed, "Time to go!"

He glanced at his watch and saw that it was indeed time for him to get out of there. Which meant he couldn't be of any more help to Jack—not at the moment. No, like it or not, that would have to be left to Bennie.

Smith shook his head, and silently added, *Sorry for* this*, too, Jack.*

Then he stepped back into the shadows, leaving Bennie and Jack alone in the middle of the living room.

"What should we do?" Bennie repeated.

When no answer came back, Bennie looked up and around and realized he was alone. He started to call out for the other man, but he never got the chance.

The front door exploded in.

4:

A short while earlier: Dr. Howard Torrens clicked off his computer and stood, stretching. It was time to go home.

No, scratch that–he remembered with annoyance that Xaveria Denali had all-but-ordered him to go and visit Jack Gael that evening. Sighing, he ran his hand through his graying hair, took off his white lab coat and put on a heavier overcoat, then exited his lab. He allowed himself one last glance back at the big, silver orb that rested in one corner. Taller than a man and just as wide as it was tall, that strange object had occupied that space–and his thoughts–for many years. It had been discovered in one of the earliest "mining" operations, and had proven to be utterly impenetrable and impervious to any forms of probing, up to and including explosives, lasers, particle beams and good old-fashioned mechanical compactors. No, nothing had so much as scratched or dented its perfect, mirrored surface.

He shook his head at it as he did nearly every evening before he left his lab, as if acknowledging that it remained a complete mystery to him, just as it had to everyone before him who had possessed it.

Closing the door, he made his way out of the building and down to the garage, where he located his hovercar and fired it up. He did not immediately turn on the news–and therefore, at first, he had no idea of what had just happened at the Newport Arena across town. When he finally bothered to check the headlines, he put two and two together and stomped on the accelerator.

Minutes later, his hovercar swooped down at reckless speed and came to a halt at the address Denali had given him; the current location of Jack Gael, the mysteriously impervious man. He was somehow not terribly surprised to see the front door shattered and dislocated. He hopped out of the hovercar and ran up to the now-open doorway. Inside he saw two men in rumpled suits standing there, looking around, while a larger man in an industrial laborer's jumpsuit stood across from them with his hands up. On the floor lay two further items of note: an apparently unconscious man in a jumpsuit, a bloody wound in his side, and a blanket covering… *something*… that was also exceptionally bloody.

Torrens felt himself growing sick. He took a step back from the doorway, but then one of the men in suits turned and saw him.

"Stop right there," the man called out. As he turned, Torrens saw he held a pistol in his right hand, and now it was pivoting around to point at him.

Torrens raised both hands. As he did so, he nodded toward the shattered door. "Was that necessary?"

"What?" The one with the gun frowned.

"Was it necessary to blow up the front door? He doesn't look in any condition to have denied you entry."

The one with the gun continued to frown. The other one said, "Do you know who this guy is? What he can do?"

Torrens thought this over and nodded. "Fair point," he said.

Both men ignored this concession. "So," the one not currently aiming a weapon at him said, "who are you, then?"

By way of response, Torrens started to reach into his jacket with his right hand.

"Hey. Careful there," the man in the suit said, tensing.

Smiling, Torrens brought out a small leather case. He opened it, revealing his identity and rank within the Union bureaucracy. He doubted they got to see that level of clearance very often. "I'm Dr. Howard Torrens," he said. "You two are detectives, I take it?"

"That's right," the nearer one replied. "I'm Lieutenant Hoyt." He nodded toward his partner, who sported a big, dark mustache. "That's Lieutenant Rodriguez." He still hadn't lowered the gun.

"I'm glad to meet you," Torrens said. "And–stop pointing your weapon at me."

Now that Hoyt understood that this man was his superior, his nanites and his Union conditioning caused him to react to the command as if Grand Overlord Gorvag himself had issued it. He blinked, as if only then realizing he was holding the pistol, then lowered it and almost set it down on the floor, before apparently coming back to his senses and simply putting it away in his shoulder holster.

"We work for Sub-Administrator Denali," Rodriguez said, in a tone that indicated he felt that should make an impression on Torrens, no matter how high up the bureaucratic ladder he happened to reside.

Indeed, the scientist nodded at this, then replied, "So do I. Which means we're part of the same organization." He smiled again at the two cops; the smile held no warmth. "But you might notice the purple chevron next to my picture there. That means you're working for *me* now."

"But–" Hoyt began.

Torrens met his eyes briefly. "Yes? Detective?" He looked away, as he rested his hands on his hips. "You have an objection?"

Hoyt glanced at Rodriguez, then back at Torrens. "Well–it's just that we were ordered by the sub-administrator to keep a watch on the Gladiator–Jack Gael–personally."

Torrens nodded impatiently. "Yes, yes. That's fine. I'm not ordering you away." He looked at them again. "Unless you're causing me a problem–?"

The two detectives looked at one another. Hoyt shrugged. He looked back at Torrens. "No, sir. No argument here, sir."

"Good," Torrens said. "And it's 'Doctor,'" he added absently as he moved into the living room. He gave Bennie a quick glance; the big man stood stock-still, almost at attention. Torrens frowned, then ignored him and looked down at the two bodies–one covered and one uncovered–on the floor. He pointed at the unconscious blond man. "That's Gael there, yes?"

"It is," Hoyt said. Then added, "Doctor."

Torrens nodded to himself. Then he motioned toward the bloody blanket, and the stains steadily spreading out from under it. "And what's the story here?"

A pause, then, "We're not exactly sure," Rodriguez answered. "It looks like she was cut in ha–" He stopped in mid-utterance and stepped toward Torrens, waving his hand, as the gray-haired man was squatting down and reaching out. "You don't want to move that blanket, Doctor. You–"

Torrens ignored him, grabbed one corner of the blanket and attempted to toss it aside. It was stuck. Grimacing, he pulled it up and away.

To their credit, the two police detectives managed to remain stoic, but it was obvious to anyone who might be looking on that they were sickened by the sight. Torrens, on the other hand, exhibited no reaction whatsoever. He looked down at the remains of the redheaded woman for a few seconds, pursed his lips, nodded to himself as if he'd just figured something important out, and laid the blanket back over the body parts again.

Torrens stood, ran his hand through his hair, and thought for a long moment, while the two detectives stood there waiting.

"Call in a disposal team for the body," he ordered.

Hoyt nodded.

The scientist turned his attention to Jack. "He's still alive, right?"

"We–we *think* so, Doctor," Rodriguez answered. "But it's hard to be sure of anything, with him. We can't…"

"You can't touch him. Yes. I know." Torrens was tapping on Jack Gael's leg like it was a solid marble tabletop. It certainly felt more like a piece of stone or metal than it did like a human leg. "Remarkable," he muttered. He looked up at them. "But you can pick him up, right?"

"We–haven't tried."

"Try."

The two men squatted down and reached underneath the prone figure. Their hands popped up in the air when they tried to grip him.

"It's like trying to get a grip on ice," Rodriguez said after their third failed attempt.

"Slick as glass," Hoyt added under his breath. "I wish I knew what the deal is with him."

Torrens thought quickly. He believed he needed to get Gael back to the lab quickly, and for more than one reason. Yes, he feared the man might bleed to death if something wasn't done soon, and he figured he had a much better chance of addressing that problem with his equipment around him. But also, he worried that a platoon of Kratons might roll up at any moment and try to take over the case. Or just end the case by blowing everyone away. Yes, they all supposedly worked for the same government, the same masters. But if the Kratons would just wantonly assault one of the arenas—and during a live broadcast—as they'd done that evening, and killing any number of civilians in the process... Well, who knew what they might be capable of, or what agenda they might now be following?

"A bedspread or blanket," Torrens said. He looked around and decided where the main bedroom was. He pointed. "Get one."

One of the cops dashed into the bedroom and emerged moments later with a broad, blue and yellow comforter that had to fit a king-sized bed. He stood there, holding it, staring at Torrens.

"Put it under him," the scientist instructed.

"Oh! Yeah."

Rodriguez knelt down and started pushing the heavy cloth under Gael's body. Hoyt got down in one knee and grabbed it. He pulled it until roughly half was on either side and underneath the unconscious body. Then they both stood, reached down, grabbed the comforter with all four hands and lifted. Up went Jack Gael, stiff as a board. The field around him—whatever it was—didn't seem to extend very far out from the surface of his skin. At least, not at the moment. Blood flowed in rivulets, but didn't drip; not a single drop. Instead they appeared somehow suspended in midair, close about him.

"I'm worried about that wound he's suffered," Torrens said, mostly to himself. "Alright, good—carry him out to your car. Then follow me back to headquarters."

The cops looked at each other again. They appeared as if they were about to object.

"I'll call Ms. Denali," he said soothingly. "I'm sure she'll appreciate all your hard work this evening."

Another second of hesitation, and then the two officers carried Jack Gael toward the blasted-open doorway.

"Oh," Torrens said, looking back at Bennie, who hadn't moved or spoken the entire time. "What's the story with this guy?"

The two detectives stopped and looked back at him, but neither said anything.

"You interrogated him, right?"

"We, uh–we just got here ourselves," Hoyt replied.

Torrens stepped toward the big guy. "Who are you?"

"I'm Bennie. I'm Jack's friend. I came over and saw he was hurt, and…" His voice trailed off and he looked around, as if suddenly wondering where someone else had gotten off to. Then he straightened again. He looked down at the other bloody body—the one covered by a blanket. "And I saw other stuff, too."

Torrens considered the guy for a few more seconds. His skin was starting to crawl, and he figured it was because he was so sure the Kratons were on their way. They could come swooping down at any moment, just as they had at the arena.

There surely wasn't time to adequately question this man here and now. Did he want to drag him to headquarters, and keep him locked up there for who knew how long, while Torrens dealt with far more important and pressing things—like the invisible barrier around Jack Gael?

He made a quick decision. He hoped he wouldn't regret it.

"Get out of here," he told Bennie.

Oddly, the big man didn't instantly bow or salute or spout the typical, "Yes, sir," as usually happened when Torrens or some other official caused a worker's nanites to trigger. Instead, the big man just gazed back at him for a moment, frowning dully.

"You mean—I can *go*?" he asked at length.

Puzzled—but not enough to risk exposure to the Kratons a second longer—he nodded and waved dismissively. "Yes," he said, his tone now conveying annoyance and weariness. "Go home."

The big man raced out the door.

Torrens looked around one last time, then exited the house himself. He heard the sound of a siren approaching. That wouldn't be Kratons, it would be the clean-up crew he'd ordered the detectives to call.

Go home, he'd told the strange guy back there.

He wished he could go home, himself.

But the thought of figuring out Jack Gael's mysterious invisible shield did put a little bit of a spring in his step.

He was in his hovercar and headed for his headquarters, the detectives' car trailing along behind, a good forty-five seconds before a phalanx of Kratons descended on the now-empty house.

CHAPTER 8

THE BLACK KRATON – DIAGNOSTIC MODE – KRENZ – EXIT

1:

Dr. Erich Krenz felt the presence behind him before he saw it. The little whining sounds he associated with the servomotors of the regular Kratons weren't emitted by this one. No, this Kraton moved silently, and quite stealthily when it wanted to.

Of course, that was only one of several very obvious differences between it and the other robotic servants of the Union.

For one thing, this Kraton was jet black, which made its burning crimson eyes stand out visually in ways Krenz found terrifying.

For another, this Kraton was taller than the others–more than seven feet tall, and correspondingly bigger overall. More menacing. Again–terrifying.

Sitting at his control console, Krenz could feel the robotic monster looming over him. Slowly he turned around and saw that he was facing its stomach area, so he looked up, until his eyes met those burning coals that gazed down at him.

"Dr. Krenz," the Kraton's mechanical voice droned, *"we await your latest update on the project you have been assigned."* The robot clenched one fist and shook it for emphasis. *"The Union*

wishes for greater control over the human labor pool. You will accomplish this."

Krenz blanched. "I–I have been researching several ideas; considering a number of approaches. But they all turn out to be too dangerous to the population."

"Dangerous?" the robot rumbled.

"Every version I have tested results in a high possibility of fatality for the human subjects. I am attempting to reduce that side effect to an acceptable level."

"Acceptable?" The robot sounded personally offended. *"Who decides what is acceptable? You?"*

"I–err, no, of course not," Krenz stammered. "But we can't just kill off two-thirds of the human population in an attempt to force them to work harder." He attempted to tack on a smile at the end of that sentence, but it failed miserably.

"That is the trouble with you humans," the big Kraton said. *"You are simply not ruthless enough. That is why you have lost control of your own planet."*

Krenz said nothing to this.

"Continue your work, Doctor," the black Kraton commanded. *"Regardless of your projected fatality rates."*

Krenz blinked, then turned back to his console and tapped quickly on the screen.

"Yes–very well," he replied. "I'm sure I'll have a breakthrough for you soon."

The black Kraton leaned even further forward, and one of its massive arms reached down and gripped the back of Krenz's chair, as if to steady itself.

"Good," the robot replied. *"See that you send an update to the central server before the end of the day. One that satisfies the requirements of this stage of the project."*

"Of–of course," Krenz replied.

The Kraton released its grip on his chair, stepped back, turned and stalked away.

Krenz realized he was sweating profusely. He also realized the black Kraton had left smooth fingerprints permanently embossed into the metal frame of his chair.

Swallowing with some effort, Krenz got back to work, redoubling his efforts.

2:

Jack was awake, though he wished he wasn't.

He kept his eyes closed tight and his head turned away, as they'd warned him to, so he wouldn't go blind. Even so, the utter intensity of the light made him grimace.

An energy beam fired from a device the size of a small cannon was striking an invisible spot just below his right foot, then diffracting into a thousand shards of light, flaring brightly across the laboratory. He could feel the tiniest bit of warmth on his big toe, where it struck his invisible shield, but nothing remotely painful. In truth, he wondered if that sensation was entirely his imagination.

After another two minutes of this, orders were barked and the beam shut off.

"It's safe," a voice called out over a speaker set into the wall. "You can open your eyes."

Jack did this. He looked up.

An older, gray-haired man in a white lab coat and glasses was sitting in a chair just outside the clear cube containing Jack's hospital bed. He spoke to Jack over an intercom.

"Is it hot? Warm, even?" the man was asking.

Jack dutifully sat up, reached out and gingerly touched his foot, then ran his fingertips over the inside of the invisible shield there. He drew his hand back quickly.

"It's hot?" asked the man in the lab coat. He seemed inordinately excited by the prospect.

"No," Jack said, reaching for his foot again, this time more confidently. "I was just nervous it might be." He gave a little laugh as he felt of the inside of the bubble that surrounded him. "It's fine. Same as always."

This told Jack that even while being hit at close range by some kind of laser cannon, his shield had still completely protected him. For the thousandth time since he'd acquired it, he gave silent thanks for the silver belt he wore.

The scientist looked up from his computer screen and his eyes met Jack's. He shook his head in wonder.

"That's some force field you're surrounded by," the man said. "I assume it's coming from that belt. Where did you get it?"

Jack said nothing. He contemplated the many ways he knew he could assault this man and then go about busting out of this place—wherever it was. But he held back, in part because he was curious. Also because his livelihood was currently tied to performing as a gladiator in the arenas of the city and the region, and he worried that preemptively busting up the place might get him kicked out of the league. Then he remembered the Kraton attack on the arena and he began to wonder if that hadn't already happened.

His attention was brought back to his immediate circumstances by the scientist.

"What harm could there be in telling me where you acquired it?" the older man asked. "You've got it now, and clearly no one can take it away from you. I'm just curious about its origin. Who made it, when, why, and so on. How it works."

Jack met his eyes. "I don't know," he said. "Who are you, again? And when am I getting out of here?"

The gray-headed man smiled flatly at him. "My name is Howard Torrens. Dr. Howard Torrens." He swept an arm around to indicate the big room they occupied—though Jack's hospital bed was isolated within a much smaller, clear-walled, cubical sub-section of that room. "This is one of my labs. Where I try to figure out ancient technology." He smiled. "And, in the case of your belt, very *mysterious* technology—since I've never seen its like before and have no idea from where or when it came. Which returns me to my original question: Where did you *get* it?"

"I found it," Jack said with a half-shrug.

Torrens took this information in and then nodded. "I am inclined to believe you," he said. "Found it where?"

"In one of the mines," Jack replied. He considered mentioning John Smith but decided against it, at least for now. Information like that might come in handy later, if things didn't go his way. "I don't know which one. I don't really keep up with the mines, you know? I was an agricultural laborer, right up until my last day on the job. The Kratons ordered me to search a mine and I found it."

Torrens chewed this over for a second. "That's fine," he said. "I can have the Union techs trace your labor assignments in the days prior to when you started fighting in the arenas. We'll zoom right in on where you were that day."

"I doubt that'll do you much good," Jack said.

"We'll see."

Torrens stood and began to pace back and forth, just outside the cubicle.

Jack had woken up for the first time only a couple of days earlier. Everything after the Kraton attack at the arena was a blur. From what he'd managed to glean from his nurses and doctors and this man Torrens, he'd been stabbed in his home, more than a week earlier. He had a vague recollection of a woman being inside his shield with him. Obviously letting her in had been a mistake. The woman was dead now, apparently, though they weren't very clear on what had happened to her, and Jack had no memories of it himself. He'd been told his friend Bennie had found him, called for help, and the paramedics had come. They'd brought him to this lab after discovering they couldn't treat him, due to his shield and his unconsciousness.

He'd nearly died of blood loss before he'd randomly woken up just long enough to grasp his dire condition. At that point, he'd mentally caused his shield to retract away from his wound. The doctor had tended to the slice in his side, after which Jack had reinstated the full-body protection, though now at a much closer distance to his body. He wasn't exactly wearing the shield like a wetsuit, but then again it wasn't that far from it, either.

Soon various lab-coated men and women had started showing up, coming and going, bringing various instruments with them to test his shield. This new scientist seemed the oddest of the bunch, though Jack wasn't entirely sure why—yet.

"So—when do I get out of here, Doc?" Jack asked. "I'm not bleeding any more. I must be doing better. On the mend. Now I'd like to go home."

"Yeah, I'm not so sure about that," Torrens replied. He moved to a computer terminal and began to type on it. "We have a few more tests to run. *I* have *several* more tests to run."

"Tests on *me?*"

"Yes," Torrens said. "On you, and…"

"On my belt," Jack said.

"Of course."

"You want it."

"Of course. Who wouldn't?" The scientist shrugged. "But, at the moment," he said, not looking up from the computer display, "I'd settle for understanding how it works."

Jack pursed his lips. "I'm not under arrest, am I?" He spread his hands. "I didn't do anything wrong, as far as I can remember."

"No," the scientist said. "You're not under arrest." That funny smile returned as he typed. "But you are being… let us say, *detained*. Briefly. Because the Union is considering declaring that belt to be their proprietary property, and demanding you hand it over."

"They're welcome to try to take it," Jack said.

Torrens raised a hand, deflecting this argument away. "That's a legal matter and well outside of my purview." He shrugged at Jack. "The other reason is because there are things we need to know," he added.

"We," Jack repeated. "By *we* you mean the Union. The *aliens*."

"Yes, they were indeed aliens the last time I checked," Torrens said, his attention focused firmly on his typing.

Jack looked from the scientist to the luxurious space around him. Torrens was in possession of a veritable Taj Mahal of a laboratory—very different from what most human beings these days could command. Most people were lucky if their labor gang assignments only took a few years off their life, rather than leading to almost immediate death. Jack felt his stomach sicken at the thought.

"Nice place you've got here," Jack said. He looked directly at the scientist. "It marks you as a collaborator, doesn't it? Dr—?"

"Torrens," the man in the lab coat said again, distractedly. He still hadn't looked up from his work. The implied insult appeared to sail right past him.

"Yeah, that's right," Jack said. "Howard Torrens. Collaborator with the Union. Most people don't have a choice–they're controlled, forced to obey. But you…" He shook his head. "You work for them willingly, don't you? You're paid to carry out their orders against your own kind." He looked around at the fancy surroundings again. "Paid pretty well, I suspect."

The scientist finally looked up and met his gaze. "I do my job," he said. "I earn my pay." He stared back at Jack for a long moment.

Then, "I know exactly who and what I am," he said, "and you know nothing about me."

"I think I know all that really matters about you."

Torrens glared back at him in silence for a very long moment. He appeared as if he were searching for some kind of verbal comeback. But then his expression changed and he looked closer at Jack.

"You said most people are controlled. I would take issue with that phrasing–not *controlled*, more like *guided*, I think. It's a relevant point. But semantics aside–" Torrens leaned in closer, studying Jack. "—you're not, are you? Not at all."

"No," Jack said, feeling a vehemence rising up inside him that he'd never known before. For the first time he began to consider if perhaps John Smith had been right; if there was indeed more to life than using his belt to get rich and famous. "No," he repeated, "I am a free man."

"And yet you work for the Union, too, don't you, Mr. *Gladiator*? By fighting in the arena."

"I work for myself," Jack snapped. "I destroy their Kratons and knock out their champions."

"For the entertainment of our alien overlords," Torrens said. "And for their pay."

"For *myself!* And for the people watching. The *people!* That's different from what *you* do!"

Torrens shrugged. "Perhaps. In any case, I didn't mean to step on a sore spot."

"It's not a sore spot," Jack almost shouted, before trailing off into sullen silence.

"You were pointing out that you are free," Torrens said after Jack had calmed down a bit. "And I agree with you about that. It's quite obvious that you are." From his spot outside the transparent cube, he continued to study Jack like a microbe on a test tube slide. "And how *is* that?"

Jack said nothing.

"The belt, again, of course." Torrens made a snorting sound that came across as more appreciative than dismissive. "I've just got to get to the bottom of that fascinating device."

"You won't," Jack said.

Torrens frowned.

"Let me be clear to you," he said. "I'm trying to figure out the mysteries of your belt in a relatively gentle fashion. You will note I never aimed the laser cannon directly at your body. There are others who work in this building, and nearby, and for the same boss as me, who are *not* gentle. Not at all." He flashed that smile again. "So I hope you understand now that it is not in your interest to stonewall me, or to try to provoke me. The more information I get from you, and the faster I can get it, the less information will have to be brought out of you through far less pleasant means."

Jack shook his head. "I'm sorry, Doctor," he said. "I hate to break it to you, but I'm not feeling all that afraid right now—not of you, not of anyone or anything else you keep around here." He lay his head back on the pillow. "I'm pretty sure I could leave here any time I wanted to, and there wouldn't be much you could do to stop me."

"You might be surprised," Torrens replied.

And then, as Jack watched, the scientist reached out and typed a couple of instructions into a keypad fitted to the outside wall of the cube. For a second, nothing happened. Then Jack could hear a hiss coming from several directions around him at once.

"What do you think you're doing?" he asked, frowning. "We've already seen that you can't get inside my bubble. Not unless I want you to."

"I'm not trying to get *inside* it," Torrens said over the intercom. "Quite the opposite. I'm keeping something *out*."

Jack frowned deeper, blinked, and then realized what was happening.

He couldn't *breathe*.

Torrens had sucked all of the air out of the cubicle.

The force field around him kept some things out—bullets, energy beams, fists—but let others in, such as air and visible light. But it couldn't let something in that wasn't out there to begin with.

He started to panic, thrashing about on the bed, trying to get up.

"Now, now," Torrens told him over the speaker. "You don't want to reopen your wound."

"I'll tear this whole place down," Jack was saying, but his voice was growing weak, trailing off. Spots flashed before his eyes, and the room seemed to be spinning madly.

"You know what might be really interesting?" Torrens was rubbing his chin as he watched Jack's struggles lessen by the second. "If I pumped in some kind of poison gas now. I wonder if your bubble—your belt—is sophisticated enough that it would know to allow some molecules in, but keep other ones out." He chuckled. "Of course, if you die now, we might never find that out."

Jack tried to say something back to him, but couldn't. He couldn't breathe at all.

Torrens must have typed in another set of instructions, because air hissed back into the cubicle.

Jack was lying flat on his back, but he was breathing. Torrens spoke over the intercom again. "You see," he said, "you're not quite as invulnerable as you thought you were. You can resist a laser cannon, but you can't go long without oxygen." He chuckled. "Sometimes the old-fashioned ways really are the best."

As Jack regained his breath and sat up, he realized that another person had entered the room. A woman. A very tall, slender woman.

"Mr. Gael," she said, her strong voice carrying easily across the room. "I hope you are doing better today. I understand it was touch and go there for a while."

"It was, yeah," Jack replied, studying her. "In fact, I nearly suffocated."

The woman's sharp features furrowed at that, and she glanced at Torrens, then back at the man in the hospital bed. She moved on as if nothing untoward had been said.

"I have brought you some fresh clothing," she said. "Between the blood stains and the hole in the shirt, your previous set was at the end of its lifespan and has been sent to the incinerator." She motioned and a mustachioed man in a dark suit approached the cubicle. He carried a set of folded clothing, red in color, and a new pair of boots. He stood outside the door to the cubicle and waited.

"I have noticed you prefer your standard laborer's jumpsuit to fancier clothing, and that is how the audiences for your bouts know you. So that is what I have brought you," the woman continued. "I trust you will allow Detective Rodriguez to bring them inside your little room there, without doing him any undo harm."

Jack motioned for the man to enter. "Sure," he said. "I appreciate it. I was getting a bit tired of my rear end hanging out the back of this hospital gown."

The door slid open and Rodriguez moved inside, set the stack of clothing down on a rolling table at the foot of the bed and backed out quickly. The whole time, he wore an expression that clearly said he expected to be swatted by an invisible hand at any moment.

Jack slowly got out of bed and stood somewhat unsteadily at the side of it, steadying himself with one hand. He moved to the foot and looked down at the clothing, then up at the woman and at Dr. Torrens.

"A little privacy, maybe?"

The woman nodded to Torrens. He tapped a couple of buttons on the outside of the cubicle and its walls turned opaque.

"Now, don't be up to anything untoward in there, Jack," the woman called to him through the now-dark gray walls.

Jack hadn't been kidding; he was happy to get out of the gown and back into real clothing. He started to grab the folded jumpsuit but then hesitated. He thought for a moment, then looked down at the silver belt around his waist and whispered to it, "If you're about to say something, say it *quietly*, huh?" Then he reached out with his right hand, the bubble still surrounding him at a distance of about three millimeters, and touched the clothing.

"Diagnostic mode operational," the belt squawked, but this time in a soft tone that Jack himself barely heard. Apparently it had listened to him!

"Foreign objects detected," the belt added a moment later. *"Potential hazard—initiating purge in three...two..."*

So they *had* infused his new clothing with nanites. Either these Union collaborators had figured out the belt had removed his old ones, or they weren't taking any chances, sending in reinforcements to control him.

"One..." And a sizzling sound came from the new clothes, followed by the slight smell of ozone.

Well, that was too bad—they'd just wasted another batch of nanites.

Another moment and the bubble around Jack expanded to include the now-nanite-free clothes. He quickly donned them. As he was lacing up the new boots, the woman's voice came over the intercom.

"I trust you're done," she said.

The walls became transparent again.

Jack sat there at the foot of the bed, now clad in a fresh new red jumpsuit and boots, the silver belt as always around his waist. He smiled at them.

"How would you like to give me that belt, Jack?" the woman asked.

"This belt?"

"Yes. That belt."

Jack pursed his lips. He looked from Denali to the belt and back at her again. "Umm… Just give it to you? Like a present?"

"Precisely that way, yes," Denali replied.

Jack appeared to be considering this for several seconds. Then he asked, "What would I get in return?"

The woman smiled back, but now there was a hint of uncertainty in her eyes. "A medal," she said. "Status as a hero of the Union. Money. Fame. Women. Whatever you might desire."

Jack again appeared to be considering her offer.

"Nah," he said at last, shaking his head. "I mean, I've already got money and fame. The last woman tried to kill me. You can stuff your medal. And 'hero of the Union' sounds to me like 'biggest collaborator creep.' So I'll just keep the belt, instead."

Frowning now, Denali held his gaze for several seconds that seemed to Jack like an eternity. The longer he stared back without looking away, the better he felt about himself. At last the woman broke away and glared at Torrens.

"He wasn't affected. Not in the least."

"What?" Torrens said, surprised.

"It's plain to see."

"But—how can you be sure?" Torrens asked, looking from the woman to Jack and back.

She shook her head dismissively, then added, "Just get that belt off of him. Immediately. Whatever it takes. No more excuses."

And with that, she swept out of the lab, the detective in the dark suit hurrying after her. The effect with her leaving was akin to a storm passing through and dispersing.

Torrens stood there, staring at Jack, uncertain. Jack suppressed a laugh. He could guess what the man was thinking: *Has he really done something with the nanites in the clothes? Has he defeated them somehow? Is that possible?*

Oh, it's possible, Jack thought to himself.

Then he had an idea.

He wasn't sure how it would work out. A lot would depend on what kind of person this Dr. Howard Torrens really was. And Jack had no idea about that. Was he truly an opportunistic collaborator, who thought nothing of selling out the human race to these aliens and their pet robots, in exchange for wealth and power?

There was only one way Jack knew of to find out. And he didn't really have much to lose. He assumed Torrens planned to hold him there, threaten him with suffocation again, and meanwhile mix in the threat of starvation and dying of thirst.

Jack had been thinking of simply using the field around him as a battering ram, to try to smash his way out of this place. But he wasn't at all certain he could succeed. He didn't know what material this cubicle around him was made of, much less the walls of the lab beyond. And brute force seemed to him more like a last-ditch option than the first thing he should try. Especially considering the wound he carried.

Thus it was that Jack called out to the still-grimacing Torrens and made him a proposition.

"Dr. Torrens," he said. "I appreciate you saving my life. I shouldn't have been so harsh with you before."

Still clearly upset from his interaction with the woman, Torrens acknowledged the words with a nod. He picked up an instrument and fiddled with it a bit.

"I'll tell you what," Jack said. "I'll let you study me and my belt as much as you'd like. I promise not to do anything to harm you." He raised his right hand. "My word of honor. My pledge as a gladiator."

Torrens looked up at him from the device and frowned. "You'll let me come in there, and won't try anything?"

"I absolutely promise to do nothing to harm you," Jack said. "My word of honor—you will leave this cubicle no worse than when you entered."

Torrens appeared to consider this.

"It would be helpful for me to run a few tests up close, instead of remotely," Torrens said, as much to himself as to Jack.

"Run them all you'd like," Jack said. "Only, have them bring me a sandwich or something when you have a second. I'm pretty hungry. And I know you're not planning to starve me out or anything."

"No—no, of course not," Torrens said, too quickly. "I'll have them bring your dinner in a few minutes. But first—"

Still carrying the small device, Torrens chose another one from a nearby table and then walked over to the door to the cubicle.

"You really do swear not to hurt me if I come in there, right?"

"I absolutely do so swear that."

Torrens nodded. "Okay. For some reason, I believe you."

He keyed the lock and the door slid open. He came inside and approached Jack where he was sitting up on the foot of the bed. He held up one of the scanners and said, "Please hold out your right arm."

Jack held up his right arm. Torrens leaned forward and ran the device over it—or, rather, over the invisible energy field some three millimeters beyond Jack's skin. "Fascinating," the scientist muttered. "That's truly fascinating. There's a matrix, and it's invisible to normal light and most other wavelengths, but if I adjust the—"

He carried on like that for a few seconds, then used the other device to scan Jack's same arm.

"Ah," he said. "Yes. So there is a self-perpetuating field of varying size and depth, and it has—"

Jack had had enough. Torrens was right there. To carry out his plan now would be simplicity itself.

Smiling, he raised his left arm and reached out, touching Torrens' right shoulder. Touching it with the bubble of energy that surrounded him.

The scientist blinked, looked at what Jack was doing, and started to object.

Before he could say or do anything, however, another voice—a third voice—spoke up. And it said:

"Diagnostic mode operational."

3:

Guards came for Jack Gael at midnight.

They were humans, not Kratons. They burst through the door of his cubicle, dragged him out of bed and hustled him into a smaller transparent box before he could react. Then they sealed it closed and loaded it onto a rolling cart, which they proceeded to push along darkened hallways until they reached a room very similar in some respects to Dr. Torrens' lab—and very different in others.

Where the lab Torrens ran resembled the inside of some kind of spaceship, this room resembled nothing so much as a Medieval dungeon. And instead of computer consoles and laser generators, this room contained what looked like the products of the feverish mind of an agent of the Spanish Inquisition, brought forward a dozen or more centuries and updated using the best in state-of-the-art equipment.

And standing at the center of that space was a tall, hunched-over man in a lab coat, with a shock of blond hair and thick-rimmed glasses. As Jack was led into the room, the man bowed and said, "Welcome, Mr. Gael. I've followed your exploits in the arenas with great interest and I'm so glad to have you here in my laboratory." And when he said his name, Jack involuntarily shuddered, for it was a name that had been used to frighten children for as long as he could remember. "I am Erich Krenz," the man stated. "And I have been given the task to remove that belt from your waist—by any means necessary."

"You're welcome to try," Jack said, summoning up all the bravado he could muster. Much of it was pure bluster, however. Not even a few weeks of safety and security provided by the belt could quite overcome a lifetime of terror at the mere thought of Erich Krenz and his torture dungeon.

The guards had slid Jack's new containment box off the cart and left him standing there in the center of the room, surrounded by Krenz's implements of torture.

Krenz himself approached now, leering at Jack through the transparent box and Jack's transparent shield inside it. He tapped at the box with one finger.

"Ingenious, eh?" he asked. "I designed this substance myself. It's grown from a single crystal, as was the cubicle you've spent the last few days inside." He grinned. "Oh, I'm sure if you put your mind and your back into it, you could eventually crack and open this box or that cubicle. But it would take you a good bit of uninterrupted time and effort, and we have denied you those two things since your arrival. I have made certain of it."

"So you've made a box that can hold me. That's fine," Jack said. "But sealing me inside here doesn't get you any closer to taking away my belt."

"This is true," Krenz replied. "Fortunately, the other new feature I've developed is one I will demonstrate for you now."

He motioned and two Kratons strode forward from the shadows. Jack hadn't even noticed their presence before that, given the rather distracting nature of the other items that filled the lab.

The Kratons opened the door on the front of the box and reached inside, pulling Jack out. As they did so, Krenz moved behind a computer console and began tapping various buttons.

As soon as Jack was free of the box, he turned on one of the Kratons and chopped his hand horizontally. The robot staggered back, sparks flying from a crease that had been opened in its neck. Jack meanwhile turned halfway around and kicked, and the other Kraton stumbled backwards. After three shaky steps it collapsed.

The first Kraton used that moment to recover. It advanced on Jack again. He punched it in the face and the robot's head separated cleanly from its shoulders, bouncing across the tile floor. The body stood there a moment, sparks and flames spraying up from its torso through its jagged neck, then toppled over and lay still.

Jack started to go after the other one, which was struggling to regain its footing. He took one step toward it and froze. The room had become filled with a low but powerful humming sound. And the heretofore-invisible bubble surrounding him had just become quite visible.

He looked around and could see a sort of glowing blue matrix of intersecting lines tracing his own shape, simply extended outward in every direction by several centimeters. He frowned. Something Krenz was doing was causing the bubble to change in this way. What else could Krenz do to it?

That question was answered only a few seconds later, when the humming sound grew louder. At the same time, the matrix around Jack shimmered and almost—but not quite—vanished.

"Just a little more, I think," Krenz was muttering as he adjusted the controls. "Almost…"

The other Kraton stood there, staring at Jack, murder plain in its emotionless electronic eyes. It appeared to be waiting for the last of the field around him to disappear.

"It's all about harmonics, you see," Krenz told him as he continued to make adjustments at the console a few meters away. "We can't penetrate your shield when it's at full strength, so I needed to find a way to reduce its strength."

The blue matrix was faint now, but it was clearly still there.

"Ah well," Krenz said. "I was hoping to be able to eradicate it entirely, but it truly is an exceptionally well-made artifact and continues to resist." He gave a half-shrug. "Still, that level of vulnerability should be good enough for my purposes."

Krenz motioned and the surviving Kraton advanced on Jack. He responded to its movement by punching it. His fist impacted the metal surface with a dull thud; the Kraton scarcely noticed it, while Jack withdrew his now-reddened hand and held it to his mouth.

"Thank you, Mr. Gael," Krenz said. "You have shown me just what I wanted to see." He motioned to the Kraton. "Seize him. Hold him securely."

The robot complied, grasping Jack by the back of the neck before he could attempt to run—not that there was anywhere for a lone, now-unarmed man to run in this building.

Krenz shuffled out from behind the console and chose a few implements from his vast collection. He held up a piece of silver metal with one terrifyingly jagged edge. "We'll try the sonic saw first," he said, grinning. "If it won't cut through the belt, it will most certainly cut through *you*. Cut you in half, in fact. Then I can fish the belt out from what remains."

"How goes it?" came the voice of the woman that had been ordering Dr. Torrens around the day before. Dangling in the grasp of the Kraton, Jack was just able to look over in that direction. He saw her gliding in, the gray-haired Torrens following behind her. Today she wore a dark green version of the skintight suit she'd worn the day before.

"Ah, Sub-Administrator Denali," Krenz greeted her. "And Dr. Torrens. Welcome to my laboratory." He gestured toward Jack. "As you can see, the force field projected by the subject's belt has been drastically reduced in coherence. I was about to take actions to separate said belt from said subject."

Denali strode up to Jack and looked him over. She did not appear at all impressed.

"Excellent, Dr. Krenz," she said. "I can hardly wait to see what happens next. Proceed."

Standing behind Denali, Howard Torrens continued to behave like the sycophantic lackey he'd been all his life—the scientific genius who put his gifts to work in service to the Union—the alien cabal that ruled Earth. Such a thing had always seemed perfectly normal and natural to him. After all, those aliens held all real power on the planet. And Torrens wanted to conduct his research and tinker with his inventions. How better to do that than in the service of the Union, who supported him and funded his work? Meanwhile, any real concern for the plight of all the laborers out there in the city and beyond—well, they'd never really been a concern of Torrens. If the Union had decided one day to wipe them all out, the Howard Torrens of yesterday and before probably wouldn't have lifted a finger to save any of them. They simply dwelt below the minimum level of his concerns as he saw them. Beneath his notice.

That had all changed the previous day, when Jack Gael had touched him—or, rather, when the force field projected by Gael's belt had touched him. Torrens had blacked out, apparently stumbling back and falling into a chair next to the hospital bed Gael had occupied. He could not have been out for long, because no one came in to check on him before he awoke.

When he'd opened his eyes and looked up, he'd seen Jack Gael sitting there on the bed, his arms crossed, studying Torrens carefully. Torrens had started to follow the many years of his ingrained habits and training, and sound an alarm. But then something strange, something unexpected, had occurred:

Torrens had decided he didn't *want* to sound the alarm.

In fact, he had decided he could suddenly see things from Jack's point of view.

He *was* a collaborator. He'd always *been* a collaborator. Working for the aliens, against his own people.

The mere thought of this had caused Torrens nausea the day before, and it made him feel even worse now.

The nanites, he'd understood upon waking up in that chair the day before, had deceived him. The nanites with which the Union infected every human at birth had effectively manipulated him his entire life. They weren't just to provide protection from disease and to increase worker productivity, as the aliens always claimed. They were about rendering humans more docile; more susceptible to the power of suggestion.

And, somehow, Jack Gael and his amazing belt had managed to fry every single nanite that had infested Howard Torrens.

Torrens had sat there for a long while, mulling it all over. He had understood then that his life had reached a crossroads; perhaps the single most important one he would ever face. He could choose to continue to serve the aliens, of his own free will. Or he could take advantage of this one opportunity—this one time in his life that he was free of their influence—to choose a different path. He needed to think it over and be sure he knew what he was doing, and what he'd be getting himself into.

He'd not even spoken to Gael at that time. He'd simply gotten up out of the chair, gone home, and slept on it overnight. Part of him worried that the nanites might somehow reinfect him during the night, while another part of him figured that, if that happened, it represented his choice being made for him, with no further need for angst.

But, upon waking that morning, it hadn't happened. In fact, his head felt clearer than he could ever remember it. Layer upon layer of imagery, memories and compulsions had been washed away. He had a freshly-laundered mind and, with it, fresh perspectives.

And so now, as Krenz and Denali loomed over Jack and prepared to kill the man in one of the most grotesque ways imaginable, in order to obtain the belt he wore, Torrens took action. Not much was needed, and he was determined that what he did would not be visible to any people or Kratons in the room, and would not appear as anything noticeable on surveillance recordings later.

Torrens was standing back from the other two. They paid him no attention whatsoever. He drifted back another couple of steps, being sure not to get anywhere near Krenz's control console. He put his hands in the pockets of his lab coat, waited a moment so the connection wouldn't be too obvious, and then keyed a small transmitter in his right pocket.

A loud beep sounded from Krenz's console, immediately followed by a robotic alert message: *"Warning—harmonics field de-powering. Harmonics field de-powering."*

Krenz was leering at Jack, reaching toward him with the sonic saw. When he heard the warning message, he looked back in surprise at the console, his expression conveying the sense that he felt the machine had somehow betrayed him on a personal level, robbing him of a great victory—or at least delaying it. He put down the saw and shuffled back behind the console, looking at the controls.

Denali, meanwhile, appeared confused by the turn of events. She reluctantly took her eyes away from Jack, or rather from his belt, and turned around to look at Krenz, frowning. "Doctor?" she asked. "Is there a problem?"

"A slight one," Krenz replied distractedly as he tapped away at the controls. His frown deepened, changing into an expression of deep concern, followed by outright fear.

"What is it?" Denali asked.

Torrens slowly but deliberately made his way toward the exit.

"Warning—harmonics field dropping below critical levels. Shutdown is imminent."

Torrens looked back before he went out the door. He wanted to signal Jack somehow; to let him know exactly what was happening. But he was afraid he'd give himself away. He settled on a very slight nod in Jack's direction. He *thought* Jack saw him, but couldn't be sure.

As he stepped through the door, he could only hope Jack could figure it out for himself.

4:

Jack figured it out for himself.

The blue matrix that identified the location of his force bubble faded and vanished. But the bubble wasn't gone. Oh, no. Quite the contrary. It was back, and back with a vengeance.

Jack reached over his right shoulder and the field around his right hand expanded until it surrounded the head of the Kraton holding him by the neck. He gently squeezed, and the Kraton's metal head popped and imploded.

Tearing himself free from the dead robot's grasp, he took two steps toward Erich Krenz, who still stood at his console, frantically pressing buttons. Clearly the physically-challenged Krenz had more faith in his ability to get the harmonics field working again than he did in his ability to flee the room before Jack could get him.

The harmonics field, however, did not cooperate. Consequently, Jack got him.

"Now—hold on one moment, young man," Krenz began to say as he backed away from his controls, having accepted at last that the system was somehow dead and would not be coming back up. "This was nothing personal. I am a professional, merely doing my job, and—"

Jack threw a punch. Ten feet away, the invisible field extending out from his hand impacted Krenz's jaw and floored him.

Movement to his left. Jack looked away from the stocky scientist to the other person still in the room. It was the woman. Denali. She had backed away, but was still some distance from the exit. Jack wasn't done with Krenz, but he turned to deal with her.

An energy blast sizzled past Jack's right ear. For a moment it disconcerted him, until he realized it wouldn't have gotten through his shield and hit him, even if it had been aimed properly.

Another blast confirmed that. Denali had hidden herself behind some equipment and was shooting at him. At? She was shooting *him*. She just couldn't get her firepower to actually make contact with him.

Jack kicked out and the blocky machinery she was crouching behind leapt up into the air. As she tripped and fell backwards, the massive objects came down on her right leg, making an awful, crunching sound.

Denali screamed.

The pieces of machinery continued to tumble and rolled off of her, freeing her. She gathered herself enough to limp backwards until she came up against the wall behind her. There she looked frantically left and right, saw a white cylinder attached to the wall a couple of feet away, grabbed it and pointed it at Jack.

"That's not going to help you," Jack said, walking in her direction. "It's a fire extinguisher."

Denali keyed the cylinder and unleashed a blast of foam and gas in Jack's direction. The clouds momentarily obscured his view. Shouting wordlessly in anger, he lashed out with his right hand and then his left, and did manage to knock the cylinder from her hands. But she had accomplished what she'd intended; visibility in that part of the lab was now almost zero. By the time he ran across the room and waved away enough of the clouds to be able to see at all, the woman had vanished.

Jack cursed, then turned back to look for Erich Krenz.

He didn't have to look very hard.

The big, hunched form of Krenz barreled out of the mist and bore down on him, a jagged knife in one hand and a whirling motorized blade in the other.

Jack held nothing back as he swiped his arm from left to right.

The blow nearly tore Krenz in half as it hurled him across the laboratory.

Jack Gael exited the Union lab building some minutes later. He'd easily torn his way through a small army of Kratons, chopping them into shrapnel and scrap. The human guards had fled as the famed Gladiator approached. No one there, man or machine, had come close to slowing him down.

Dr. Torrens, meanwhile, kept well out of the way and watched from a safe distance. He marveled at the power and the sheer effectiveness of the belt. And it was clear Jack was still figuring out the most basic ways to use it, both for offense and defense. Surely he would only become more proficient, and more deadly, the longer he possessed it.

Torrens found himself wondering what Jack would do now; where he would go. Clearly his career as a gladiator in the arenas was finished. Now he was an outlaw. Surely there must be others in such a condition—? Torrens assumed Jack would find those other outlaws and live on the periphery of society.

And that was a shame, he thought, because that belt gave Jack the chance to make a real difference. It was too bad he was just a simple laborer, with no real grasp of the strategic situation on the planet. If only, Torrens mused, someone were in a position to offer Jack Gael real guidance.

Thus it was that, three days later, as the repair crews were finishing up their work of restoring the building to its previous, pre-Gladiator condition, Torrens received a message.

It seemed someone wanted to meet with him. To talk with him about Jack Gael.

Someone by the name of John Smith.

BOOK TWO:

THE CENTURION AND THE ANGEL

CHAPTER 9

WELCOME TO THE REBELLION – THE TEMPORAL TRANSPORTER – HELP – REBIRTH

1:

Jack's escape almost came to quite the anticlimactic end, before it had barely begun.

He'd walked casually out of the building where he'd been kept prisoner, with nothing and no one able to touch him. He'd emerged into the nighttime, and the streets around the lab were deserted. Even so, he'd wanted to get out of there, so he'd started to jog, then to run. Scarcely two blocks later, however, his pace had drastically slowed, and eventually he'd stumbled and fallen to the pavement.

Pulling himself up to a sitting position, there beneath the blue-white glare of a street light, he'd looked down and realized he was bleeding again. And badly. As he'd feared, all the frantic activity had reopened the knife wound.

His head was spinning. He needed to do something, but he wasn't sure what.

"Well, look who we've found," came a voice from behind him.

Painfully Jack turned and looked.

It was the two detectives. He'd encountered them multiple times of late, from the arena to the laboratory where he'd been held. He couldn't remember their names, but he knew they worked for the Union. Not that they made any effort to conceal that fact.

"Be careful," one of them said to the other. "You saw what he did to the Kratons back there."

"But look at him now," the other cop said. "He's barely conscious. One foot in the grave." He moved in a little closer, until the outline of the bottom of Jack's bubble was obvious, because it held a quantity of red fluid. "Look at all the blood!"

"That lady did a number on him," the other said.

"Not quite like the number he did on her," the first cop said. "Although…" His voice trailed off.

"Yeah," the other said, picking up the train of thought. "Maybe in the long run it will amount to the same thing."

Jack wanted to punch the two guys. He wanted to knock their heads off—and it was very likely he *would* knock them off, if he succeeded in punching them. But all his strength was deserting him. Instead, he slumped slowly to the sidewalk, groaning.

His eyes open now only as slits, he could just see the two detectives cautiously approaching him. His first thought was that he was going to wind up right back in that stupid laboratory building. His second thought was that he might not be alive by the time they got him back there.

But then some sort of commotion was happening around him; he wasn't sure what it was. Voices, shouts, a couple of shots fired— from what kind of weapon, he wasn't sure. The world was morphing into a tunnel of darkness that threatened to swallow him up entirely.

Hands came at him, but not in a threatening way. Trying to pick him up. He looked at the faces attached to the bodies that were attached to the hands, and didn't recognize the people. They were young, not in uniform, and scruffy-looking. So—probably not Union.

Jack thought about the fact that he might be on the verge of death. He mixed in the thought that these people were possibly not working for the aliens. And on top of all of that, he concluded he stood a better chance of survival and freedom by not dying here on the spot.

Having considered all those factors, he mentally issued a series of orders to the belt. First, the shield reshaped itself around him until it was about six inches from his body. Then it opened in the area of his wound, to allow access to anyone who might wish to apply medical treatments. That having been accomplished, he passed out. The last thing he remembered was seeing hands reaching down and trying to pick him up again, and this time succeeding.

Jack Gael awoke in a hospital bed for the second time in only a few days.

The bed occupied a small room that couldn't have provided more of a contrast to the high-tech medical prison he'd awoken in previously. This place looked beaten-up and run down. And yet somehow it gave the impression of being far safer.

He attempted to sit up but felt bandages pulling at his side. Looking down, he saw an IV tube that ran in through the invisible opening he'd created in his invisible bubble. It turned a corner at his elbow, ran down his forearm, and connected to the back of his hand.

The room came into focus around him, revealing itself to be as plain and entirely unmemorable as he'd first thought. That was when he noticed a familiar figure in blue clothing sitting hunched over in a chair to his left.

"Hello," he said.

The figure started and looked up.

"Well. Awake at last, are we? I was afraid you were going to sleep a bloody month."

As he'd suspected, it was John Smith.

"You," Jack said.

"Me," Smith replied.

"How?" Jack asked.

"Those two detectives that work for Xaveria Denali found you on the street, after you broke out of their evil crime laboratory." He paused. "In fact, that may be what they have on the sign up over the door to the place: *Evil Crime Laboratory*." He shrugged. "Anyhow. They were about to take you back inside, when my own team intervened. That resulted in a different outcome."

"Did it?" Jack nodded slowly. "I appreciate the help, then," he said.

Smith waved the thanks away. "I assure you, I did it entirely for my own selfish reasons. But I will accept such credit as I may be offered."

Jack frowned. "You were watching me?"

"When the Union people took you, I stayed close by, hoping for a chance to bust you out." He grinned. "It turned out you didn't need me."

"Before that, though?"

Smith shrugged. "Yeah, a little bit. Just keeping tabs on you, in case you changed your mind about things. Or in case the Union decided to escalate things. Which they did."

Jack nodded slowly at this, but his expression made it clear that he wasn't entirely sold on what Smith was selling.

After that, the two sat there for a short while in silence, looking everywhere but at each other. When their eyes did meet at last, Smith said, "So now you've seen what they're really like. The Union and their human lackeys."

"I have," Jack agreed.

Smith's expression grew intense. "Are you still staying neutral? Keeping out of the fray?"

Jack looked away, then shook his head.

"No, no. You were right about them. I see that now."

Smith looked at him skeptically. "Just like that?"

Jack shrugged. "They tried to cut my belt off of me. They tried to suffocate me. They did a lot of stuff. And for years they've been filling us full of little machines to make us want to obey them. So, yeah, they're pretty bad." He met Smith's eyes, and his own were burning with anger. "I'm ready to pay them back," he said. "I'm ready to kick them off this planet."

"About damned time," Smith said under his breath. Then he added, "Well. That went better than I expected. I guess I wasted all that time putting together the slideshow for you."

Jack snorted a laugh, then sobered when he realized Smith's expression had not changed and was as flat as ever. "You're not serious."

"Completely serious." Smith waved his hands around. "I had pictures of the strip mines; of the dry river beds. They've been consuming our planet's resources in a bigger way and at a faster clip than the human race, at its worst, ever considered doing. And the labor gangs. There aren't a whole lot of us left, we human beings. But the ones who survived the initial invasion so long ago, their descendants now mostly work in the labor pits, in the mines, or working in some other fashion to exploit the world's resources far beyond the failsafe point."

Jack stared at him. "It's that bad?"

"It's worse than that. You saw how nuts their top scientists are."

Jack nodded slowly. "That I did."

"You saw it up close and personal."

"Very true. Why are they doing it?"

Smith pursed his lips. "I've looked into that, over the years—and through so many replays, for lack of a better word. And I have a theory, if you're interested."

Jack spread his hands. "It's not like I'm really going anywhere right now."

"True. A captive audience." Smith sat back in his chair. "I suspect the reason the aliens came here in the first place is that they lost a war, somewhere out in space."

Jack frowned. "They *lost* a war?"

"Yeah. Bear with me." He gestured with his hands as he spoke, doing so more quickly now. "They're called the Union, right? But mostly we see the Kratons, their robotic servants."

"And their human collaborators," Jack said.

"Exactly. But what about the aliens themselves? Do we even know what they look like?"

Jack considered this, then shook his head. "I've seen a couple on the vids, but…"

As he trailed off, Smith interjected, "But always in the background, in the shadows. Hidden."

Jack nodded, conceding this point.

Smith leaned forward, more intense now. "I think it's because they're from several different alien races. And because there aren't very many of them. From what I've pieced together, they used to make up a big, interstellar empire of multiple alien races. But they lost a big war to some other force, and there are only a few of them left from each race. Maybe just a handful. So they stay out of sight, behind the scenes, pulling the strings—as they use Earth as a resource base and a staging ground for building up their military might again."

Jack thought about this. "Yeah," he said, "it makes sense. But, if they're building up their forces again, that means they must be planning to start another war. And Earth will be caught right in the middle of it all."

"If there's even anything left of Earth by that point," Smith said.

"We've got to get rid of them," Jack said, growing more animated now, as well. "Get them off the planet, and quick–before they bring down God knows what onto our heads!"

"That we do, lad," Smith said. "And that's what I've been trying to do. But I can't do it alone." He stood and walked over to the door. "The aliens call themselves a Union. Well, there's no reason we can't have a union of our own."

He opened the door and waved at whoever was outside. One by one, three figures filed in. Two men and a woman, all seemingly in their twenties, each wearing a modified military uniform.

"Jack Gael, meet three leaders of the army we're going to assemble." Smith introduced them as Thompson, Liu and Rossi. They each nodded.

Jack looked back at them. Something was bothering him. Then he realized what it was.

"Wait," he said. "The nanites—"

Smith raised his hands as if to fend off the concern.

"They're clean," he said.

"But—how?"

"We've developed a process of our own for dealing with them," Smith said. "Now, admittedly it is a little crude, but those who survive are free of the nanites for a period of several months, at least." Smith nodded to the newcomers. "These three all had their treatments within the last two months. They're good."

Jack mulled this over. "You just said, 'Those who *survive*.' You mean your treatment can *kill* people?"

Smith glanced at the others; they all looked away. He nodded slowly. "It involves essentially electrocuting the patient until the nanites are all fried or evacuate their host. The trick is accomplishing this without frying the *patient* at the same time." He frowned. "We have suffered a few casualties, yes."

Jack was frowning. "I think I can do that for them, and do it a lot safer," he said. "For them, and for anyone else."

"I'm counting on it," Smith said. "I'm *very much* counting on it." He grinned. "For a whole lot of people."

2:

"We have a whole lot of people now," John Smith had said to Dr. Howard Torrens when they'd first met. "But we need you on board, too."

And they'd gotten him. With his nanites fried by Jack Gael, Torrens had been quick to agree to secretly cooperate with the new resistance. But their working relationship over these past few weeks had not been a smooth one.

Now, weeks later, Torrens sat at the table in the Blue Dolphin, his eyes darting from the drink in front of him to the front door of the establishment to the man in blue sitting across from him. He'd left his ubiquitous white lab coat folded on the back seat of his car, parked outside.

"You seem nervous, laddie," John Smith said, sipping at his beer. "Honestly, though, that's probably wise. You work for some very bad people."

"I've done some bad things myself," Torrens said, looking down at the table.

"You weren't responsible for that. The nanites–"

"The nanites are a convenient excuse," Torrens said. "But they don't absolutely control people. They just make you more susceptible to suggestion. And more docile."

"That seems like a pretty fine hair to split, as far as I'm concerned," Smith said. He waved a hand airily. "But it's behind you now. You're free."

"I'm not free as long as I'm still working there with Xaveria Denali and the Kratons and the rest," Torrens said. "I'd like to just go away–go as far away from here as possible, and get away from all of them."

"But they control the entire planet," Smith pointed out. "There's nowhere else to go."

Torrens nodded slowly. He was looking off to the side, now, but was not really focused on anything in particular.

Smith was growing concerned about the man. He seemed despondent. That wasn't good, considering the things he still needed from the former collaborator.

"But," Smith said, "if we succeed, they *won't* control the planet any longer. It will be *free*."

Torrens nodded again, but he didn't seem terribly convinced.

"Oh," Smith said. "One other thing. How is the new machine coming along?"

Torrens shrugged. "The parts that can be built using technology that currently exists, I've built. Just as you requested. But it will never work without certain other components. And those, well…" He shook his head. "I don't think I even understand what I don't understand about them."

"I'm well aware of the parts you still need," Smith said. "And I think I can take care of that for you."

Torrens simply stared back at him. After a second, he found his voice. "You're serious about that?" he said.

Smith smiled flatly. "Of course I am. What—don't I strike you as an eminent supplier of specialty parts to mad scientists everywhere?" He paused, looking at the scientist through narrowed eyes. "If you possessed those last few parts, do you believe the machine will work?"

"Who knows?" Torrens said with a nervous laugh. "This is all pie-in-the-sky." He looked at Smith and blinked. "Isn't it?"

Smith said nothing; he merely stared back at Torrens.

"You're not saying you actually *have* the last few components I need, are you?"

Now Smith smiled a genuine smile. "Just follow me out to the car and I'll get them for you," he said.

"But, I mean…" Torrens frowned. "I've been thinking of this as entirely theoretical. I never dreamed those very specific pieces of equipment actually existed anywhere–or that I could get my hands on them if they did."

"They exist," Smith said. "And you're about to have them in those very same hands."

"But–where did you *get* them?"

"Not a good question to ask me," Smith shot back. "About anything."

Torrens blinked at that, then finished off his drink and paid the check. Smith tossed the last of his back and stood. No one else in the Blue Dolphin paid them the slightest bit of attention. Smith was known to frequent the establishment; likely it was assumed that anyone with him was okay, too.

As they exited the bar and stepped out onto the sidewalk, Torrens shook his head and laughed.

"What is it?" Smith asked as he unlocked the trunk, opened it, and revealed a pile of small and medium-sized boxes. He rifled through them, reading over the labels stuck to each of them. He selected one, set it aside, then dug around some more.

"We're actually doing this," Torrens said. "We're actually building a machine that will–"

"Don't say it out loud," Smith said.

"You think someone is listening out here?"

"I think they're listening *everywhere*. But also, I don't want to jinx it." He handed two medium-sized boxes to Torrens and closed the trunk.

"And you're going to go through with it? You yourself?"

"I am." He offered Torrens a sardonic smile. "After all the time trips I've made, what's one more?"

"I'll need to test it first," Torrens said, "to make sure it works properly."

"There won't be any way to tell, from this end, if it worked or not," Smith pointed out. "And, anyway, when you activate it the first time, there will be a strong electromagnetic reaction. I'm sure Denali and her bully-boys will detect it. It probably won't take them very long to figure out that it happened in your lab. They'll come running, and that will be the end of it." He shrugged. "So I'm thinking we'll only get one chance."

"But–we will need a guinea pig," Torrens protested. "Surely we have to test it at least once."

"No," Smith said, shaking his head. "When you have it ready to go, contact me through the usual channels and I'll come in. And then you can use me as your guinea pig."

"Just like that?" Torrens said.

Smith nodded. "Just like that."

Torrens thought it all through for a moment. "But–what about this resistance army you've built? If you're gone, who will lead them against the Union?"

"Jack can lead them. That's part of the reason I chose him at the start; why I always choose him at the start. He's always creative with the belt, *and* he tends to blossom into a pretty decent guerilla commander, when the chips are down."

Torrens considered this.

"So–if your resistance army *can* get the job done and overthrow the Union, why take this trip yourself?"

Smith shrugged. "Just in case the resistance fails, I suppose." He paused, then added, "Plus, I'm not entirely certain any of this happens the way it has, if I don't go back and make it happen. Again."

Torrens was looking at him quizzically. "I'm not sure I follow."

"Neither am I, to be honest," Smith laughed. "Think of it this way: We arrived at the point we are at now, where the resistance has a decent shot at winning, because originally I went back in time and made things happen a certain way." He paused, pursed his lips and added, "Though, admittedly, it took me quite a few tries to get it this right."

"Okay," Torrens said, "I understand so far, though I'm not sure I see it the same way you do."

"Perfectly fine," Smith said, holding up both hands. "This is all mostly guesswork on my part, though of course I do have the advantage of having experienced it all multiple times now."

Torrens nodded, conceding that point at least.

"But here's the thing," Smith continued. "That first trip took me way back, much further than any of the later ones. I ended up around 700 AD. And in a few days, we arrive at the date where I first went back in time. What happens if I don't go back *again*, and kick things off the way I did before?"

Torrens ran his hands through his hair. "I give up," he said. "What happens?"

"I don't know either, you nit, and that's the point!" He spread his hands. "For all I know, if I *don't* go back again, maybe everything reverts back to as if I never did."

Now Torrens simply stared at him. "But—but that would mean—"

Smith nodded. "Yes. You see it now, don't you?"

"I think I do," Torrens said. "It would mean you're trapped in a long loop. You keep having to go back. Over and over."

"Forever. Yes." Smith stared at nothing for a long moment, then blinked and met the scientist's eyes. He smiled. "But we don't know it for certain—not just yet. Even so," he added with a shrug, "I think it's better that I go back."

For nearly two full minutes, the two men simply sat there, saying nothing to one another. Finally Torrens sighed heavily and gave Smith a look. "None of it makes logical sense," he said.

"You're telling me. But after everything it's cost me to get this far, well…" He chuckled and shook his head. "...Let's just say I'm not taking any chances."

Torrens considered this and nodded. "Sure," he said. "That makes as much–or as little–sense as anything else in this mess."

"It's the only way to even halfway wrap your head around it," Smith said with a grin. "So—I'm doing it. *We're* doing it."

"I'll have it ready," Torrens assured him. "And it'll work."

Smith clasped his hand. "I know you will," he said. He didn't speak the rest of that thought: *You always do.*

And with that, the two men climbed into their cars and went their separate ways. For the time being.

3:

Days later: Xaveria Denali stormed into Torrens' lab like a tall, slender tornado. The limp had nearly vanished when she walked; it seemed she'd quickly gotten used to her new, bionic leg. Behind her came two Kratons, servos whining as they moved, along with two human scientists.

"Ah. Sub-Administrator," Torrens exclaimed, not bothering to look up from the computer where he was working. "How good to see you up and around again."

Denali ignored his salutation. She stopped only a short distance from him and glared. "Torrens," she said. "Our situation is growing intolerable. What are you doing to make it right?"

Now the scientist did look up. She was gazing at him imperiously, as though weighing whether to have him shot.

"I have several projects underway at the moment," he replied casually, keeping himself from rising to her level of intensity. That didn't seem to him a place he'd want to be for long, or one he'd long survive. Instead he smiled flatly at her, ignored the Kratons and the other scientists, and said, "There's one I think you will find to be of particular interest."

Denali ignored this entirely. "Have you found a way to nullify Gael's shield yet?" she demanded.

"Not beyond what the good Dr. Krenz accomplished with his wave harmonics, I'm afraid," Torrens replied. "But the equipment is bulky and requires a massive and continuous source of power, so creating a portable unit is quite out of the question, at least for now." He chuckled. "So all you have to do is capture him and bring him into this building, where we can strap him down and use that machine on him again."

Denali's sour expression darkened.

"You *were* able to do it once before," Torrens noted.

"It was a fluke," the woman growled. "We slipped an agent under heavy mind control into the audience at his arena match, waited until she had gotten close to him, then sent in an army of Kratons to force him to protect her. Once she gained his trust, he let her inside his bubble." Denali sighed heavily. "Stabbing him was only one option. I'm still not certain why she opted for it, and did it so soon in their relationship."

"And we can't exactly ask her, can we?"

Denali's dark eyes bored in on Torrens. "No, Doctor," she hissed. "We cannot. But if there is one thing I'm certain of, after the way it all worked out, it's that Gael is unlikely to allow anyone else into that bubble with him. Not anytime soon."

Torrens nodded at this.

"We were speaking of Dr. Krenz," Torrens said after a moment's silence. "Is there any word on his condition?"

Denali looked away. "Krenz's body could not be saved. His intellect is being preserved, however. But he is not yet conscious. And we have no idea of when he might wake up." She turned back to Torrens. "And that means you are in charge here. At least for now. Until Krenz has recovered, you are the best we have available." She leaned in. "And that is why I am here, demanding progress. Krenz would have succeeded by now. You have nearly infinite resources at your disposal. My patience, however, is *not* infinite. I demand results."

"What's the rush, Sub-Administrator?" Torrens asked. "Gael is just one man. How much damage could he be doing?"

"More than you might imagine," she growled. "And he's not just one man anymore. He's building an army. A resistance force. They're calling themselves 'the Union.' Can you imagine? The Union! In direct provocation of our leaders. It is entirely unacceptable."

"Oh?" Torrens pretended to be surprised by this news, and to consider it. "Even so, surely they cannot represent much of a threat to the *real* Union—" He nodded toward the two hulking robots behind her. "—or to our mighty Kratons."

"They have been costly enough," Denali replied. "In recent days they have attacked our military bases and work camps. Freed many of our laborers. Cost us time and money and resources. And evaded all attempts to capture even one of them."

"But—how many of them can there be?" Torrens stroked his chin. "Even if Gael and a few confederates kidnapped workers from the labor camps, their nanites should be keeping them docile and subservient to the Union."

"We... think they've found a way to overcome the nanites," Denali admitted reluctantly. "More every day appear to be freeing themselves of Union influence."

"How can that be possible?" Torrens asked, feigning shock, knowing he himself was one of the lucky humans that Jack Gael had freed from the alien nanites.

"That, Dr. Torrens, is one of the many things *you* are supposed to be figuring out for us." She rested her hands on her hips and glared at him. "Or else you will be sent to the labor pits and someone else will be promoted to Chief Scientist. Do you understand?"

Torrens remembered the old protocols. He stood up straight and saluted. "I understand and I obey, Sub-Administrator."

"Good," the woman said. And with that, she swept out of the room. She moved as gracefully as she was able, given her new mechanical leg. The Kratons followed along silently in her wake. The two human scientists, however, remained. They stood at rigid attention across the room from Torrens, who looked at them in puzzlement.

"Why are you still here?" he demanded.

The three looked nervously at one another, and then the tallest of them replied, "Sub-Administrator Denali has reassigned us to your lab. We are to assist with your work."

"You mean you are to spy on me and report back to her on everything I do," Torrens corrected.

The three lab-coated newcomers looked at one another but said nothing.

"Very well," he said at length. "I could certainly use some help here." He paused, thinking. Then, "And—you may have noticed, the Sub-Administrator demanded I spare no efforts and no expense to stop Jack Gael and end his rebellion—correct?"

The three blinked and pursed their lips and looked at one another.

"Well?" Torrens demanded loudly. "Did she or did she not?"

"Those were not her precise words, Doctor," one of them began to say.

"Then let us call her back in here," Torrens suggested, strolling over to them and inspecting them closely, like a drill sergeant in the Marines. "Let's inform her that *you three* are unclear on the orders she just issued. I'm sure she'd be very happy to stop whatever she's doing and return to go over it with you one more time. Imagine the reward you might all receive for that."

The three appeared very uncomfortable now.

Torrens stepped over to the communications unit on the nearest wall and made as if to punch the main button. "I should call her back for you—yes?"

"No," the tall one snapped. "No—that will not be necessary, Doctor." He glanced at the other two quickly, then looked back at Torrens. "I—I believe you summed up… the *spirit* of her orders… very effectively." Sweat was running down his face by the time he got those sentences out.

Inside, Torrens was laughing. Outwardly, he continued to regard the three with a carefully-calculated combination of contempt and condescension. "Very well," he said at last. He motioned the three to follow him across the laboratory to a new assembly of machinery he'd been working on when Denali had first arrived. "I believe this device will be able to solve all our problems, once it is in full working order," he told them. "It combines existing human and Union technology with a few components with which we have only recently come into possession." He thought of John Smith handing over those components a few days earlier, but kept that part of the story to himself. "It doesn't work yet. But we simply must complete its construction soon, in order to satisfy our superiors."

The three gathered around the machinery and examined it visually, being careful not to touch it. The main body was a dull gray box, about a meter's width per side. A gray metal loop extended out from and back into each of the surfaces not touching the floor. A control panel covered in multicolored lights flickered at waist level on one of the sides.

After a few moments, the tall scientist looked at Torrens with a frown. "What will it *do*, Doctor?" he asked. "Disrupt Jack Gael's force field?"

"Nothing of the sort," Torrens said.

"Then what—?"

Torrens grinned. "This, my new young friends, is the solution to all our problems." He patted one of the metal loops.

"You see, this is nothing short of a temporal-based transporter."

At their blank expressions, he laughed before elaborating:

"It's a time machine."

4:

"Can you hear me, Dr. Krenz?"

The voice floated in the ether, buoyed by dark dreams and fantasies.

A jolt of electricity. The ether thinned, parted.

"Dr. Krenz?"

"Wurrr…"

The sound that came in apparent response to the repeated question was puzzling. It sounded more like a mechanical whirring than a vocal utterance.

"Dr. Krenz, can you wake up?"

"…Urrrrrr…"

Another bolt of lightning ran through—the ether? The world itself? No—through his *brain.*

What was that feeling?

Was it… *pain?*

That seemed right. And yet it also seemed very wrong. It wasn't pain exactly—not the way he remembered it. But somehow he knew it served the same purpose.

Did that mean… Was he feeling pain in a *different* way than before?

How could that be?

"Dr. Krenz, we can see you're partially conscious, but there are still no signs of body control. So we're going to up the voltage and try to bring you to full awareness."

What was that voice saying? What was it droning on about? Why couldn't it just go away and leave him alone?

Lightning.

His wishes suddenly no longer mattered. He was dragged virtually kicking and screaming out of the well of darkness within which he'd floated, and back into the real world.

He opened his eyes.

"Dr. Krenz! Welcome back!"

Erich Krenz, without moving his body at all, looked around at what lay within his immediate field of vision.

He saw scientists in lab coats, and behind them the unmistakable slender form of Xaveria Denali, all staring at him—some in anticipation, some in wonder, and some in what might very well have been horror.

Horror? Why should *that* be?

Then he started to remember.

The man in the bubble. Jack Gael.

There had been a fight.

Gael had punched him. He'd hit Krenz with the full force of that impenetrable force field.

And then… what?

Nothing.

Darkness.

Unconsciousness.

…Coma?

And if so—for *how long?*

By sheer force of will, Krenz caused his right hand to come up off the—hospital bed? Surely it was a hospital bed he lay upon. He angled his head enough that he could look down at his hand.

What he saw was not a hand. Not a *human* hand, anyway.

It was an intricate construction of silver metal parts.

He flexed his "fingers" and watched in wonder as the metal parts moved with clockwork precision. A soft whirring sound came from them as they shifted about.

"Your body," came the voice of the doctor who had been speaking to him, "was damaged beyond all repair."

Beyond all repair? Then how was he alive?

"Sub-Administrator Denali authorized the transplanting of your mind—your consciousness—into a different body."

"Whrrr—" He tried again to speak and still couldn't form an actual word. His mouth felt different. Wrong.

Wait—his mind had been placed into a different body? Exactly whose body did he now occupy? The thought washed over him with the force of a mental storm. What new frailties and vulnerabilities had he inherited?

Then he put two and two together and thought maybe he understood. The metal hand. That was *his* new hand. So perhaps his entire *body*…?

"Thssss bdyyyyy…"

The doctors and scientists surrounding him moved in closer, hearing him trying to speak. What he intended to be whispering, however, came out as a mechanical whine. He paused, gathered himself, and tried again.

"This… body," he said, the voice grating and electronic. *"What… is it?"*

The scientists and doctors looked at one another—nervously, Krenz felt. They looked guilty. Probably because they hadn't asked his permission to put him into this body.

"A Kraton," the main doctor replied at last. "You were placed into the shell of a Kraton that had not yet been activated."

Krenz flexed his robotic fingers again, watching the parts move as he ordered them to move. Then he looked up at the doctor with eyes he now knew were electronic—and which burned with crimson fire.

"Good," he said.

They all looked at each other with a strange combination of relief and alarm. Relief that, apparently, he wasn't angry at all; alarm that he seemed somehow *pleased* about having the body of a Kraton now.

At that point, the woman responsible stepped forward. The scientists parted like the Red Sea to allow her to stride up to the side of the bed.

Krenz wanted to laugh: She'd lurked in the background until she knew for sure how he would react. Probably she'd feared he would lash out violently.

"Welcome back, Dr. Krenz," she said.

He wondered if she'd been about to say, "To the land of the living," and had stopped herself. And well she should have. He wasn't entirely sure that was true anymore.

Having figured out how to move his hand, subsequent movements became much easier. He forced himself to sit up in the big bed, which he then saw wasn't a bed at all, but a metal slab holding up his metal form. He didn't mind; it felt no different to him.

"Sub... Administrator," he droned. *"I am happy... to be back. And... I have much... to think about."*

She frowned at this but then nodded. "I understand," she said. "You have to come to terms with this new body."

"No," Krenz replied immediately. *"Not... about that. I am... pleased... about that."*

"Then what—?"

"About how... to destroy... Jack Gael... and his rebellion," Krenz said in his flat monotone.

Her eyes widened. "Oh?"

"Yes," he said. And, *"Give me... one hour. One hour... to learn... this body. One hour... to think. Then return. I will... have... your answer."*

Denali considered this for a moment. She smiled a very tiny smile and nodded.

"I will see you in one hour, then," she said.

And she swept out of the room, ushering the various scientists out as well.

The large, powerful robot that now carried Erich Krenz's mind sat there on the edge of the bed, moving its limbs, practicing its vocal functions. It stood and, slowly at first but with growing confidence, walked about the room.

When one hour had passed and Xaveria Denali and the team of scientists returned, the big metal form stood there in the center of the room, head bowed, mechanical hands clasped behind its back, in a pose Krenz himself had assumed many times over the years.

"This is not my *laboratory building,"* Krenz said. His voice was now much smoother, without the electronic stuttering, though it still sounded hollow and synthetic.

"No," Denali replied. "We are at the Union's medical/surgical facility approximately two kilometers from your old lab building."

"Torrens is running the labs now, I assume."

"He is," she said.

Krenz said nothing for a moment. He was thinking; remembering what had been drifting through his mind as his mind itself had been floating over into and filling this new body.

As he ran through the multitude of threads and followed each to its natural conclusion, one of them presented itself to him as the preferred option.

With startling suddenness, he turned directly to face Denali. She started, then regained her imperturbable icy veneer.

"I have it," he told her.

The other scientists looked from Krenz to her.

"Have what?" she asked, her expression uncertain. Clearly she had not yet decided if she could work with this cyborg being that had once been one of her chief scientists. Well, he would show her.

"I have been puzzling over the current situation with the rebellion."

"Yes? And?"

"And I believe I have determined how to end that rebellion in one single stroke."

She raised one eyebrow. "Go on. I'm listening."

"Nanites."

Both of her eyebrows plunged down, reflecting profound disappointment.

"Dr. Krenz," she intoned, "I did not go to such a tremendous amount of expense and trouble to resurrect you, only for you to recommend to me the process we have been using on the native inhabitants of this planet for at least two hundred years."

The robotic face of Krenz didn't flinch, and the blazing red eyes didn't move from her.

"I am not speaking of the weak nanites we have employed during all of that time, Sub-Administrator," Krenz said, his new robotic voice resuming some of its harsh tone. *"The nanites that merely cause humans to be more vulnerable to suggestion. That make them slightly more docile. No,"* he said, *"The day when those measures were adequate to our needs has passed."*

Her eyes narrowed. "Then what—?"

"We must have new nanites," he replied. *"Nanites that will give the Union direct and total control of every human on this planet."*

She was obviously taken aback by this. She moved forward and leaned in over him. "Tell me more," she purred.

He considered the various simulations his new computer mind had run while he had been acclimating himself to his new body. This took less than half a second. Then he told her, *"They require no new advancements. They can be made now. Production can begin in this very facility. Though we will need the maintenance and delivery systems available only in our old laboratory building to properly send the nanites out into the global ecosystem. Obviously we want to be sure we can infect the entire species, and not miss a single person."*

Denali blinked at this. Her veneer of icy calm almost, almost cracked. She looked around for a moment, then back at Krenz, and replied, "Yes—of course."

Inside his metal box of a skull, Krenz laughed at this. Surely, at this very moment, Denali was coming to understand that Krenz, now essentially a Kraton, was free of the nanites forever, while she in her human body was not.

Another thought raced through his mind then. Would she or the Union leaders suspect his loyalty, if he could no longer be influenced by nanites? He concluded that, not only was that likely, but he calculated a ninety percent likelihood that these very scientists that had transferred his consciousness to this body had also rigged it up with a self-destruct, which he would probably be told about if he ever exhibited any signs of disobedience. Or perhaps they would simply trigger it immediately, out of fear. Fear of what he had become. Of what they had made him into.

Krenz laughed at this. He ran a quick internal scan—quicker than any human could ever notice—and detected the device he was expecting to find. It rested in the lower left portion of his torso. Instantly he caused it to be deactivated.

It wasn't that he wished to be disloyal to the Union. To the contrary, he had always enjoyed being a part of the ruling cabal of this planet, and he had every wish and desire to continue to serve them faithfully and true.

He just didn't like to be threatened into it. And he certainly had no desire to carry around a potentially fatal weakness. Not when he could simply shut it off.

Once the self-destruct unit had been neutralized, he returned his attention to Denali. He calculated that approximately three seconds had passed since their last verbal exchange—not enough time to cause her to become suspicious, he determined.

"There is one side effect of the new nanites I've designed," he added. *"Though I doubt this will be enough to dissuade you from employing them. Still, I feel I must divulge the information to you and to our superiors, so that an informed decision can be made."*

"Yes?" Denali asked, wariness returning to her features. "What side effect?"

"Upon release of these proposed new nanites," Krenz said matter-of-factly, *"a very large number of humans will simply die."*

"Die?" Denali took this in, then nodded. "I see. A large number?"

"At least half of those who remain," the robotic voice answered. *"Probably many more."*

Denali for once appeared shaken, though she cast it aside quickly. "And the rest?"

"Not just susceptibility to the power of suggestion, as we currently enjoy. This would mean complete and total obedience."

Denali thought this over for no more than two or three seconds, then nodded.

"I will take this to the Union," she said, "with my full endorsement for its employ."

"I was certain that you would," he said.

She started to leave. Krenz called her back.

"Yes, Doctor?"

"There is one other thing. You may already know about it, of course. But, just in case…"

She said nothing, waiting.

"Moments ago I interfaced with Dr. Torrens' laboratory," Krenz explained. *"To be certain its facilities could handle the full distribution of the new nanites."*

"Yes?" She was growing slightly impatient. Which was funny to him. She had no idea the amount of patience he was exercising with her. After all, his mind was now moving hundreds of times faster than hers. Thousands of times faster.

"While my consciousness was inside Torrens' lab, I detected a new device that has been set up." He paused, then, *"One that will draw a vast amount of power, when it is activated."*

Now he had her attention. "Oh? And what exactly is the function of this new device?"

When he told her his suspicion, she didn't believe him.

When he backed it up with all sorts of mathematical and theoretical evidence, she still didn't believe him.

"Then, perhaps, you should ask him *about it,"* Krenz said. *"Before he does something to change history itself."*

CHAPTER 10

I ALWAYS GO BACK — THE TIME COMMANDOS — A STRANGER — THE LEGATUS

1:

Seated across the broad conference table in the Union's new lab building, Xaveria Denali steepled her long, slender fingers under her chin and gazed at Howard Torrens.

"When, exactly, were you planning to tell me you'd invented a *time machine*, Doctor?" she asked. "Or were you planning to save it for yourself?"

Torrens was taken aback. She *knows. But—how could she know?*

He'd sworn his lab assistants to secrecy. Now he suspected they'd immediately gone and spilled their guts about it.

Despite himself, the scientist started to sweat.

It's okay, he reminded himself. *You knew this could happen— that she would find out. You're prepared.*

He offered the woman a casual smile and said, "Save it for myself? Oh, you are always so delightfully amusing, Sub-Administrator." He offered her a weak smile. "Quite honestly, I've never been hopeful it had a prayer of actually working. I didn't want to waste your time until I knew for certain it would actually function, and wasn't just a pipe dream."

She looked back at him for a moment and matched his smile. "And when exactly do you suppose that would have been?" She didn't bother to wait for an answer. She looked past him and into his lab, as if she could figure out with but a glance which of the many banks of machinery constituted this alleged time machine. Behind her, the servos of the two huge Kratons whined as they shifted subtly in position.

"Does it work yet?" she asked.

"Not entirely, no."

"Not entirely? So some portion of it *does* work?" She leaned in closer, increasingly interested. "What part of it yet eludes you?"

"Well, it's extremely difficult to test," he said. "You see, so far, it only works in one direction. *Backwards*. I'm not able to send something *forward* in time at all, and when I send something *back* in time, I'm unable to return it to the present. It's just gone."

"But—wait. Did you say you *can* send something *back* in time?"

"I…*believe* so, yes," Torrens admitted reluctantly. "But—again—it's hard to be *sure*, when I can't bring the test object back to examine it."

She waved a dismissive hand. "That's fine. Good enough. That's all we need."

"All you need? Need for what, Sub-Administrator?"

"For my plan. I'm going to have you send a commando unit back in time. There, they will prevent this resistance from ever forming. And they will acquire that silver belt for me—before it ever falls into the possession of Jack Gael."

Torrens took this in without any visible reaction. Inside, however, his mind was churning. He had been concerned that Denali might discover the time machine before he and Smith had been able to use it as they intended. He had *not*, however considered that she might actually want to *use* it, and use it *immediately*.

Denali went on a little longer about her grandiose plans—and about how Torrens would benefit from them, thanks to his continuing good work for her and for the Union. Meanwhile, he felt as if he were about to explode. He needed to contact John Smith immediately.

After several long, excruciating minutes, the tall, slender woman stood up from the conference table and smiled a bone-chilling smile at him.

"I'm quite pleased, Doctor," she said. "You have done well. These are all very positive developments. I anticipate ending this so-called Resistance very soon. And that reminds me." She leaned in and lowered her tone. "You may not have heard yet about what Dr. Krenz has achieved."

"Dr. Krenz? Then he's—?"

"He is back among the living, yes—in a manner of speaking. His mind is now housed within the body of a Kraton."

The thought of such a thing horrified Torrens beyond description, but he managed to keep the look off his face.

"And his intellect is already paying dividends for us," Denali continued. "He has developed a new type of self-replicating nanite. One that can control human minds more effectively, and is more resistant to outside interference."

"He has, has he?" Torrens felt ice cold daggers jabbing his insides at the mere thought.

"There are admittedly a few drawbacks," Denali added. "A rather high mortality rate, for one thing."

This startled Torrens so much he couldn't keep the look off his face. "*Mortality rate?*"

"Yes," the woman replied. "It seems some sixty percent of humans exposed to the new nanites die an agonizing death." Utterly misreading the look on Torrens' face, she nodded understandingly. "I know," she said. "It will be unfortunate to lose such a large portion of the labor pool. But I believe it will be worth it, because Dr. Krenz's tests show that the remaining forty percent will obey! Unquestioningly!"

Torrens wanted to throw up. Instead he forced a bland smile onto his face and said, "Ah, I see. Please give him my congratulations."

Torrens contacted John Smith the moment Denali left the building. They arranged an emergency meeting for as soon as Torrens' work shift ended.

Over drinks at the Blue Dolphin, the scientist laid out for the man in blue the terrifying new information. When he'd finished, a grim Smith stared ahead, thinking.

"We have to move all of our timetables up," Smith said at length. "I don't like it, because it won't match the exact day I originally went back. But I don't see that we have a choice now." He shook his head in frustration. "This is what you get with time travel. Things change uncontrollably every single time, no matter what you do—but never in the ways you want them to change!" He sighed heavily. "So, this is what we have to work with, and we don't have a choice. I'll pass the word to Jack. I'll tell him he and his new army will have to attack immediately."

"But the Resistance isn't ready yet—at least, not from what little I've heard."

"No, it's not," Smith said. "But we don't have a choice now. We can't let the Union use your machine. *We* have to use it once—to send me back—and then you have to disable it. Blow it up. Whatever it takes to prevent it from ever being used again."

Torrens stared off into the distance; he was thinking of ways to disguise the time machine so the Union wouldn't be able to recognize or use it, but he could still activate it at some future point, if necessary.

"Dr. Torrens? Did you hear me? Do you agree?"

Torrens blinked. "What? Oh–yes; yes, of course. Destroy it afterward." He nodded reassuringly. "But–the time and place you've told me you want to be sent. Why there? Why then? It seems so… obscure."

Smith chuckled mirthlessly. "Obscure is right. But you have to trust me–that's the time and the place where I need to go. It's the time and the place I went to the first time, when this whole thing started, and I believe it's the only way to bring it all to a satisfactory conclusion. I think it's a nexus moment in history. It's drawing me back. I can feel it, even now."

"But–what about everything going on *now?* Jack Gael and the Resistance, and–"

"That's all critically important, yes," Smith said, nodding. "I wouldn't have spent so much time getting Jack to where he is now, if I didn't believe he has a crucially important role to play in defeating the Union and liberating the Earth. But–" And at that,

Smith sat back and regarded the scientist with broad, bloodshot eyes. "—I think if I don't go back to where it all started for me–back to that place, at the dawn of the Eighth Century–and make sure things get going again the way they *have* to, then nothing that happens after that will matter, because it could all change. It almost certainly *will* change."

Torrens sifted through this. He shook his head. "But it could change for the *better*," he observed.

"No, I don't think so," Smith replied. "Now that time has almost caught up to the moment when I first was sent back, I think I have to start the cycle over again. If I don't go back and get the ball rolling just like before, maybe Jack never gets the belt, and the Resistance never forms, and the Union completes its rape of this world and its extermination of the Human race." He laid his palms flat on the table and met Torrens' eyes. "Do you see, Doctor? I have to go back–because I think I *always* go back."

The scientist did not look convinced, but he nodded his head slowly. "If you're that certain it's the only way, then that's what we'll do," he conceded. Then he paused and offered Smith a confused look.

"We have to get you into the building. Into the laboratory. How? Ever since the incident with Jack, the Kratons have locked everything down. You say you have to use the time machine. How do you propose we get you into the room with it?"

"Leave that to me. I'll be there. In your lab. When the time comes. Just have the machine fired up and ready to send me back." He smiled grimly at the gray-haired scientist. "And then, as soon as I'm gone, not only must you destroy that machine—you have to erase any plans, diagrams, schematics, and whatever other instructions that you may have left."

"I understand," Torrens said, frowning. He stared down at the table.

"I know it was a lot of work and you're proud of it, Doctor," Smith said. "But it's too dangerous to leave around for the Union to seize."

"I can't bring you back," Torrens said quickly, looking up. "It will be a one-way trip."

"I know," Smith said. "I've been on a lot of those. This is just one more. I'll get back eventually."

Torrens stared back at him and shook his head. "That's all very hard to believe," he said.

"Indeed it is," Smith replied. "I don't know that I entirely believe it myself, and I've lived every single second of it."

He thought for another moment, then met the scientist's eyes. His own burned with a pale inner fire that verged on madness.

"This is it, Doctor," he said. "Everything is on the line here. And we can't have any mistakes. Because we'll only get one shot." He smiled flatly. "This time around, anyway."

2:

Gladiator smashed through the Union lab building's defenses and led his little army inside just as Dr. Howard Torrens was powering up his Temporal Transporter for the first time.

Alarms shrieked. Kratons stationed in various locations came to life and advanced on the intruders, weapons blazing. Torrens feigned surprise and barked orders at the Union commando team assembled in his lab: "They're coming! Get ready. I'm sending you all through no matter what happens!"

The leader of that commando team, a particularly scaly gray alien called Juvus Naxam, had been about to issue that same order. Standing over seven feet tall, with one large eye on each side of his reptilian head, he closed his broad mouth and motioned angrily at the six other members of his Time Commando team. Each of them was an alien as well, and part of the planet's ruling cabal; the Union dared not trust so critical a mission to semi-enslaved humans or robots. With sharp gestures Naxam urged them to squeeze in closer on the golden metal square set into the floor. The square Dr. Torrens had told them was the Temporal Transporter's "send" zone. A golden square situated right next to a silver circle of similar dimensions.

Sounds of battle came to Torrens and Naxam from outside the lab and down the hallway. The sounds grew louder very quickly.

"Activate the machine," Naxam barked at Torrens. *"Quickly!"*

Torrens looked out through the transparent doors, trying to spot the oncoming attackers. Nothing yet. He turned back to the alien.

"Yes—yes, I will, as soon as the computer finishes calibrating the target coordinates precisely."

"It does not have to be precise," Naxam shot back. "Our goal is to go back in time to before the first Union invasion, and clear the way for it to proceed even more successfully—and to locate and retrieve for our superiors the silver belt currently worn by Jack Gael, before ever he acquires it. This requires no precision. Any time within approximately a fifty-year window prior to the Union's arrival on Earth should do nicely." He snarled as he raised his left hand, which was covered in a gleaming golden gauntlet. "And with this weapon, I will have no difficulties fulfilling my mission." The alien jabbed a gray finger from his right hand at Torrens. "Now, *activate the machine!*"

"Yes—very well," Torrens said, fumbling at the controls and very carefully *not* activating the machine. He looked back up at Naxam, saying, "You do remember this machine cannot bring you back to this time, yes? It can only send you *back* in time—a one-way trip. Returning to this period of history is up to *you.*"

"Yes, yes," Naxam said tiredly. "We were briefed on all of this. We will construct hibernation units using materials we are taking with us—" He patted two large black plastic cases being carried by one of the other Time Commandos. "—and materials we should be able to acquire in that era. Then we will seal ourselves away until awakened in this time again. Gael will no longer possess the belt— *we* will! Whereupon we will hand it over to our masters, and complete victory will be ours." Naxam nodded in arrogant satisfaction at the plan he'd laid out, then glared across the short distance to Torrens, still manning the control panel. "Now—again, Doctor—*activate the machine!*"

Torrens had begun to panic. He was running out of ways to delay. *Come on, Jack,* his nanite-free mind thought to itself. *Hurry up and get here! Solve this problem for me, now!*

And just as he was thinking that thought, the Resistance army burst into the hallway at the far end and advanced rapidly on the doors to his lab.

Naxam saw them coming, Jack Gael—the Gladiator—at the vanguard. The slender man in the red jumpsuit chopped at Kratons left and right, his blows severing heads from bodies and arms from torsos. The men and women behind him—*free* men and women,

Torrens reminded himself with a swell of pride—fired their pistols and rifles and blasters left and right, cutting down any other remaining defenders.

The cavalry had arrived!

But the enemy had a cavalry of its own. An army of Kratons—dozens of them; far more than he'd suspected occupied the building at the moment—appeared from a side corridor and rushed in. They counterattacked, forming a barrier—a wall of powerful robots—separating Gladiator's attackers from the Time Commandos.

Before Torrens could say or do anything else, however, a strong, muscular, and very scaly gray arm reached out and a scaly gray hand seized him by the throat, lifting him a couple of inches off the floor. "ACTIVATE. THE. MACHINE."

Gasping for breath as Naxam leapt back onto the gold square in the floor alongside the half-dozen other commandos, Torrens reached down and touched a purple square on the control panel. "Powering up," he announced. Instantly a deep, resonant hum filled the air.

"Yes," Naxam barked. *"Yes!* Send us *back!* Our *destiny* awaits!"

Torrens touched the button again, knowing it wouldn't work. "Sending!"

Nothing happened.

The scaly gray alien looked around, scowled, and turned to Torrens. "What is wrong? Why have we not moved?"

"One second," Torrens said, feigning confusion. "I'm working on it."

At that moment, Jack Gael smashed his way past the last remaining Kraton and rushed at the commandos. He leapt forward, arms wide, and if Torrens understood anything about Gael's tactics, he suspected the invisible force bubble surely was expanding in front of him, like a bulldozer blade.

Sure enough, Jack managed to tackle all of the Time Commandos at once, knocking them all off the golden square and onto the floor. That done, he had to fight to extricate himself from them, as they sought to pin him down and overpower him.

Meanwhile, with absolutely no one looking at Torrens anymore, the scientist nodded to a figure who stood alone in the shadows, practically invisible himself.

"You're up," Torrens said.

A figure all in blue stepped out into the light. He nodded at the mass of aliens fighting Jack.

"The golden gauntlet again. No surprises from that bunch. All the creativity of a head-butt to the face." He held up a small device the size of a button. "They'll find that this time I'm prepared."

As usual, Torrens had no idea what the man was talking about. He simply motioned to the silver circle. "Good luck, Mr. Smith," he said.

Smith pocketed the small item, stepped onto the disk and nodded once.

Torrens tapped the purple button again. The hum grew louder still.

John Smith's figure shimmered and vanished as he was hurled back in time. Or, at least, that's what Torrens *hoped* had just happened to the man.

Guinea pig, indeed.

But then, as Torrens reached out to tap the button one last time, turning it off, the Time Commandos managed to regain their footing and charged into Jack Gael. Together they formed a scrum of bodies, with Jack stumbling backwards and the Commandos surging into him.

Jack was knocked back, until he inadvertently stepped onto the silver circle. He vanished.

The alien commandos tumbled after him, and none of them fully registered that he was gone until it was too late. The entire mass of them fell onto the silver circle and vanished as well.

Now Howard Torrens stood alone in the lab—a lab that moments earlier had been filled with battling soldiers and rebels and robots.

He looked at the silver circle in horror for five long, full seconds.

"Well, crap," he said to himself.

At that moment he noticed something else: The silver circle–the time travel gateway–wasn't empty. There was an object resting on its surface.

"Uh oh," Torrens muttered. "Oh, no."

The belt. The silver belt that created the force field bubble around Jack Gael. It sat there, all alone, on the time travel gateway circle. It hadn't gone back with Jack when he and the Time Commandos had passed through.

How strange. Why might that be? Did it possess some property that disrupted the time travel effect? He supposed that must be the case, though he figured he could do a few tests later to try to find out for sure.

Then he thought of something else: This did not bode well for Jack Gael.

Wherever and whenever he emerged, Jack would be entirely defenseless–and in the company of six powerful and vicious alien warriors.

No, not good at all for Jack.

Torrens walked over and picked up the belt. For a long moment he seriously considered putting it on himself. But then he thought of all the trouble it had brought poor Jack. And about the people willing to saw Jack in half to get it. That, he decided, was trouble he did *not* need. No, he had plenty of trouble of his own at the moment. No need to ask for more.

An indicator light flashed on his main workstation: Someone was entering the building. He glanced at the security monitor. It was Xaveria Denali, along with a team of Kratons and a couple of human scientist types.

Torrens blinked and looked down at the belt he was holding–the object for which so much chaos had erupted over the past few months. The object Denali and her masters craved. The object they'd gone to such lengths to try to acquire.

Torrens hurried around the big silver sphere that still filled one corner of his lab. On the far side of it was a row of metal lockers along the wall. He opened a random one and stuffed the belt inside, then closed the door. He didn't bother to lock it. If anyone suspected an object of such power and value lay inside, no mere lock would even slow them down in getting inside.

That done, he switched off the time machine. He stared at it for another couple of seconds, marveling that it had apparently worked. He'd never entirely believed it would. Then he dropped into his big swivel chair next to the silver sphere and waited for Denali and her entourage to arrive.

The humming sound he'd noticed before had faded, which relieved him somewhat–but now it was slowly building back up again.

He didn't notice it at first. He was lost in his thoughts.

He'd just sent John Smith back in time, as the two of them had privately arranged earlier. That had gone according to plan.

The machine's hum grew louder still.

Torrens reached for his pipe.

The problem, of course, was that he'd also just sent seven Union-serving Time Commandos back with him.

And, of course, the Gladiator—Jack Gael.

The Resistance was already going to have to get by without Smith. What would it do without Gael?

What have you done, Howard?

He fumbled at his pipe, getting it filled with tobacco, and reached for a match.

The hum at last became so loud it brought him back from his reverie.

"What the devil is that?"

He looked over at the control panel. The temporal energy readings were off the scale.

"Oh, no," he whispered.

"Torrens," came a shouted voice from just outside his laboratory. "We have to talk. *Now!*"

Xaveria Denali glided into the room, her Kraton bodyguards surrounding her.

Torrens was just setting down his pipe and starting to get up when the time machine exploded.

3:

Centurion Julian Alexius Lascaris threw the bloody helmet down on the floor of the ersatz throne room, then glared up at his exiled emperor.

"Spies!" he hissed. "Spies sent by Leontius. Perhaps assassins as well."

Justinian II stared down at the scarlet-streaked object that lay before him. He started to speak, but halted before he'd gotten two syllables out. His eyes met those of Lascaris briefly before he looked away, one hand going to his mouth in shock.

"The time to move is *now*, great Caesar," Lascaris said. "We have the forces here, now, at the ready. Leontius must scarcely suspect the power you can marshal, merely awaiting your command to march."

"Leontius must suspect *something*," wheezed Radolus, the elderly advisor to the exiled emperor. "Why else would he send these alleged spies of which the centurion speaks?"

Justinian looked at Lascaris again. "Yes—what of this, Centurion?"

"That traitorous fool, Leontius, surely must not suspect much, my lord. Otherwise he would not have sent spies or assassins—he would have dispatched a *legion*, with orders to eradicate us all!"

Justinian furrowed his dark brows above darker eyes. Beneath them, the ghastly opening where his nose had once protruded reminded all present of how much the exiled ruler must want revenge—must want his throne in Constantinople back. And yet, he hesitated. Always he hesitated.

"Your soldiers stand ready to return to the capital and make it your own once more," Lascaris pressed on. "In addition, the chief of the Khazars has vowed to contribute many of his finest horse-mounted warriors to your cause." Lascaris looked from the former emperor to the aged advisor, then to the half-dozen other senior military officers gathered there in that tiny shack that they all pretended was a palace. "Will you march, sire?" Lascaris all-but-demanded. "Honor demands it. *God wills it!*"

"Keep silent, Lascaris," snapped one of the generals; the one called Tiberius the Younger. "The emperor will decide when it is time to march—and what exactly God wills!"

Lascaris shut his mouth reluctantly and began grinding his teeth. *These jackals,* he thought. *They sit here in this fly-infested cesspool of a Crimean town, Cherson, and pretend it's Constantinople. They make-believe they're still Roman officers and not disgraced exiles—just like me.*

But we can change that—if they'll show the backbone necessary to take action.

"I am sorry, General, but I cannot keep silent," Lascaris said after several seconds of doddering by the officers there assembled. "I believe the opportunity we have waited for has arrived, and we should seize it. Now!"

The generals and the advisor looked to the emperor, who blinked as if coming out of a trance. He turned his frowning attention on the centurion, then made a single quick motion of dismissal with one hand.

"We thank you for your words, Centurion," Justinian said. He looked down at the bloody helmet again, curled his lips, and motioned with one hand in a dismissive fashion. A servant swooped in and retrieved it, carrying it away. Justinian fanned himself for a moment, then shifted his gaze to Lascaris. "We will take this all under advisement."

And with that, Lascaris found himself hustled out the palace doors, which closed resoundingly behind him.

He stood on the side of a muddy street. People in all forms of colorful clothing walked past, moving in every direction, going about their daily tasks.

Palace? The Centurion scoffed at the thought. Cherson was a garbage dump. And, as much as it pained Lascaris to admit it to himself, Justinian and his generals were the garbage.

And Lascaris had no intention of becoming garbage himself.

Still grinding his teeth, he made his way along one sodden street after another, dodging merchants and beggars and prostitutes the entire way, until he arrived at his own meager dwelling. His woman, Lhaza, met him at the door.

"Home early, are you, Julian?"

The centurion shook his head bitterly.

"Those fools," he muttered. "They're condemning us all to spend the rest of our lives here, cut off from power, from wealth, from anything that makes life worth living."

Lhaza reached up and stroked his rough cheek. "Come inside and relax," she said. "I will prepare drinks… and perhaps we can find at least *one* thing to do, that makes life worth living."

Lascaris smiled down at her. He opened his mouth to speak. Before he could get a word out, however, a cry came up from somewhere nearby. Shouts, a crash, and more people shouting. Lascaris turned away from the blonde woman and gripped the pommel of his gladius as he strained to see or hear anything that might indicate what was happening.

Just then a messenger darted around the corner, obviously headed the way Lascaris had just come–toward the emperor's "palace." Lascaris reached out with one powerful hand and halted the man in his tracks.

"Impede me not, sir," the man croaked, almost breathless, "for I bear intelligence destined for the emperor!"

"Tell me this intelligence," Lascaris barked.

"I must not tell it to anyone before I have delivered it to the great Caesar," the messenger replied, trying to catch his breath.

"I am a Roman centurion in Caesar's service," Lascaris shouted. "Divulge your information now!"

"I–very well," the man said. "A stranger has appeared just outside of town."

Lascaris stared at him dumbly. "*That* is your message for the emperor?" he demanded. "Strangers come and go every day."

"You have missed the important part, lord," the messenger said, still breathing heavily. "This stranger *appeared*. As if from nowhere."

Lascaris's eyes narrowed. "What do you mean by this—he appeared, as if from nowhere?"

"Just that, O great centurion of the Empire. One moment the street was empty, and then came a strange flash of light–accounts of its exact nature and color vary from one witness to the next–and the next thing anyone knew, this man, this stranger, was standing there."

"Who is he?" Lascaris demanded. "What does he look like?"

"We do not know, sire," the messenger said. He squirmed as if desperate to get away. "That constitutes all that I know, and the sum of my message. May I now please proceed to the imperial residence to deliver it?"

"You may," Lascaris said, releasing him.

But no sooner had the messenger run off toward Justinian's ragged and flea-bitten excuse for a palace than another commotion came from the direction of the earlier disturbance. Lascaris decided to investigate for himself. Scarcely had he turned two corners, however, than he ran headlong into a small unit of his own troops, surrounding and escorting a man he'd never encountered before.

The prisoner was clad in strange garments–strange even for the cultural crossroads that was the Crimean Peninsula. He wore blue from head to toe. He had long, dark hair and dark eyes, and his nose was long and straight.

"You there," Lascaris called. "Halt!"

Seeing the centurion and hearing his command, the troops halted and saluted.

Lascaris approached and looked the stranger up and down carefully. Indeed, his outfit was unusual, to say the least.

"What is your name, and from whence do you hail?"

The man in blue met Lascaris' gaze and smiled. He said something under his breath, in words the centurion could not make out.

"Speak you only the barbarian tongues?" Lascaris demanded.

"No, no–I speak your language well enough," the man replied in a rough and odd-sounding form of Greek. "As to my name, I suppose 'John Smith' wouldn't work here. You may call me Constantine Vlahos."

A Roman soldier on either side held John Smith firmly by the upper arms. Meanwhile, this new officer was studying him closely.

"Vlahos," the Roman said. "A common enough name, for a most uncommon stranger." He rubbed his square-jawed chin as he squinted at Smith. "Why have you come to Cherson?"

"Cherson?" Smith considered the name and nodded to himself. "Then Torrens' machine worked even more precisely than I'd hoped. Excellent." He returned his attention to the centurion. "So the exiled emperor is here, then?"

"The emperor is here, yes. Justinian II."

"Very good. I have come bearing information for him. And counsel on matters most grave." He nodded once. "And you are–?"

"I am Julian Alexius Lascaris, centurion to the emperor."

"Yes, yes, I remember now," Smith said. "Well, that's fine, then. Take me to the emperor, if you please. I have much to say. And then much work lies before us." His eyes twinkled as he met those of the centurion again. "I fear I was not the only one to undertake the journey to your city, centurion. Others may be hot on my heels. If so, they'll likely be along sooner rather than later. We need to be ready."

Smith was thinking of the Time Commandos, who'd been in Torrens' lab when he'd departed. He'd told Torrens not to send them back–to destroy the machine instead. But he did not trust that man to carry out the task. Perhaps out of treachery, perhaps out of cowardice or incompetence, he did not trust Dr. Howard Torrens at all. Which meant he had to assume the Time Commandos would be coming after him, and he had to make such preparations for them as he could.

"Yes," he said aloud, "I fear they are coming. And could be here quite soon."

The Roman soldier was staring back at Smith. He shook his head. "You make little sense, stranger," he said. "*Who* will be along?"

Smith laughed out loud at this. "I cannot in all truthfulness call them *men*. Let's call them *demons*," he said.

The soldier recoiled at this. "Demons?" he gasped.

"Oh yes. Demons from the outer darkness." Smith looked up at the sky and added, "Quite literally."

4:

Weeks had passed, and the exiled emperor had made no moves toward defeating his rival in Constantinople and reclaiming his rightful throne. Because of this, Centurion Julian Alexius Lascaris was now back in the throne room, once more pressing the exiled emperor to take action.

"Again, I make this assertion, mighty Caesar," declared the centurion. "You must order the attack *now*. Already have we squandered much of our opportunity. Conditions may never be so favorable again."

Murmurs, mostly of disapproval, arose from around the flea-infested throne room.

"This again?" complained old Radolus, the elderly advisor. "Exile this man, my lord."

"Already do we dwell in exile here, Radolus," Lascaris snapped.

"This is true," the emperor noted.

"Then order him to commit suicide," Radolus said. "Anything to end this constant and repetitive—"

Lascaris moved directly in front of the old advisor, glaring down at him. "Some would say it is suicide to threaten me so," he growled.

"Gentlemen! Gentlemen!" called the emperor. "I will have peace and decorum in my court."

Lascaris glared at the old man for another long moment before stepping back and bowing to the emperor.

"Besides—Radolus is no longer my only advisor," Justinian noted. "We have a new one. One who, in his weeks with us, has demonstrated great wisdom." He looked across the room to another figure; a hooded one, who wore dark blue robes and dwelt deep in the shadows. "Legatus! Legatus Vlahos. What say you of the centurion's claims? What do *you* advise?"

Legatus Vlahos stepped forward and bowed to the emperor. Straightening and turning to face the centurion, he spoke—careful to infuse just the right amount of authority and command into his tones, without sounding impertinent or disrespectful. He was, of course, quite literally a past-master at such things.

"The centurion's words carry much wisdom, my lord," he said. "The usurper Leontius is away from the capital, and all signs indicate the people of Rome are increasingly unhappy under his reign and would welcome your return. They would, in fact, fight for it—for your restoration."

"You cannot know this," one of the generals shouted. "Why should we believe you?"

"Have I not amply demonstrated my knowledge these past few weeks, at your service, lord?" Vlahos bowed again to the emperor. "The people of the empire hunger for your restoration, my liege. You must seize this opportunity to reclaim your birthright and destroy the usurper once and for all."

The centurion—Lascaris—looked upon the hooded figure with a degree of visible appreciation. "The Legatus's speech is rough, but he speaks words of wisdom, great Caesar," he said.

"These two men will lead us to ruin," the general cried. "My lord—you must trust your officers! We are not at all convinced it would be wise to risk everything in such a foolhardy move."

"You wish the emperor to trust you?" the centurion said, turning to the general. "You generals who have done absolutely nothing to improve our condition from the moment we were sent into exile here? You generals who have proven time and again to be too timid to exploit the tiniest of opportunities that have presented themselves?"

"How dare you speak to us that way?" The general had one hand on his sword hilt. He turned to the emperor. "Say the word, my lord, and I will have this man scourged."

Vlahos, in his blue robes, stepped in between the two men. He addressed the emperor in a smooth tone.

"While I'm certain we all appreciate the caution the generals of your staff favor, my lord, this centurion in his brashness does express a worthwhile question: Do you wish to remain safe, or do you wish to be bold? Would a time *ever* come that your generals would consider *safe* enough to strike our enemies? Or are you all content to simply sit here in this godforsaken wasteland and rule over a tiny realm of farmers and barbarians until one of the usurper's assassins finally slips past our defenses and manages to kill our great Caesar?"

The generals stammered but offered no real reply.

Justinian's distorted visage looked from hooded Vlahos to the generals to the centurion and back as he considered all that he'd heard. After several seconds of this, he shook his head. "My generals have kept us all alive this long because I trusted their judgment," he said, his voice high and nasally. "Impertinent as it might be, your counsel is appreciated, Legatus—but I dare not disregard their counsel now."

The meeting broke up a few minutes later and Legatus Vlahos followed the centurion out of the building and down the path a short distance before overtaking him and pulling him aside.

"You are of course quite correct in everything you said back there, centurion," he said. "And I admire the boldness with which you presented it. Frankly, I'm surprised they're not preparing to crucify you as we speak."

"They may be," Lascaris replied. "But what of it? To die now, having spoken my mind and the truth, or to waste away here until disease and boredom claim me—which would truly be worse?"

"Yes, yes," Vlahos said, nodding inside his hood. He'd known from previous experience that there was an opportunity in this place and time to begin the process of building a world that could resist the invasion of the Union aliens and their Kratons. It was, as he'd described it before, a *nexus* in time. Now he was becoming increasingly certain that he'd found the man to tie his fortunes to—and that man was not the exiled emperor or one of his generals, but this common soldier that stood before him.

"I will share a secret with you, centurion," Vlahos said then. "I suspect great enemies are coming here soon."

"The demons you spoke of when you arrived," Lascaris replied with a wary look. Vlahos could not tell if the man believed him or not. Probably somewhere in between.

"Yes, the demons," he said, "but that is not the secret. The secret is that, if they come, they will likely carry with them a weapon of great power."

"A weapon?"

"Yes." He smiled. "And I would like for you to *take* it from them."

"Would you now?" Lascaris considered the other man's words. Then he drew forth his sword and brandished it; the setting sun gleamed off its immaculate surface. "And this weapon you speak of—is it mightier than my gladius?"

"Very much so, yes."

The soldier's eyes widened at this. "Well, then. What sort of weapon might it be, Legatus?"

"It may be a belt. It may be a metal glove. Or it may take some other form. If the time should come, I will indicate it to you—and then you must strike, swiftly and brutally and ruthlessly. Faster than anyone can react. If you do, great power will be yours, and the chance at even greater glory." He gazed up into the eyes of the centurion. "Can you do this?"

Lascaris sheathed his sword and beat his fist on his chest in salute. "It will be as you say, Legatus. Swift and brutal."

"Excellent," Vlahos replied. "If you succeed, you may be able to conquer not just this obscure territory, and not just the Roman Empire itself, but the entire world."

The Roman centurion stared at him for a long moment, eyes wide, and then broke the tension with a hearty laugh. "You are a wise man in many ways, Legatus. But–and I mean you no offense, of course, but–sometimes you sound like the silly foreigner you are."

Vlahos was taken aback. "And how is that?"

"Because the Roman Empire *is* the whole world," he said. And with a chuckle he strode away.

Vlahos watched him go, quite pleased with himself for one of the few times since he'd arrived there.

And for the first time since he'd left the Twenty-Fifth Century, Constantine Vlahos—the man who would in ages to come be known as *John Smith*—began to hope the alien Time Commandos actually had succeeded in following him into the past.

CHAPTER 11

MISSING — A NEW RULER — DO NOT HESITATE — EVERYTHING GETS CRAZY

1:

Another week had passed in miserable, flea-ridden Cherson. Smith was glad he'd caught up on all his vaccinations and medications back in 2468, before he'd stepped through Torrens' time machine and ventured back to the Eighth Century.

Another week and still no sign of pursuit from that far-flung year. That was fine–it was all according to plan. He'd instructed Torrens to delay the alien troops–Xaveria Denali had called them Time Commandos–for as long as possible, before sending them back. He'd also told Torrens to send them back using the golden square transport pad, not the silver circle. He and Torrens had set the gold square to arrive some two months after anyone using the silver circle. That would give Smith time to set up a proper welcoming committee for the Commandos, so that he could capture or kill them and take their weapons.

Of course, the aliens might not arrive at all, or they might arrive at any moment. Smith had no way of knowing if or when they traveled back, and if they had, whether they'd used the gold square or the silver circle. And he had no way of finding out or being sure about any of it. All he could do was trust that Torrens had carried out his portion of the plan properly.

Therefore it was a great and terrible surprise for John Smith—for Legatus Constantine Vlahos—when the Time Commandos arrived way too early, and accompanied by Jack Gael.

The commotion had the entire town in an uproar. Cries and shouts came to Smith from the streets outside. Donning his blue cloak and hood, he raced outside, to see people fleeing in his direction. They were trying to escape from something disturbing that was happening just outside of town.

Smith hurried along the streets of Cherson until he reached the outskirts and saw a strange group of figures headed his way. He stopped and looked them over. Yes, he realized with a start—it was Xaveria Denali's Time Commandos. One of them was clad neck to toe in a smooth, gleaming, almost skintight suit of golden armor. And they had at least one prisoner among their ranks. With a start, Smith realized that the prisoner was Jack Gael.

How could that be? How could they be here so much earlier than he and Torrens had planned? And how had these commandos been able to take Jack prisoner, when he had that amazing belt around his wai–

Smith's musings came to a sudden and complete halt as the procession drew closer and he became aware of one other critically important thing about Jack, besides the fact that he'd been taken prisoner:

He was not wearing the silver belt.

2:

Minutes earlier and many centuries later:

The reptilian Juvus Naxam and his Time Commandos had been about to travel back in time on their mission when they'd been attacked by the accursed Jack Gael and his invisible force field. In the process of fighting him, Gael had passed through the time machine's portal. A moment later, they had done the same.

Consequently, they'd all been sent back to—to whenever and wherever this was, which was definitely *not* when or where they'd planned to go.

Now Naxam picked himself up off the muddy ground, got a quick sense of the tactical situation, and began shouting orders to his troops.

Then he realized they were not alone.

A short distance away, and appearing very disoriented, stood the scrawny human form of Jack Gael.

A shock of panic—a panic he would never, ever admit to his team—ran through Naxam. *The Gladiator is here, waiting for us.* What to do?

He had to act fast. He had to be bold. Perhaps the mission might still be salvaged somehow, if only his team could disable and capture Gael.

Naxam raised the gauntlet he wore on his left hand and mentally activated it. Instantly he was covered over in a gleaming, almost skintight layer of metallic golden armor. Only his head remained uncovered.

He rushed forward just as Gael was dazedly looking up at the new arrivals.

Leaping, Naxam smashed into the human and drove him backwards, into the ground.

Gael gasped for breath, the air driven out of his lungs. Naxam got up and stood over him, prepared for a very violent battle. He was under no illusions; he'd seen some of this man's bouts in the arenas. He knew how difficult he would be to beat. But he was prepared to give it his all, in the service of his Union masters.

But Gael just lay there, eyes closed, struggling to breathe. Their collision seemed to have taken quite the toll on the slender human.

Naxam considered this and frowned in confusion.

When he'd tackled Gael, the man had *felt* it? He'd had the wind knocked out of him? How was that possible, given the force field that always surrounded him? The impenetrable bubble Naxam's superiors assumed was generated by the silver belt he wore around his wai—

Naxam did a double-take. The silver belt–it was missing from Gael's waist.

Missing.

The seven-foot-tall Time Commando retracted the golden armor back into the gauntlet; clearly it was not needed after all. Not against one lone pathetic human with no defenses. He reached down and grasped Gael by the collar of his red jumpsuit. He lifted the blond man easily into the air and glared at him. "Human!" he shouted.

Still struggling to catch his breath, Jack managed to open his eyes.

"Where is the belt, human?" the alien demanded. "What have you done with it?"

Jack blinked, blinked again, then looked down at himself. He became aware that the silver belt he'd worn constantly for the past several weeks was gone. He stiffened, then sagged, almost lifeless.

"Where is the belt?" Naxam demanded again. "You arrived here before us. Time travel is strange—you could have been here hours or days already. What have you done with it?"

"Honestly, I got here just before you did," Jack managed to say.

The monstrous alien bent down until his fangs were mere inches from Jack's face. "Then where is the belt?"

"I wish I knew," Jack muttered.

The Time Commandos marched toward the city they could see in the near distance. They pushed and prodded Jack along as they walked.

They'd put questions to him a few minutes earlier. "Where is the belt?" the leader of the aliens had demanded, over and over. "Where did you hide it?"

To which Jack had answered, "Why would I *hide* it? If I had it, I'd be *wearing* it—and beating the stew out of all of you right now!"

Instead, the aliens had beaten the stew out of Jack–to the point that he had to remind them that, if *he* couldn't find the belt, no one could; and that if they killed him or seriously wounded him, he wouldn't be much use in helping them search for it.

Reluctantly Naxam had to admit the logic in this–though Jack Gael was a human, and humans were notoriously illogical.

So they'd stopped beating him to death, looked at their surroundings and started marching toward the city, with Jack in tow.

"Our only way home," Naxam barked to his team, "was to construct hidden cryogenic chambers and freeze ourselves until our time comes around again." He glared at Jack. "But we do not know how far back we have been thrown."

"It appears much farther than we had planned," one of the other commandos observed. "But—who can be certain, on this backward, barbarous world?"

"Quite so," Naxam agreed. "And, in any case, we have our orders, and our mission. We cannot return to our present until we have the belt in our possession. It therefore seems to me that we could be here a while, searching for it." He pointed at the town they were approaching. "We will need a base of operations, and this one will do for now."

The party of seven, including six extremely alien beings, marched along, arriving soon enough at the outskirts of the small city. There an ancient and nearsighted Kazakh in brown robes, who'd been walking away from the town, stopped and greeted them. When he at last drew near enough to them to get a somewhat clear look at Naxam's alien visage, he cried out in fear and tried to hurry away. The Time Commandos stopped him. The man regarded them with wild, terrified eyes.

Naxam waited a moment while translation nanites issued in an invisible cloud from his golden gauntlet and rendered everyone's speech understandable to all present. Then, "What is this place?" he demanded.

"Cherson," the Kazakh replied in halting tones. "The city wherein dwells Justinian II, deposed emperor of the Romans."

"Oh?" Naxam exclaimed. "Well, you have a *new* ruler now."

And with that, the commandos proceeded into the city.

3:

The commotion outside brought blue-robed John Smith into the street, along with other members of Justinian's court and dozens of locals.

Someone was approaching, along the same road he'd first followed into the city. A group, it looked to be. Smith recognized them quickly. All of them were tall; some were oddly-shaped; a couple had reptilian scales. Yes, the Time Commandos had arrived. So they'd managed to come back, too.

This was what had concerned him all along. Torrens had not been able to keep them from using the time machine after he had. Perhaps Torrens had even done it for them willingly. Smith was still not sure what to think about that man.

So, here they were, in the Crimea in the year 701 CE–or AD, as Smith still called it. What had caused them to come here? It could be any of a number of things. They could have a specific mission in this time and place; perhaps they felt the same sensation that a great historic nexus intertwined here and now—as did Smith.

Perhaps they were actively searching for him! Perhaps the Union knew more about him than he had realized, and had sent the Time Commandos in hot pursuit.

Or perhaps they'd simply come through using the same coordinates Torrens had programmed for Smith. Maybe they'd expected to come out somewhere entirely different, and were presently quite shocked at their surroundings.

Whatever the case might be, Smith concluded the thing for him to do was to lay low, keep out of sight as much as possible, and try to learn what he could from the alien warriors.

That made sense to him right up until he saw the seventh figure among them. At that moment, his heart sank.

It was Jack Gael. A very roughed-up Jack Gael, clearly their prisoner.

And a roughed-up Jack, held prisoner, could mean only one thing: no force field bubble.

Sure enough, as they drew nearer Smith could see Jack no longer wore the belt.

"What now?" he groaned inwardly. If Jack was here, now, and without the belt, then he wasn't in the future, leading the rebellion against the Union.

Did the *aliens* have the belt? Either here, now, or those still in the future?

It all made Smith feel ill.

He looked down for a moment, his stomach churning, then snapped his head up again at the sound of a bellow–one that came from no human throat.

"Where is the so-called *emperor*?" one of the aliens loudly demanded. "Bring him here, that he might learn who now rules this land."

As Smith looked on from one side, watching the six aliens approaching from his right, a group of Roman soldiers marched up the street from the other direction. Their leader he recognized: Lascaris.

The centurion brought his squad to a halt a few paces away from the bizarre newcomers. There the two groups squared off, facing one another. Smith meanwhile lurked in the shadows nearby, watching it all, his hood now up and pulled forward, camouflaging his face in shadows.

"What manner of creatures are you?" the centurion demanded.

"Your new masters," the leader of the Time Commandos replied, his slender tongue darting in and out of his wide mouth. "Bow before me, human."

Lascaris stared back at the alien, dumbfounded.

"Speak you nought but that incomprehensible dribble?" he asked.

Smith realized then that, while he had possessed language nanites for many, many years–to the point that he took them for granted–these Romans couldn't understand a word the aliens were saying.

The leader appeared to realize that, too. He raised the golden gauntlet high, triggering the release of a cloud of translation nanites.

This was a mistake on multiple levels.

Centurion Julian Alexius Lascaris watched as the bizarre figure before him raised his armored fist high. Instantly he braced himself for the attack that had to be imminent.

At that exact same moment, he became aware of the hooded blue shape of Legatus Vlahos standing in the shadows to his right. This in turn caused him to remember the legatus's earlier warning: *Demons are coming.* And along with it, the legatus's admonition that, when the opening came against that enemy, to *strike*–and strike swift and hard.

Lascaris was a man of action. He needed no more prompting than that. What he beheld there before him was a horrific foe, to his eyes clearly supernatural in origin and probably very, very deadly. The legatus's words now made perfect sense to the centurion: *Do not hesitate.*

Faster than the eye could follow and in one smooth motion, Lascaris drew his gladius from its sheath and leapt to the attack.

And so it was that, even as Juvus Naxam raised his golden-gloved fist over his head and triggered the release of translation nanites into the air, a figure leapt at him. One of the humans–but moving so quickly.

Naxam was a fierce and powerful soldier of the Union. But he had spent his entire life learning lessons that served him poorly on this day, in the far distant past of Earth.

The humans Naxam had bullied and butchered since birth were a defeated people. Their militaries had been long since destroyed and disbanded. Their collective will had been broken centuries earlier. And then, on top of all of that, the Union's nanites had rendered them all docile, obedient slave creatures.

The thought of a human defying his will was preposterous to Naxam.

The thought of a human–and a primitive, zero-technology human at that–actually *besting* him in combat? Well, such an idea was beneath contempt.

Thus Juvus Naxam–who thought of himself as a warrior without peer–found himself in no way prepared for the reception he received from Centurion Julian Alexius Lascaris.

The human leapt at him. There came a silvery blur.

Do not hesitate.
Lascaris brought the broad cutting blade around in a smooth arc, driven by the force of his powerful muscles. It caught the demonic being's left arm just below the elbow and continued on in its path.

The golden gauntlet–still containing the scaled and clawed hand–fell to the ground.

The creature only stared at its missing limb, gaping.

Lascaris again wasted no time. He saw the gauntlet lying on the ground, pale blood issuing from the forearm still inside it. He dove into the mud and came up with it. Standing again, he reached for the grisly portion of the arm that protruded out. Grasping it, he yanked it free, then tossed it aside. As the other bizarre creatures looked on in stunned immobility, the Roman centurion pulled the glove down over his own right hand.

Nothing happened.

The leading demon stumbled back, clutching at its stump, which was now spouting grayish blood. It fell to the ground, groaning.

The other five creatures overcame their shock and moved to advance on Lascaris, weapons at the ready.

It all happened so quickly, Smith was barely able to process what he'd witnessed.

The centurion had chopped off the commando's arm! The Roman soldier had the golden gauntlet now!

Now Smith knew the time for action on *his* part had arrived.

He stepped out of the shadows, moved toward the centurion, and said to him in a low but fierce tone, "Visualize a suit of golden armor, covering your body!"

Lascaris was holding his ground, clearly prepared to lead a fight against the entire squad of aliens. At the sound of Smith's voice, he looked over at him.

"This is combat, Legatus," he called out, hefting his blade. "I require no lessons from a foreign diplomat, no matter how much of a sorcerer he fancies himself."

Smith cursed. "No—you have to *listen* to me," he shouted. "You don't know how that weapon works!"

Ignoring him, the centurion motioned for his men to advance, then rushed at the other aliens.

+   +   +

Lascaris again dismissed the annoying words of the man in the blue robes. He had no time for that one's prattle. Did the legatus not see that he faced a formidable force of enemies?

Around him, the other Roman soldiers clashed with the demonic interlopers. Swords struck gray armor; flashes of magical light streaked here and there. Lascaris could make no sense of any of it. He simply wanted to kill these bizarre invaders as quickly and efficiently as possible.

At the cries sounding behind him and to his left, he glanced over and saw one of the demons blasting a Roman in the chest with brilliant green light. The human soldier dropped to the ground, lifeless, a smoking hole in the center of his bronze chest plate. The light burned—and hotter than any fire! Two seconds later, another of his men was killed. And then another.

The centurion cursed again and swung his broad-bladed gladius in a killing stroke. It clanged off the gray armor of the creature directly in front of him. Lascaris immediately had to hurl himself to his right to avoid one of the killing blasts of light that had taken down two—now three—of his men.

Another strike of the gladius; another failure to do any damage. What was this demonic armor made of?

And then the demon with which he struggled struck him with its long, curved claws, renting jagged holes in his Roman bronze chest plate. Lascaris staggered back and cried out. So, too, did yet another of his men, who fell dead at the centurion's feet.

This battle was not going well. Lascaris backed away from the invaders, trying to think quickly as he moved.

At that moment he heard a voice from behind him. It was the legatus again. Would the man never quiet down?

But what he was saying finally started to get through to the centurion: "The gauntlet will create magical armor for you—just hold it high and visualize it!"

Magical armor? Well—what did he have to lose?

Lascaris turned back to the attacking aliens and, as he did so, he raised his golden-gauntleted fist over his head. In a flash, a nearly skintight suit of smooth, metallic golden armor spread over his entire body, up to the neck.

Involuntarily he gasped. He looked down at himself, astonished. This was no ordinary suit of armor—that much was obvious from the fact that it had appeared as if by magic. No, it had almost no weight to it at all, and it fit him perfectly, as if it had been molded to his body shape when it was still being forged. Though what strange forge could have brought forth something like this, he could not imagine.

The five other demons stopped in their tracks when they saw the armor covering him now. One brought up a weapon of some kind and fired it. A beam of the deadly, blinding light shot out and hit him square in the chest. Lascaris winced, remembering what that light had done to his comrade moments earlier. But he found he didn't feel the blast at all. It made pretty rainbows as it deflected away.

"Magical armor, indeed," he muttered.

Vlahos still stood nearby, and he was saying something. Lascaris looked over at him again. "What is it, Legatus?"

"How to describe it for you?" the man was saying. Then, "I know–think of Zeus! Throwing lightning bolts! Try to imagine that, and then try to do it yourself."

Lascaris regarded the man in blue robes as if he were a lunatic. But–why not? Again, he'd been right about everything so far. And the armor was indeed proving to be quite magical in its properties.

Lascaris casually brought his right hand up and motioned toward the five attacking demons. As he did so, he imagined the father of the gods, hurling bolts of lightning at his foes.

No sooner had he done this than a blinding bolt of lightning shot out from his fingertips. It struck the demons and fried the nearest one, leaving it a smoking mass of metal and flesh. The four behind it were scattered like leaves in a storm by the force of the blast; they tumbled away, head over heels.

Astonished, the centurion turned halfway round to check if his own men had seen what he'd just done. The few still standing were all staring at him, slack-jawed, dumbfounded.

"I suppose I'm Zeus now," Lascaris said with a laugh.

He turned back to face the enemy. He knew he'd done well so far, and had caught them all by surprise, defeating their leader and stealing his prime weapon. Even so, the battle wasn't over.

He watched the demons as they attempted to regroup and rally.

Again he remembered Vlahos' words: *Do not hesitate.*

He did not hesitate. Lightning flew.

4:

John Smith looked on in amazement as the Roman centurion charged into battle against five deadly alien killers.

It seemed as if, once Smith had gotten through to Lascaris with the suggestion to visualize what he wanted the golden armor to do, the Roman had taken that advice to heart. He raised his gladius high over his head and a shimmering aura appeared around it. Lascaris then swung the blade and, this time, instead of deflecting off the alien armor, the sword cut through it easily. The head of one of the aliens was separated from its body and sent rolling along the street, to end up at Smith's feet. He looked at it, shuddered, and moved deeper into the shadows, watching.

It took the Roman only a paltry few minutes to finish off the Time Commandos. Once the other five had been dismantled and dispatched, Lascaris advanced on the one who had been their leader. The now-one-armed lizard-man lay in the mud, clutching at his still-bleeding stump. Smith wondered how near to death the Union alien was.

Not long at all, as it turned out. The centurion took two long steps forward, swept the glowing gladius around, and beheaded the alien commando in one simple movement.

"*Ha*," he cried once the last of the aliens was dead. "These demons were no match for good Roman steel."

Smith suppressed a laugh. The aliens had done perfectly well against Roman steel until Lascaris had activated the gauntlet's armor—and then had listened to him about how to use it!

Smith hurried up behind the surviving Romans and pushed his way through until he stood in the midst of the dead aliens. He surveyed the field of the brief but deadly battle and nodded to himself. Excellent. The biggest threats to his plans now all lay dead. He shifted his gaze from the deceased aliens to the live Roman who now wore incredibly high-tech armor. He started to wonder if the second-biggest threat to his plans now stood before him, clad all in gold.

"Who might you be?" Lascaris was demanding of the slender blond man in the red industrial jumpsuit who sat on the ground a few steps behind the battlefield. He held the gladius ready, its silver blade still shimmering with power.

Smith rushed forward and stepped between them.

"His name is Jack Gael," Smith told the centurion quickly. "He is no threat."

Lascaris frowned. "You know him, then?"

"Yes," Smith replied, kneeling down to check on Jack, who seemed extremely disoriented. He pulled back his hood and Jack's eyes focused on him.

"Smith," he said, his voice unsteady. "It's you."

"It is."

"He called you 'Legatus.'"

"He did. My name here is Vlahos. I am serving as a *legatus*—ambassador, advisor, official—to the emperor."

"The emperor? Seriously?"

"One of them, anyway."

Jack shook his head in confusion. "What is this place?" he asked. He frowned and added, his tone low but incredulous, "Did we travel in time?"

"We did," Smith replied, keeping his own voice down.

He looked back at the big, golden-clad Roman standing behind him and said, "This man is a friend. Let us help him up."

Lascaris took this in, nodded once, and leaned down to help Jack to his feet.

"If you are a friend of the legatus, then I welcome you to Cherson," Lascaris told Jack, once they were all back on their feet. He looked Jack Gael over carefully, perhaps checking for broken bones or other injuries. "You were a prisoner of the demons?"

"Demons?" Jack looked confused enough already; this word only seemed to confuse him further.

"The demons that held you captive, yes," Smith said, returning Jack's look with one that clearly said, *Go along!*

Jack now seemed utterly bewildered, but he gathered his wits as best he could and nodded. "Yes, a prisoner." Then his eyes focused for the first time on what the Roman was wearing and he visibly reacted. "That's impressive armor," he said.

"I liberated it from the demons," the big man replied. "It is magical."

Jack took this in and nodded again. "Right," he said. "Clearly."

"You can minimize the armor now, if you want," Smith told the Roman. "I believe we are out of danger, at least for now." He nodded toward the man's right hand. "Just focus on the gauntlet alone. That should do it, if I remember the schematics correctly from last time."

Lascaris had reached the point where he was letting most of what Smith said go right past him without even trying to understand it. But he must have gotten the gist of this suggestion, because he raised his fist and stared at it, and an instant later the rest of the golden armor had vanished. Only the gauntlet on his right hand remained. He stood there a moment, patting himself down to reassure himself the armor was gone. Then he summoned it back again, and repeated the process.

"He has a new toy," Smith told Jack, moving further away. "He'll be occupied for a few minutes. We need to talk."

Smith led the blond man off to one side of the road. There they found a bench carved from gray stone and only partly covered in bird droppings. They sat down.

"The rush of battle and the newness of his new toy will wear off in a moment or two," Smith said, nodding toward the centurion, who stood some thirty feet away now, still activating and deactivating the armor from the gauntlet. "Once he starts thinking straight again, he'll realize the enormous amount of power he has acquired, because of that glove. He's going to need guidance, just as you did."

Jack nodded absently. He appeared absolutely miserable. His red jumpsuit was muddy, his skin bruised and cut in numerous places. All of that, of course, likely paled in comparison to how he felt about having lost his belt. Smith asked him what had become of it.

"I don't know," Jack replied, shaking his head and staring at the ground. "I had it on when I was fighting the aliens back in the laboratory. I tackled them and we fell down and the next thing I knew, we were all here. And my belt was missing."

This seemed very peculiar to Smith, not to mention inexplicable. Had the belt simply been unable to travel through time? Did it possess some characteristic that blocked the process–that kept Torrens' time machine from being able to send it back? He supposed it was possible. In that case, the belt was likely sitting on that silver circle on the lab floor, and Torrens was probably picking it up and wondering what had just happened. Of course, that was many, many centuries in the future.

He looked back at Jack, a man now so despondent. He realized how much of his own self-worth Jack must have invested in that belt. Of course he had, Smith understood. He'd been a simple laborer his entire life, his world controlled by aliens. The belt must have represented everything to Jack: liberation, power, the ability to shape and determine the course of his own life. To lose something like that…

"I'm sorry it's gone, Jack," he said. "If I can find it and return it to you, I will."

He didn't know what else to do or say about it, so he set it aside for a moment. There were other things they needed to speak of. For one thing—

"You're not supposed to be here," he told Jack.

"You've got that right," the blond man said.

"You were supposed to lead the Resistance, the rebellion, back in your own century. I planned it all so carefully."

"But here I am," Jack said. "And I'm stuck, right? There's no way back, is there?"

Smith stared back at him. "No," he said. "Other than the old-fashioned way. Which is the way I'm planning to go back: One day at a time." He looked away, thinking. "But that only works for me, because I never seem to age. For anyone else—no, there's no way back to the future now, instant or otherwise. Torrens' machine was a one-way deal. The alien commandos were planning on constructing freeze-pods for themselves, once their work was done—but they weren't planning on traveling back to Ancient Rome. I'm pretty sure there's nowhere around here we could look and find the components needed to finish their pods."

"Fantastic," Jack muttered.

"There is one other way, I think," he added after a moment. "But, to do it, we'd need one thing."

Jack looked up at him, a spark of life in his eyes for the first time. "Yeah? What's that?"

"Your belt."

Jack appeared to crumple before Smith's very eyes.

"Ah. Well. If you happen to find it, let me know, huh?"

Smith nodded, helpless.

After a few seconds, Jack looked at Smith again. His voice carried with it a strong tone of skepticism. "Is this where *you* wanted to come back to?"

"It is," Smith replied.

"Why?"

"There are a number of reasons, many of them involving this time and place being a nexus spot in history. But there's no point in going into all that right now." He shrugged. "And if you really are stuck here with me, we'll have plenty of time to talk about it later."

Jack looked away, his expression vacant. Then he pointed to the centurion, who was still experimenting with his golden armor while the other Roman soldiers looked on in amazement. "What about that guy?" he asked. "You're okay with him having that weapon from our time?" He paused a second, thinking about what he'd said. "Or I guess I mean from *my* time. Because I don't know *what* time is *your* time."

"Honestly, neither do I, anymore," Smith replied. "But, yes— I'm okay with him having the gauntlet. I've studied him carefully these past weeks I've spent here. I think he's the person I was supposed to find here. I'll guide him; help him learn how to use the gauntlet the proper way. And together, if all goes well, he will be one instrument—one very powerful and important instrument—in building the world I think we will need in the future. To fight the Union and their Kratons."

Jack absorbed this and then laughed in amazement. "You can't be criticized for not thinking big enough, Smith," he said. "Or, I guess I mean, Legatus—what was that name?"

"Vlahos," Smith started to reply. But he never got to finish speaking because, at that very moment, a blinding light flared to life in front of them, and everything got crazy again.

CHAPTER 12

ONE DAY AT A TIME — THE ANGEL — THE LONG WAY HOME — 1700 YEARS

1:

Howard Torrens' ears were ringing so loudly he did not at first hear Xaveria Denali shouting at him.

The time machine had exploded. He understood that immediately, even as he slowly picked himself up off the floor.

"How am I still alive?" he wondered aloud–though he could not yet hear himself speak.

He picked his way over the smoking debris until he was back where the machine's control center had stood. He looked at the blackened remains of it, then back over at where he'd been sitting. He couldn't see his chair from there. It was blocked from view by that ten-foot-tall silver sphere.

The mysterious, ancient, *impenetrable* silver sphere.

He understood what had happened: That big, indestructible object had saved him. It had deflected the force of the blast, along with the metal and plastic shrapnel, away from him.

He sighed with relief, then frowned.

Radiation. What about radiation? That would've filled the entire room, regardless of the sphere. Temporal radiation, for sure. Other kinds as well.

He tapped out commands on the nearest console and looked at the results. Yes—this laboratory had indeed been flooded with extreme levels of radiation mere moments earlier, though it had entirely dissipated by now.

A deep fear gripped him: What exactly had he just been exposed to?

Torrens felt himself grow weak in the knees. He reached out and put his hand on the nearest console to steady himself. Then he cried out and jumped back. A spark—massive and powerful—had jumped between him and the metal unit.

He blinked rapidly, thinking. Static electricity, surely.

"Torrens!"

This time he heard the voice. He turned unsteadily—it felt as if his knees were turning to jelly—and saw Xaveria Denali standing at the entrance to the room. Two of her Kratons were still standing, and had taken up defensive positions on either side of her. The other two were in seated positions on the ground, and Torrens could tell they'd suffered damage, presumably from the explosion.

"Can you hear me, Doctor?" Denali asked, striding forward. Her skin-tight purple jumpsuit was scorched and damaged in places.

"Yes—thank you, Sub-Administrator," he replied, nodding to her. "My ears are ringing something fierce. But—are *you* okay? It looks like you took more of a hit than I did."

"I am fine," the woman replied. "The Kratons shielded me." She looked at him askance. "How is it that *you* survived?"

Torrens gestured toward the big silver ball. He noticed—but the others did not—a spark that shot from his fingertips as he moved his hand. "I happened to be over there when it happened," he said. "I think the sphere must have blocked the worst of it for me."

"How…fortunate," Denali said. She glanced at the silver object, then at the ruins of the machine. Then she asked a few basic questions about what had happened. The main thing she wanted to know: Had the commando team been sent back in time? Yes, he assured her, it had. He omitted the part about how the team had traveled to where John Smith had just gone, not to where she had wanted it to go. He would let the Time Commandos tell her all about that themselves—if they ever found their way back to the present. And, knowing where and when Smith had gone, he doubted they ever would.

Eventually Denali seemed to satisfy herself as to what had occurred in the lab.

"Repair the machine, then," she ordered. "I'm certain we will find more uses for it soon."

"I will do my best, Sub-Administrator," Torrens replied–knowing full-well there was no way he would ever be able to repair this one. It was well and truly toast. Likewise, he knew he couldn't build another one without the help of John Smith. And Smith had been sent somewhere many centuries in the past.

Denali and her entourage exited. A couple of minutes passed as they made their way back down and out of the building entirely. During that time, Torrens sank back into his chair and stared at his hands. He was starting to grow concerned. At three different moments during his conversation with the sub-administrator, electricity had arced along his fingers. It was a miracle the woman hadn't noticed. No, he realized. Not a miracle–she simply thought so little of him, and so little of all other humans besides herself, she hadn't paid him enough attention to notice it.

He was in the process of devising a series of tests to investigate what had happened to him when a voice came from the shadows nearby.

"Torrens," the man's voice–and a familiar one at that–said. "It's nearly time."

The doctor nearly jumped out of his shoes.

"What the–?!"

He whirled and stared into the darkness between towering pieces of equipment, trying to see who had spoken. Simultaneously his hand moved to the desk to his right, fumbling at it for a weapon–or anything that might be used as a weapon. Of course, nothing remotely useful presented itself. He was reduced to taking two steps back and calling out, "Who's there?"

A figure stepped out of the shadows. His nose was long and straight, his hair dark, and he wore a blue jacket and blue pants. Torrens recognized him instantly, despite the fact he looked a little worse for the wear.

"Smith!"

The scientist moved towards him.

"You're here! So–it didn't work after all."

"To the contrary," Smith said—and now Torrens could see wrinkles on that narrow face that he hadn't noticed before, and a strange madness lurking behind the eyes.

"What?" Torrens said, though he was afraid he understood now, all too well. "What do you mean?"

"I mean it worked," Smith told him. "Your machine worked perfectly. You sent me to the Crimean Peninsula in the year 701 AD." He smiled. "And now I'm here."

Torrens shook his head, confused. "But how–? The machine only operated one way." He met the man's burning eyes. "How did you get back?"

"One day at a time," Smith replied. "One day at a time."

2:

Cherson, the Crimean Peninsula, 701 AD:

"You can't be criticized for not thinking big enough, Smith," Jack Gael was saying. "Or, I guess I mean, Legatus—what was it?"

The man who had been called John Smith and was presently called Legatus Vlahos started to reply. He never got the words out of his mouth. For, at that moment, a blinding light flared to life in the middle of the muddy Roman street.

Smith grunted and raised his hand to block the glare. What could this be? Some new threat? Had Torrens failed to destroy the time machine, as Jack had ordered him to do? Was some new enemy coming back to attack them?

As the glare faded somewhat, Smith squinted his eyes and tried to peek—to see what was happening.

It was a man-shape, taking form right there in front of them. A human body, floating several feet above the muddy street. Its face was completely indistinct within the bright glare.

A voice came from it then, and the voice was a cacophony of many voices blended together. "Jack Gael. Where is Jack Gael?"

Despite the blinding light, Smith's eyes widened. Who was this strange being? And—it knew Jack? It knew of a man from the far future, who had existed within this particular time and place for less than a day? How? How could that be?

"Who are you?" came a voice from nearby, that Smith quickly recognized as the centurion, Lascaris. "If you seek to harm anyone in this city," the Roman said, his sword at the ready, "I will stop you."

"I wish to harm no one," came the shimmering voice from the ethereal body. "I have something for Jack Gael. Something I'm sure he would very much like to have."

Silence for a moment, and then Jack—standing just to Smith's right—spoke up. "I'm here," he said. "I am Jack Gael."

"Ah. Jack," the voice said. "There you are. I'm glad to see you're still alive. And that you've survived so long without this."

The blazing-white body descended until its feet touched the ground. There was no noticeable reaction when it landed. The mud didn't boil away; the ground didn't sprout blossoms. Smith knew he wouldn't have been surprised if either thing had happened.

Still he couldn't make out the man's features—though he was confident now that it was a man, at least. A human man, though blazing with white light, possibly internal, possibly external, or perhaps both at once.

Jack was standing before the apparition now, and didn't appear to be fazed by its radiance at all. He simply reached out both hands, and the strange, glowing being handed him something.

Jack appeared amazed, and not just by this angelic figure appearing to them in Ancient Rome and knowing his name—but also by what the being had just handed him. Smith tried to see, though the light made it difficult. But then it faded just a bit, and Smith realized what Jack had just been given. Involuntarily, he gasped.

"There is one thing you must do with it," the figure told Jack. "The man called John Smith will explain it to you," he added, looking straight at Smith.

Smith felt his knees go weak, but he nodded. Seeing now what Jack had been given, yes—he knew exactly what he was supposed to tell Jack. He didn't have a clue as to *how* this was all happening, but he definitely knew what Jack was supposed to do next.

"Where did you—?" Jack started to ask. He wasn't able to finish his question.

The blazing figure flared brighter still, until everyone there had to look away. The next moment, he was gone.

Jack's eyes were dazzled. He blinked furiously. When his eyesight cleared, he looked down at what he now held–what the angelic being had given him. He had to be certain what he'd seen before was true.

It was.

How it could be, he had no idea. But it was.

In his hands, Jack Gael held the silver belt.

3:

This new John Smith that had simply appeared from the shadows inside Howard Torrens' laboratory spread his hands wide. "Your time machine worked, Doctor," he said again, though Torrens wasn't sure he believed it. "It's been minutes for you since you last saw me, but it's been many centuries for me."

"You were in Ancient Rome?" Torrens asked, his tone skeptical.

"They called it that. You'd call it the Byzantine Empire," Smith replied. He waved a dismissive hand. "Doesn't matter." He laughed humorlessly. "I survived, yet again. And I've lived it again. All of it, all over again." His eyes grew distant; he stared a thousand yards away, there inside the lab.

Sparks leapt from Torrens' fingers. Self-consciously, instinctively, he hid them behind his back. Meanwhile he struggled to come to grips with Smith's claim. He was not at all certain he believed a word of it. Surely it made much more sense to think that Smith had somehow failed to go back in time, and then the explosion in the lab had knocked him out–and knocked him silly, apparently.

Intellectually, Torrens had always understood that, if Smith truly was immortal, he might well live through all the years in between where he'd been sent in the distant past and the present again. Yes, intellectually, Torrens could grasp that—just barely. But to actually *see* the man standing there before him, not half an hour after he first departed for the past... It was somehow unnerving, and a bit hard to wrap his mind around.

And meanwhile he kept being distracted by the feeling that his body was filling up with electricity, with some kind of strange energy. That the explosion had done something to him; something more than just knock him out of his seat.

"If you went back in time," Torrens ventured carefully, "what have you been doing?"

"Staying out of the way," Smith snapped. "Letting my earlier self carry out all his plans. Working a little bit, here and there, behind the scenes, to help it all come out."

Torrens shook his head. "But—why hasn't history *already* been altered? Why weren't you able to do as we discussed before?" He looked around, his arms raised. "Xaveria Denali and her Kratons were just here, so apparently nothing has changed."

"No," Smith said, gazing down at the floor again. "Nothing has changed. After all this time–" He paused there, as if realizing what he'd just said. He laughed bitterly. "After all this time, one thing I've learned for certain is that the past is extremely difficult to change. Which makes the *future* extremely difficult to change."

"Then what was the point?" Torrens asked, bewildered. "What can we *do?*"

Smith looked up into Torrens's face and his eyes burned with a pale fire. "There," he said. "You've asked the right question." He spread his hands wide. "We can't change the past. And the future resists all efforts to change it remotely. But the one thing we *can* do is change the *present*. And that's what I intend to do."

"How? How can we have any more success now than at any other time?"

"Because this is where everything finally comes together," Smith said. "Here and now." He met Torrens' eyes. "You will recall that I said I was traveling back to a critical nexus point in our timeline, back in Ancient Rome."

"Yes," Torrens said. "You did say that."

"This is another," Smith said. "The most important one yet. Everything I've worked toward, over and over, will come to fruition in the here and now." He exhaled slowly and stared at the floor. His voice, when it came, carried with it the weariness of the centuries. "And we will either succeed, or we will utterly fail." He looked up and smiled flatly. "But, as I said, this is *it*."

Torrens stared back at him, unsure of what to say. The man was mad; of that, Torrens had little doubt. But then, wasn't he, as well? Weren't most of the human beings who still survived in this awful, alien-dominated world?

"You asked what I've been doing," Smith added. "The answer is, quite a lot of things, really." He turned and gestured toward the big silver sphere. "Why, for instance, do you suppose this big sucker is sitting here? Did *you* order it put here, in this room?"

Torrens frowned in confusion. "Well, no," he said. "It was here when I started working as a scientist for the Union, in this building. My understanding was that it had been found in the mines, some years before I was born. And one of the scientists who worked here before me ordered it brought here."

"That's very true," Smith said. "And what I did was make certain that all of that happened, just as you described it. I made sure it was found there, in the mines, and that it wound up here, now—in this place and time."

Now Torrens was certain the man had lost his mind. "Why on earth would that matter?" he asked, incredulous.

Smith smiled. "You'll see four yourself in…" He checked his watch again. "…just a couple of minutes, actually."

Torrens could make little sense of this talk. He ran his hand through his gray hair, looked around again as if hoping to find answers somewhere there in his lab, then asked, "So—what about Jack Gael? What about the Time Commandos? What happened to them?"

"Ah, yes. The Time Commandos. I hadn't known they were coming back, too. But we dealt with them easily enough."

Torrens reacted to this with wide-eyed astonishment. "You *dealt* with them? *Easily*??"

"Oh—not me, specifically," Smith said. "I was there, but I couldn't do much against them. It was the Roman that finished them off."

Torrens was baffled now. "A *Roman*? A Roman defeated a whole team of Union commandos? How can that be?" He thought back for a second, remembering the team of alien warriors that had passed through his time machine portal—and recalling what one of them had been carrying. "One of them had the golden gauntlet— one of the most powerful artifacts we have!"

"He was wearing it when we encountered him, yes," Smith said. "The Roman has it now."

"The Roman?" Torrens repeated. He simply gaped at Smith. "What is all this talk of a Roman?"

Smith grinned at this. He looked down at the big watch he wore on his left wrist, then up at Torrens, and his eyes focused at last. He smiled, and the smile carried with it a bit more than just a touch of madness. "You'll be meeting him soon enough," he said.

"What?" Torrens shook his head. "I don't understand."

"You will," Smith said. "Our mutual friend in the red jumpsuit will be joining us in just a few minutes, along with that certain Roman I mentioned. And together we're going to change the present." Smith winked at him. "And *that*, my good doctor, is how you change the *future*."

4:

"And *that* is how you change the belt's functions," Smith told the blond man who stood before him on the muddy street. "You've learned that you can concentrate on a command, and the belt will do it." Smith said. "Well, you do that, sort of. But with a string of numbers, in a certain sequence." He smiled. "Trust me. It will work." His smile wavered. "I think."

"You *think?*"

"I have to admit I'm not entirely sure," Smith said. "I've never seen the belt used this way before. But, in theory…"

Jack looked at him. He exhaled slowly. "Alright. I'm willing to give it a try," he said. "I just want to go home."

Smith turned away from Jack and paced in a small circle, thinking out loud. He named a series of numbers, then hesitated, muttered, "No, no…" He started over, paused, cursed, and started yet again.

"Legatus," came the rumbling voice of the centurion. "What sorcery engages you now? We must report to the emperor of these happenings—and of course introduce to him your friend, Gael."

"Yes, of course," Smith replied, nodding to the big soldier. "Give me just a few moments." In reality he had no intention of introducing Jack to the emperor. Who knew where *that* could lead?

Better to send Jack on his way immediately, now that the means to do so had been presented to them.

Of course Smith was still struggling to understand exactly *how* the belt had come back to them, and *who* the strange being had been that had brought it. But those questions were of a more academic nature. For now, they *had* the belt, and the imperative was to *do* something with it.

"The problem," Smith said to Jack after a few more seconds of pacing and muttering, "is that things are playing out differently this time than they have before. That could be a good thing. Or it could be a bad thing. I'm not sure." He shrugged. "This was how I got sent back the very first time, but I was alone on that occasion. None of you people were here. I'm not sure what to think. So all I can do is push forward with the plan, and hope it all comes together in something like the way it's supposed to."

"But you think the belt can carry us back through time?" Jack asked.

Smith stopped pacing and looked at him.

"Not precisely," he said. "Not in the way you mean it. But that's not the only possibility. If I can just *think*..."

Jack nodded slowly, seeming to pretend he understood what the man was talking about. "And you have no idea who that...person...was, that brought it to me?"

Smith shook his head. "The angel? No clue. That was a totally new thing, in my experience." He paced in the other direction. "Now, leave me be for a couple of minutes, so I can sort all this out properly."

Jack nodded.

Smith continued to mumble to himself as he paced in a broad circle around the muddy street. Then, finally, he came back over to Jack, a look of triumph on his face. "Yes. Yes, I think I have it." He pointed at the belt. "I'm going to give you a sequence of numbers. You need to repeat them back, in your head, and kind of aim them at the belt as you do."

"I don't know what you mean," Jack said.

Smith frowned. "Sure you do," he said. "When you make the bubble around you to change shape, or open up, that's because you're giving it mental commands, right?"

"I suppose so," Jack replied. "I haven't thought that deeply about it, really. I just want it to do certain things, and it does them."

"Okay, well, same thing here. I'll tell you some numbers, you repeat them, thinking of the belt the whole time. Like you're telling it to change shape or whatever."

Jack pursed his lips. "I think I understand."

"Okay, let's try it." He started speaking a series of numbers out loud. Jack started moving his lips as he heard each one, though not saying anything out loud. It was obvious he was *thinking* the numbers over again.

"Are you casting some sort of spell, Legatus?" asked Centurion Lascaris, his voice filled with tension. "Here in broad daylight?" He looked around nervously. "I do not object, because I have seen the effectiveness of your magic. But perhaps we should move to a more private location, and—"

Smith, annoyed, raised a hand to halt the Roman in mid-speech. Meanwhile he continued spouting out the numbers without pausing. Soon he'd named aloud a whole string of numbers, several dozen at least. When he got to the last one, a beep sounded. Smith realized the noise had come from Jack's belt. That was a good sign. They were making *something* happen, anyway.

The centurion strode over to Jack and knelt on one knee before him, looking at the belt up close.

"All this commotion over a simple silver belt?" he asked. "It does not seem particularly valuable or noteworthy."

"Think of it as similar to your gauntlet," Smith said to him, in between numbers.

Lascaris took in these words from Smith and pursed his lips. "It is a powerful magical item, then?"

"It is, as we are about to demonstrate—I hope," Smith replied.

Lascaris looked at him. "And when this man, Jack Gael, completes the spell you are giving him, what will happen?"

Smith sighed and glanced at the big centurion. "Then, if I'm doing my calculations correctly, he'll be on his way back to the time and place he came from."

Lascaris reacted visibly to this. "But—if he will become as powerful as you say, because of this belt, perhaps we should not let him leave us yet. He could be of great help in—"

"That's the last number," Smith said, interrupting him. He studied Jack closely. "It should have worked."

"The belt isn't doing anything," Jack replied, looking down at it. "And, as far as I can tell, I'm still here."

The centurion stepped closer to Jack, reached out—and his hand stopped, about a foot away from the belt. Nothing could be seen there, stopping him. But he had, nonetheless, been firmly stopped.

"What magic is this?" the big man demanded. "What prevents me from touching the belt?"

Jack grinned. "That's part of its power," he said. "You see why I'm so glad to have it back."

Lascaris pursed his lips and tapped gently at the invisible barrier. "Hmm," he muttered. "I do." He looked from Jack to Smith. "This is powerful sorcery, indeed. I do not believe we should be sending this man, or his weapon, away so hastily, Legatus."

"Ah!" Smith exclaimed. "I forgot to compensate for the... um..." He shook his head. "I know what I left out, anyway." He quickly reeled off five more numbers in sequence, telling Jack to repeat them. "And then, the last one—"

The Roman was looking from one to the other of them, puzzled but obviously intensely interested. "The last one?" he said. "So he is about to depart?"

Smith called out the last number. Jack nodded and looked down at the belt, to repeat it in his head as a command to the belt.

Centurion Lascaris stepped forward and grasped Jack—or at least the bubble surrounding him—in both mighty arms.

"Do not depart yet, Jack Gael," the Roman said. "We have need of you here!"

Smith's eyes widened. "No! Oh, for the love of—"

They both vanished from sight.

Smith stared at what had replaced them, aghast.

"Oh, no," he muttered. *"No no no!* You stupid Roman idiot! *You* weren't supposed to—" He interrupted himself with a couple of strong curses. "*You* were supposed to stay here with *me*, and help me on *this* end of things. *Dammit!"*

Other soldiers and various peasants of Cherson had already begun to gather around, staring at the new object that sat in the middle of their road. They poked at it and prodded it and *oohed* and *ahhed* at it. Smith ignored them for the moment. He paced back and forth, filled with anger and frustration.

After a few minutes of mulling it all over, though, his temper came back under his control. He started to rationalize what had happened.

"Maybe this could work out better, after all," he told himself. "That guy is pretty formidable, and heaven knows there will be a lot of enemies to defeat, back in the future." He shook his head. "And it's not like there's anything I can do about it now, anyway."

Sighing, he turned to the nearest Roman soldier and ordered, "Round up your men. We need to move this object into a place of concealment immediately."

The soldier beat a fist on his bronze chest plate. "Yes, Legatus," he answered, before hurrying to follow the command.

Smith watched him go, then turned back to the new object. He stood there, hands on hips, staring at it.

"I guess I'll be seeing you two gentlemen," he said, "in about seventeen hundred years…"

CHAPTER 13

ANOMALIES — MASSACRE — NO DISCONTINUITY — WIZARDS AND DEMONS

1:

Torrens was staring at John Smith with a mixture of confusion, pity and fear. The man had clearly lost his mind. Perhaps the explosion of the machine had affected him just as it had affected Torrens. But, instead of making him feel energized, as it had Torrens, it must have driven Smith insane.

Or–and Torrens hesitated to even consider this–perhaps Smith truly *had* gone back in time, nearly twenty centuries, and then lived through it all again. Could that possibly be?

He started to ask Smith if he had any evidence that what he was saying was true. Smith, though, had turned away and was walking towards the far side of the lab–and towards the big silver sphere.

"Yes," the man in blue said, "it should be very soon." He raised his left arm and looked at the large watch he wore on that wrist. "Less than ten minutes, in fact."

Torrens started to reply, but a beeping at his main console distracted him. He looked over at it and saw that a high-priority message was coming through.

"Yes?" he said, after tapping on the control to open the link.

"Dr. Torrens," came a strange, mechanical voice from the speaker. *"This is Dr. Krenz."*

"Dr. Krenz—!" Torrens was taken aback. "You *are* alive! I wasn't sure I should believe it."

"I… am," the strangely distorted voice replied, "…in a manner… of speaking."

This gave Torrens pause—not least because it reminded him that something strange was going on with *himself* at the moment, as well.

"Doctor," the mechanical voice said, *"I've just interfaced with the main computer systems in your laboratory. I am detecting a number of anomalies."*

"Are you?" Torrens said, glancing at John Smith. "How worrisome. What sorts of anomalies?"

"Temporal radiation, for one thing," the voice of Krenz said. *"Nearly off the charts, and increasing rapidly."*

Hearing this from Krenz only made Torrens even more nervous about what was happening, but he tried to play it off. "Yes, well, we had an accident here, earlier. I'm sure that's what you're detecting."

A pause, then Krenz replied, *"Yes… I'm sure…"*

"Well, if that's all, I have some very important business to—"

"I also note a figure standing near you. Their biometric signature does not match anyone in our databases. That should be impossible. There are no human beings left on Earth not recorded in our databases."

"Oh?" Still Torrens tried to downplay it all. He was looking directly at Smith as he said, "I don't see any ghosts or boogeymen in here, Dr. Krenz."

Smith put his thumbs in his ears, wiggled his fingers and stuck out his tongue.

The voice was silent for a moment. Then it said, *"In point of fact, Dr. Torrens, neither your nor the other person's biometrics match up with anything on file."*

This bit of information did surprise Torrens. "That makes no sense, Krenz," he said.

"Nevertheless," the disembodied voice replied, *"your own readings do not match the baseline kept in Union records, and*

indeed appear to be changing even as we speak." The tone didn't change as Krenz asked, *"Are you feeling well, Doctor? Has something happened to you?"*

"I'm quite well," Torrens said, his stomach turning somersaults and sweat breaking out across his brow. "I believe your machinery must be faulty or your connection to my lab corrupted somehow. Again I congratulate you on surviving the injuries you suffered earlier. Now, if you will excuse me, I have a great deal of work to do."

Krenz continued on as if Torrens hadn't spoken. *"I am launching a new initiative shortly,"* he said.

"How nice for you," Torrens replied, growing testy and frustrated, in addition to queasy and ill.

"I believe Sub-Administrator Denali has spoken with you about it. I have created a new generation of nanites."

"She did, in fact," Torrens said. "She also told me they could be quite dangerous. I am assuming they will be tailored to avoid any humans in the direct service of the Union—such as you and I, and the Sub-Administrator."

The voice said nothing to this.

"And I assume you will be needing the nanite lab in this facility to finalize and disseminate your new nanites into the general population."

"I will," Krenz said.

"Well, the systems are all in use at the moment," Torrens said. "Perhaps later…"

Smith shook his head at this, as if to say, "He's going to easily see through that lie, and it will only make you look bad."

Indeed, an instant later, Krenz's mechanical voice replied, *"Doctor, I am scanning your equipment remotely at this moment, and I detect no activity on the part of your nanite maintenance and propagation systems. I therefore have to conclude that either you are ignorant of how your own equipment works–and whether it is being used or not–or else you are deliberately attempting to mislead me. I calculate a ninety percent likelihood of the latter."*

"I'm afraid I don't know what you mean, Dr. Krenz," Torrens said quickly. "I'll–um–be happy to work with you on getting these new nanites out into the world, of course. Just not at the moment. Do you understand?"

"Your readings continue to vacillate wildly beyond your own baseline–and now beyond human baseline readings, Doctor," Krenz told him, ignoring Torrens' previous words. *"And I still have not found a match for the figure who is still standing near you in your lab."*

"Krenz, old boy," Torrens said, "I think you'd better go and run some diagnostics on your *own* equipment. Now, really–I must let you go."

"This attempted subterfuge is beneath you, Dr. Torrens," the robotic voice said. *"But it merely serves to reinforce the conclusion I have reached."*

"And what conclusion is that?" Torrens asked. He glanced at Smith and shrugged.

"I have determined to a ninety-seven percent level of certainty that you are working for the Resistance and against the Union. That being the very likely case, I have dispatched a squad of Kratons to your location. They will remove you from the premises and transport you to a holding facility, where you will await final judgment on your fate. Meanwhile I will be assuming control of your former facilities to launch the new generation of nanites."

Torrens felt his heart sink. Thus the words Krenz added next, as a sort of addendum, nearly knocked his feet out from under him.

"And let me be clear on this, Dr. Torrens. The new nanites are very often deadly. And I will spare no *humans.* NONE.*"* His flat robotic tone at last took on a hint of emotion. *"Within the next twenty-four hours–if you are not executed outright for treason–you will either be dead anyway, because of the nanites, or you will be utterly enslaved to the will of the Union."*

Torrens was nearly in shock from what the mechanical-sounding voice had just told him. Even so, that last bit got through to him. "But," he said, "that would mean you're rolling the dice on your *own* survival. The nanites could kill *you,* too."

"Oh, no," Krenz said. *"No, I am quite safe. You see, one must possess a human body in order to be threatened by nanites that target humans."*

Even as part of Erich Krenz's intellect was ordering a squad of Kratons to advance on Torrens' laboratory building, another part of his mind was seeking out the solution to a problem he had come to understand only moments earlier.

Upon first awakening, the idea of his mind being inside the body of a Kraton had thrilled him. The power that represented was almost beyond comprehension, compared to the painful and nearly worn-out human body he'd been trapped inside before. The few desirable human traits he had lost were more than compensated for by the power, strength and resilience he'd gained.

But after reviewing the recordings of the human Jack Gael battling Kratons in recent weeks, Krenz began to worry that even his new, monstrous, mechanical, metal body was not enough.

His enemies were everywhere–as Torrens was now proving–and he needed even more security than a normal Kraton body could provide.

Now that he was essentially a disembodied ghost, of course, he was free to search for just what he wanted.

Into the lab's data network a portion of his mind went. Out he branched, across the broader network that bound together the alien-run operations in North America and the human facilities that served them.

Through computer system after computer system he burrowed, studying everything there was to know about all of them almost instantly.

For long milliseconds he couldn't find anything of use.

Then, approximately two long, agonizing seconds after his inquiries began, he had his answer.

The Union recently had begun a program to construct Kratons out of more durable material. The Gladiator, Jack Gael, had frightened them to the point that they were willing to create a model of robot to defend themselves that was virtually indestructible.

They'd even built a prototype: the big, black Kraton that had been pushing him to develop a more improved way of controlling humans.

That Kraton was currently idle. Records showed Xaveria Denali had suggested to their Union overlords that this new model of robot might be too difficult for them to stop, if it should somehow escape their control. Subsequently they had shut it down, pending a complete reevaluation and reprogramming.

Even so, Krenz could detect it easily within the network. Given his new abilities as a ghost floating across the web of data, he had no trouble zeroing in on it.

The poor fools, Krenz thought. They'd built that body to be invincible; unassailable. Then they'd panicked and shut it down. But they'd left it connected to their network just like any other Kraton. Like any other machine in their labs.

It waited there for him as if it had been built just for him; as if it were meant for him all along.

Abandoning for good the Kraton body he'd woken up in, Krenz channeled the rest of his sentience, his personality, his memories— his *soul*, perhaps—through the fiber-optic channels and into that big, powerful body.

As he forced his way into the black Kraton, he felt its computerized mind waking up; becoming aware of his presence. Taken aback at first, it bellowed its outrage at the violation it quickly understood was occurring.

"Who–? Krenz? You? What do you think you're doing?"

"I'm taking your body," the scientist replied from the far side of the mental bridge between the two.

"What? You are doing no such thing! Get out of my mind!"

"No."

"I–I will find your human body and crush it to paste!"

"Too late," Krenz thought back at him.

Silence for a moment then, as the Kraton must have come to appreciate its fate at last.

At that moment, Krenz leapt across the mental bridge to the other side.

Then he burned that bridge behind him.

Now their two minds dwelt together inside the same metal skull. He isolated its personality traits, surrounded them, and began to crush them out of existence.

At the same time, however, the Kraton fought back. It started to infiltrate his own mental integrity.

In the process, and against the wills of both of them, the two minds slowly merged.

By the time Krenz realized what was happening, he could do nothing to stop it–and neither could the Kraton. He felt the robot's individuality melting away along with his own. Their thought patterns merged, and together they became a third thing. A *new* thing, together.

The last words Krenz heard from the Kraton's personality before it had merged entirely with his own consisted of a whispered lament: *"I should have killed you when I had the chance."*

"I suppose that was your problem," he replied to it, echoing back its earlier words to him. *"You just weren't ruthless enough."*

All of this happened in the space of a few seconds. From the outside, while that mental battle occurred, the big black robot simply lay there on a metal slab, as cold and dead and unmoving as it had been since it had been brought in and left there.

The scientists who worked there in the laboratory and were simply going about their normal day-to-day jobs, therefore, were quite startled when the huge Kraton prototype booted itself up, switched on all of its functions from the *inside*, and rose from the table like some time-lost Frankenstein's monster.

2:

"I have summoned such members of the Resistance as are close by and able to get here in time," John Smith said. "I impressed upon them the fact that this might be the last and only chance to prevent the total enslavement–or death–of the human race."

"I'm sure they will do their best," Torrens said, "but I doubt they will be able to stop the advance of the Kratons toward this building. They are, after all, merely human."

"You might be surprised," Smith said. "Jack was able to break into a couple of armories recently. The Resistance is better armed and better prepared than the Union knows, I think." He looked up at Torrens and added, "And these people know they're fighting for their very existence."

Out in the streets, a phalanx of silvery robotic Kratons ten rows deep marched toward the building where Torrens and Smith conferred. Regular citizens saw them coming and fled for their lives. Cars came to screeching halts, reversed course, and zipped away at top speed. The normal police officers patrolling that part of the city put the entirety of their efforts into crowd control–into getting the civilians out of the way and keeping them back.

But those were not the only humans to occupy the city.

Responding to John Smith's emergency call, dozens at first and then hundreds of men, women and even children flooded out onto the streets. They ignored the pleas and entreaties of the police and the dire warnings broadcast over loudspeakers along the sidewalks. They carried all manner of weapons, and they opened fire on the Kratons the moment those mechanical monsters came into view.

For the first few seconds, they even managed to damage a couple of the robots.

Then the Kratons struck back.

It was a massacre.

"As I feared," Torrens said, watching a monitor that displayed a view of what was happening outside. "They're not going to last long, despite the weapons they're carrying."

"They only need to slow the Kratons down a bit," Smith said, his eyes glued to his watch.

"And die in the process? All to buy you a few more minutes for– for whatever you have up your sleeve." He shook his head. "You're awfully cold-blooded, aren't you, Smith? Ever the grand chess master, using your fellow humans as pawns in your long-running schemes."

Smith had not chosen to watch the action on the street. He was standing next to the silver orb again, patting it gently. At Torrens' words he frowned and looked over at the scientist.

"I make no apologies for who and what I am, Doctor. Nor would I compare myself to any other men and women who have treated our fellow human beings far, far worse over the course of their lifetimes."

Torrens scowled at him. "Oh, I know my crimes all too well," he said. "And I take responsibility for all of them. I choose not to blame the fact that the nanites influenced me to do the things I've done." He nodded toward the display. "And it appears I'll be paying for it, very soon."

Even as Torrens spoke those last few words, he doubled over in pain. Smith glanced at him and saw something bizarre indeed: the gray-haired scientist actually appeared to warp and wrinkle, like a two-dimensional rendering being twisted this way and that. At the same time, electricity danced all over his body.

"Torrens," Smith said very matter-of-factly when the scientist had recovered somewhat, "would you care to tell me just what the hell is going on with you?"

"Only if you do the same for me," Torrens managed to gasp out. "You are willing to sacrifice so much of your precious Resistance just to delay the Kratons on their way here. You keep looking at your watch. Can you not tell me—what exactly are we *waiting* for?" He was still bent forward, arms clutched around his midsection, as if recovering from a severe stomach ailment. "I will share my secret with you, if you share yours with me."

"Mine won't be a secret for much longer," Smith said. "The Resistance has done their job. Only a few seconds remain now."

"Until what?" Torrens gasped, before doubling over again. This time the waves didn't just pass through his body—the very air around him appeared to ripple and warp.

Smith came over to him this time, clearly concerned. Once the effect had passed again, he helped the scientist over to his chair and sat him down in it.

Torrens, his face now bright red and drenched with sweat, looked up at the man in blue. "Don't you claim to have lived all this before? Why don't *you* tell *me* what's happening to me?"

"Because this is a new one for me," Smith said. "I honestly have no idea."

"Terrific," Torrens mumbled. "I suppose I'm dying. So I'll never find out what your secret is—what you're so anxiously waiting for."

Smith checked his watch one more time. He grinned. "Ah! You will find out... momentarily," he replied.

With that, he walked back over to the big silver sphere and stood a couple of feet from it. "Seven... six... five... four..."

"What exactly do you think you're doing?" Torrens asked, mystified.

"...Three... Two... One," Smith said.

There came an audible POP that caused Torrens to involuntarily wince. Something almost imperceptible had changed in the room's air pressure.

Then Torrens gasped.

The silver sphere was gone. After having rested there in that laboratory for as long as he could remember, it had vanished entirely.

In its place stood two figures, both clearly human. One held the other in a bear hug of an embrace.

The one doing the hugging, Torrens did not recognize at all.

The other, however… the other, Torrens knew very well.

It was Jack Gael.

And he was wearing the silver belt.

3:

Jack Gael and Centurion Lascaris experienced virtually no discontinuity whatsoever.

One moment they stood on a muddy Roman road, somewhere in the Crimea in the year 701 AD. The centurion had just followed his intuition, along with various clues he'd picked up from things said by the man he knew as Legatus Vlahos. He'd suspected Vlahos truly was a sorcerer, and was about to cast some sort of spell on the other man—the one in the strange red suit. He'd rushed over and grasped that man with both arms, holding him tight, to immobilize him and prevent him from—leaving? Disappearing in a flash of brimstone? Lascaris wasn't sure exactly what he'd hoped to accomplish.

There had been a very slight, almost imperceptible moment where Lascaris had felt he was floating in a great sea, cut off from everyone and everything else.

And then, in less time than it took to blink one's eyes, the world around them had utterly changed.

Lascaris released his grip on Jack and stood dumbfounded. Slowly he turned in a circle, looking around, taking in his new surroundings.

Gone was the stinking little town of Cherson, place of exile for the former emperor, Justinian II.

Gone were the ramshackle buildings and the stray dogs barking and the worn-down peasants engaged in their labors.

Instead, Centurion Lascaris now found himself inside a bizarre room of metal and glass and… some other sorts of unrecognizable materials. Strange lights danced on rectangles, forming images of other people and other places. A low humming sound, as of many swarms of bees far away, filled the air.

All of this he took in at first glance. Before he could study any of his surroundings further, however, he became aware of the other two men in the room with Gael and him.

One was a man he did not recognize: Older, gray-haired, seated in a fancy black chair, and wearing a long white robe of some sort. Another wizard?

The other figure he at first thought was a stranger, too. Then he recognized the facial features, and the fact that he was still dressed all in blue–though the nature of his outfit had changed from hooded robes to more form-fitting clothing he had no words for.

"Legatus," he called out to Smith. "Is that you? What has happened? Where are we?"

Smith had expected the Roman soldier to be confused and disoriented. He'd been waiting for this moment for centuries. He'd had all that time to consider what he'd say and do when the moment arrived. And yet he'd never become satisfied with any of the things he'd thought of saying.

He'd been confident the golden gauntlet the man wore had infected him with language-nanites. That otherwise-harmless variety of the little bugs should allow the man to speak and understand their language here in the Twenty-Fifth Century just as clearly as he'd understood the Time Commandos and Jack, back in 701.

What concerned Smith was what he could say that would convince the man, first that he wasn't going mad, and second, that he should cooperate—should help them in their cause.

No, in all the time he'd been waiting, he'd never really thought of the perfect response. But, then again, he'd never known exactly what the situation around them would be like when it opened— when the programming he'd had Jack feed into the belt back in 701 reached its end point, and the belt turned off its stasis field.

It was therefore fortunate, in a way, that they happened to be in the midst of a crisis–a massive battle outside. Because battles were something Centurion Julian Alexius Lascaris knew very well. And Smith knew how to appeal to Lascaris—how to manipulate him.

"A horde of demons advances on us now," Smith called out.

Lascaris frowned and approached the man in blue. "Demons? Have they followed us here? Or is this strange realm their home?"

"They *think* this is their home," Smith told him bitterly. "I'd like to change that. I'd like to wipe them all out."

Lascaris looked at the screen. He always came across as the toughest customer Smith had encountered in all of his travels through time and all over the world. And yet he was clearly taken aback when he beheld the image on the screen: A view of rows of crimson-eyed metal skeleton-creatures advancing on their building.

"This…" Lascaris gestured at the screen. "This seeing-stone shows us what is nearby?"

"It does," Smith told him.

"And they approach us even now?"

"They do."

The Centurion nodded and drew his gladius. "Then we will fight them," he said.

Smith caught Jack Gael's eye. "If they enter this building and reach this lab, it may well mean the end of what's left of humanity."

Jack looked back at him, confused. "First—just tell me how we came to be back here in this time. You said the machine didn't work that way."

"It doesn't," Smith replied. "You came back to this time the same way I did—sort of." He shrugged. "The difference was, you and the centurion got to miss all the long years in between then and now, by being conveniently frozen inside a stasis bubble the entire time. For you it was half a second. For me it was 1,767 years, seventy-nine days and eleven hours. I'll round off the minutes."

"But—how?"

"That was the other capability your belt has that I wasn't entirely sure about. Fortunately, those numbers I had you recite gave it the information it needed to know how long to project the stasis field and when to turn it off. And it worked."

"The belt froze us in a stasis bubble?" Jack asked, still not clear on what had happened.

"Yes," Smith answered. "And now you're back in your original time."

Jack nodded toward the centurion. "But with company," he said."

"Yeah, that." Smith looked sheepish. "I was not expecting him to grab onto you. The belt adjusted and swallowed him up right along with you."

Jack still wasn't fully clear on everything, but Smith waved him off. The Kratons were closing in. Further explanations would have to wait.

"You have comm links," Smith said to Torrens. "Give them each one."

"Of course."

The sweating scientist reached into a drawer, drew out two small circular items, and gave them to the two newcomers.

"They will attach to any surface," Torrens said. He looked at the man from the distant past, and added, "We will be able to talk with one another."

Jack studied the item momentarily, then brought it inside his bubble and stuck it to one of the chest pockets of his jumpsuit. The Roman shrugged—clearly none of this made any sense to him, so he was just going along—and stuck it to the side of his golden gauntlet.

Smith motioned for Jack and Lascaris to follow him out of the lab. Before they left, he said to Torrens, "Remember what we discussed before, Doctor. Keep them out as long as you can–but destroy the entire building rather than allowing it to fall into Krenz's hands."

"Destroying the building will only slow them down," Torrens pointed out. "They can always build a new delivery system for the nanites."

"I don't intend for any of them to be left to do that, when this is over," Smith said.

Torrens nodded. He turned away, wracked with tremors again.

Smith started to inquire about the doctor's difficulties, but there was no time. Instead, he led the other two men down to the lobby and out of the building. He'd expected to have to travel a good distance to get to where the clash was happening, but in the time since he'd last checked in on the battle, the situation had changed, and changed drastically. For when they got down to street level, Smith was shocked to see the Kraton army was almost at their doorstep.

And the reason why was that army's leader. He had the same general look as all the other Kratons–muscular-looking walking skeletons constructed of intricately-engineered metals. But he was slightly larger; well over eight feet tall. And all of his components, save his burning-red eyes, were jet black. He hovered in the air, some thirty feet above the army of silver Kratons that had swarmed up toward the building.

"There you are," came a grating mechanical voice Smith recognized immediately. *"The man who should not exist. The man who is only a blank spot on all our records."*

Smith looked up, saw this new kind of Kraton, and turned to the Roman centurion. "You should probably focus on that one, once he lands," he said. "Let Jack handle the others."

Lascaris looked from Smith to the black robot hovering there in the sky. Then he looked at Jack.

"This man can fight these creatures?"

"I can," Jack said. Now that he had his belt back around his waist, his personality had yet again transformed itself. He strode forth confidently, knowing the invisible and impenetrable bubble surrounded him once more.

The Roman appeared dubious, but he nodded. "So be it," he said.

The black Kraton floated closer. *"These others I will kill outright,"* he said, staring down at Smith. *"But* you–*you, sir, represent a mystery I would very much like to get to the bottom of."*

Smith started to respond, but before he could open his mouth, a streak of gold shot from the ground to his right. An instant later, something big and heavy crashed into the black Kraton. The dark figure and the gold one tumbled to the ground and landed in the midst of the army of silver robots.

Smith, wide-eyed, looked around and saw that Lascaris was gone. That had indeed been him, attacking Krenz.

"I didn't know he could fly," Smith said aloud.

"I don't think *he* knew it either, until just now," Jack Gael replied.

And with that, Jack waded into the sea of Kratons. The gladiator chopped and punched and kicked, his arms and legs surrounded by an indestructible shell, and the evil silver robots fell before him. But there were so many. So many...

The centurion meanwhile continued to fight one-on-one with the robotic Krenz. They exchanged punches and head-butts and, at one point, each had lifted the other up above his head and thrown him down, hard.

When a little distance opened up between them, Lascaris unleashed the Zeus-fury of the lightning barrage weapon in his fists at Krenz. Bolts of electricity washed over Krenz's new body, sparking and flashing and crackling. The big robot staggered back, then retaliated by kicking in booster rockets in his back and hurling himself at his adversary like a guided missile. Lascaris charged head-on to meet his foe, and they collided in midair with a deafening crash, both parties spinning away, impacting the ground and rolling to a stop.

Lascaris was up first. He pointed both fists at the downed robot and fired his lightning blast weapon again, unleashing blinding bolts that crossed the courtyard and smashed into Krenz. The dark Kraton was staggered, jerking about with mechanical seizures. When the assault ceased, he lay on the concrete floor on his back, throwing off showers of sparks by the thousands. Recovering incredibly quickly, he scrambled back to his feet as the centurion advanced on him, and again they clashed.

John Smith watched this battle taking place, and fervently hoped the time-displaced Roman could do the job. He'd never encountered an enemy like this—a human mind inside a robot body—in any of his previous trips through time. The fact that they faced one now puzzled and concerned him. He'd gotten used to history being mostly predictable, after having witnessed so much of it, over and over. He found he grew particularly antsy when things started going differently from what he was used to. And all of this–Krenz in a Kraton's body, trying to murder most of the remaining human race–was *not* what he was used to.

"Stay on him!" Smith yelled at the Roman. "Don't give him a moment to recover!"

But even as he spoke the words, Smith worried that these enemies might well be more than even the Gladiator and the Centurion could overcome.

4:

Centurion Lascaris pulled himself up to his feet after another exchange with the black metal demon. He could understand now why the legatus had wanted *him* to fight that one. Truly the demon was formidable. But so was Lascaris.

Their battle raged on, even as Jack Gael continued to serve as a mighty rock standing before the laboratory building—a rock upon which the waves of silver-gray demon creatures broke, over and over.

What the slender man in red was accomplishing was incredibly impressive to Lascaris. Somehow, he could punch and kick these metal men and do them great damage, without being injured in return. Truly it had to be a spell–surely one bestowed upon him by the legatus, who stood revealed in his eyes as a sorcerer of great power. Power enough to transport them to this strange realm, as well. The question that still puzzled him was, Why wasn't the legatus doing anything to help them *now?*

He looked back and again saw Legatus Vlahos–now calling himself John Smith–standing at the front entrance of the building, simply observing everything. And likely casting another spell, Lascaris figured.

"Wizards," he muttered to himself. Who could understand them or their ways? He supposed they had their purposes, though. The good guys needed them, to counter the ones employed by the bad guys.

Still, the Roman thought, it would be a better world if *neither* side had any.

John Smith was encouraged by the job Jack and the Roman were doing in fighting the Kratons. Still, he knew it was likely all in vain. The robots and their masters were too powerful for two men–even two as powerful as they were–to defeat.

That being the case, Smith turned and ran back into the laboratory building and dashed up the stairs to Torrens' lab.

He doubted this was a battle his side could win. But he still held out hope of winning the war.

That is, until he entered the lab and got a look at Howard Torrens–or what Howard Torrens was becoming.

The human being with gray hair, glasses and a white lab coat was gone. In his place stood a being of radiant white light.

"Torrens," he called out. "Is that you? What the hell is going on?"

The shimmering figure turned and looked at him, but said nothing.

Smith looked around. Nothing appeared any different from when he'd left earlier.

"Torrens–did you destroy the system? The nanite delivery system? As we discussed?"

For a moment there was no response. Then the being of light looked at Smith, eyes focusing for the first time, behind all that glare. "John Smith," the ethereal, even voice said to him. "No. I am sorry. I did not. I forgot."

"You forgot?"

"I… find *human* matters… less important to me now."

"Less important that what?"

"Than how I am changing."

"Changing into what?"

"I… do not know."

CHAPTER 14

ROMAN STEEL — THE CABAL — THE DEMON HORDE — CHOOSE NOW

1:

It turned out Lascaris wasn't the only combatant with a ranged distance weapon.

The black demon called Krenz hovered far up in the sky and began to fire bolts of purple light at him from a cannon built into his right arm.

The centurion dodged the shots at first, but then one connected, tagging him in the right shin. Most of the blast deflected harmlessly away, to the Roman's great relief. But still he felt it, even through the magical and miraculous golden armor he wore. That part of his leg was instantly heated so much that it burned—to the point that he seriously considered removing the armor; having the golden gauntlet reabsorb it.

He didn't, of course, because to do that would be suicide. Instead he simply gritted his teeth and bore the blazing heat until the feeling lessened, and meanwhile he endeavored to avoid being hit by the weapon again.

Lascaris reasoned that if the monster's most effective attack thus far was a distance weapon, the tactically sound counter to it would be to remove distance as a factor, and go in for close combat. Thus he willed the armor to loft him up into the sky, whereupon he zoomed into Krenz, colliding hard with the black metal being.

Flying, he'd discovered very quickly, was not hard to learn or execute. Once aloft, he could zoom around very well, simply by thinking what he wanted to happen.

The real challenge, of course, was *landing*.

But landing was a problem for later. For now, he gathered himself after that first collision and struck again, smashing an armored fist into the black metal face. The demon's blazing red eyes glared at him malevolently. He jabbed into that face with his fist, again and again. Unfortunately, he noted the blows were having diminishing returns after the first two or three. It was as if the metal being had adjusted somehow to his tactics and was absorbing the blows now, rather than being harmed by them.

Indeed, the horrific creature spoke to him then, as they grappled above the street and the horde of silver Kratons below them. And when it spoke—and despite its eerie, mechanical voice—it sounded barely inconvenienced at all by Lascaris' deadliest blows.

"You are the other one I am curious about," the voice said casually. *"Your biometric readings appear nowhere in the Union databases. As with your friend in blue, that is quite impossible—unless you both come from another world."*

"Most of your babble is incomprehensible to me, demon," Lascaris replied, "but you are quite right about one thing—I do come from another world. As far as I have seen so far, for all of its flaws, a far better world. For I find this one horrific in the extreme. In fact, I would be quite happy to return to Justinian's flea-bitten court—but for my greater desire to vanquish you in combat!"

"Justinian's court? Searching records..." A pause, as the two titans continued to struggle with one another. Then Krenz said, *"The Emperor Justinian, Roman and Byzantine Emperor who created the Hagia Sophia in Constantinople."*

"Foolish demon," Lascaris spat. "My master was not Justinian the First, but Justinian II. I served him in his exile in Cherson, on the Black Sea."

"Ah," Krenz said a moment later. *"I have it. An exiled emperor. Early Eighth Century. Well, then. So you have no idea you currently inhabit the Twenty-Fifth Century. This means Torrens*

has indeed perfected time travel, and has used it to bring you to the present, for whatever reason."

"None of what you say makes any sense to me, demon," Lascaris growled. "But my sole reason to be here now is to destroy you, and send you back to whatever Hell you escaped from!"

Lascaris used all of his might to shove the black metal robot back from him. Then he reached down, drew his gladius, held it out, and watched as its blade shimmered with the power of the armor he wore–the power of the golden gauntlet. Then he lashed out with it.

Krenz must have somehow suspected the danger he suddenly found himself in—that this might be a weapon that could harm even him. He lurched back and away from the centurion, such that only about half an inch of the sword struck his body. The blade sliced through the front panel of his torso, bringing forth great gouts of sparks and causing the robot to spasm momentarily.

Krenz emitted a shriek that sounded as if it reflected human pain as much as it did mechanical damage. Then he launched himself back into the air, getting away from the Roman as quickly as possible.

The centurion stood there, defiant, sword in hand. He shouted at the retreating black form, "You are right to be afraid, demon! Come back and finish this! I have more good Roman steel for you!"

2:

Jack Gael continued to punch and kick and chop the Kratons as they surged at him. But eventually it was like trying to punch one's way through the incoming tide. The numbers—they were simply overwhelming. And for all of Jack's invulnerability, he was also simply a man. Inevitably, unavoidably, he grew tired. Then exhausted. Then he could barely stand—much less punch and kick and chop at more and more robots.

They couldn't hurt him, of course. His invisible bubble yet surrounded him and protected him. But he found he couldn't hurt them anymore, either. At least, not until he recovered his strength and his stamina somewhat. Above all else, he needed a break.

So he fell to the ground and he lay there, gasping for breath, sweat pouring off of him. And the Kratons advanced, charging around him on either side. Some simply stepped on and over him, a few pausing to attempt a punch or blast of their own, before giving up and simply continuing on, bypassing him where he lay.

After about a minute of this, he managed to raise himself up onto all fours. But still he lacked the strength to regain his feet. By that point, the Kratons were a stream to either side, utterly ignoring him.

He managed to look back over his shoulder and saw that the Resistance army had been beaten aside as well. Among them lay the body of his recent acquaintance, Skullcrusher. The big gladiator appeared to have done some serious damage to the ranks of Kratons before he'd succumbed to their assault. As for the strange Roman soldier that had accompanied him back to the present, there was no sign of him at all now.

Cursing, he fought back onto his feet. Most of the Kratons were past him by now, though. They'd reached the steps at the front of the building—the lab building Smith had told them it was vital to keep the robots out of.

"Dammit," Jack cursed. His legs felt like lead, but he moved them anyway, hurrying after the Kratons—and knowing full well they were going to get inside anyway. There was nothing left now to stop them.

"Our combat has been memorable, Roman," the ebon machine-man said, *"but I must take my leave of you now. I believe I have distracted you long enough for my servants to have overwhelmed Jack Gael and penetrated the building at last."*

And with that, Krenz swung one of his big arms in a lightning-fast motion and knocked the centurion away. Then he turned and streaked down toward the now-undefended entrance to the laboratory building.

"Advance," cried Krenz as he hovered above what remained of his army. The Resistance fighters, as well as Gael and the Roman, had done a tremendous–a shocking amount–of damage to the Kratons. But most of the Resistance fighters were down now, not

moving and perhaps dead. Meanwhile, many of the robots still remained active. More than enough, Krenz felt, to finish this fight.

The army of Kratons stormed up the stairs and the vanguard of their ranks arrived at the main entrance to Torrens' lab.

"STOP!" came a booming voice from outside.

Instantly the Kratons froze in their tracks, as if they'd all had their power cut simultaneously.

At the same instant, Krenz halted. He, too, recognized that voice. He spun around.

A broad, circular platform had descended from the sky and hovered now above the plaza outside the laboratory building. It was surrounded in a shimmering yellowish field of energy; doubtlessly similar to the one protecting Jack Gael, Krenz figured. Though probably not as effective, given the Union's single-minded desire for that belt.

Krenz soared up above the platform and gazed down at it.

The big disk carried six chairs that might as well have been royal thrones. On each sat an alien of a different species. Human servants tended to them.

The Union itself. The cabal that controlled the Earth.

Near the edge of the platform and gazing up at him stood Xaveria Denali, now clad in a shimmering, skin-tight purple jumpsuit. Her long, dark hair was tied back in a ponytail that reached down to her waist.

"Krenz," she shouted. "The Union has come."

"I welcome them," he called down to her.

"They have come to see what you have become, what you have accomplished, and what you intend to do," she replied. "And to render their judgment upon you."

3:

Reeling from Krenz's last blow, the centurion fell to the hard pavement of the street, some distance away from where the last of the Kratons were poised to assault the building he was charged with protecting. He skidded on the surface momentarily, then brought himself to a halt and zipped back up into the air. Again he was grateful that, while the golden armor didn't cover his head the way it did the rest of him, its sorcerous powers did seem to provide an invisible shell or bubble around his head. He considered momentarily if that was what surrounded all of his compatriot, Jack Gael. Perhaps. That could explain how the frail man could do such damage to the enemy without being hurt.

Lascaris started to go on the attack again, but he was halted in mid-attack by a squawk from the small disk the man in the white coat had given him and he'd stuck to his gauntlet.

"Centurion," came the voice of Legatus Vlahos, as if by magic. "Can you hear me?"

"Indeed I can—though I cannot see you anywhere near me. How can this be?"

"It is but a simple contrivance, and not worthy of discussion at this moment," Vlahos said. "Listen to me, Lascaris: Get back here immediately. Back to the lab where you first came into this world."

"But—the demon horde stands poised at your very door!"

"That's right," Vlahos said, "but you may have noticed, they've stopped while your sparring partner there debates with our new arrivals on the disk. So this is our big and possibly only chance to pull back and dig in, here at the lab, where it matters most."

Lascaris considered this, then nodded. "A strategic retreat. I understand," he said. "I will be there presently."

"Can you give Jack a hand, as well?"

The centurion looked down, saw the thin man in the red jumpsuit struggling to rise. "Yes," he said in reply to the disembodied voice. "I see Jack Gael. I will render him assistance."

"Just get the both of you back in here, pronto," Vlahos barked, and the connection went silent.

His brow furrowed in wonder and confusion, the Roman swooped down to the ground beside Jack. The landing went much smoother this time; he was quickly getting better both at flying and at landing.

"That didn't go very well," Jack said as Lascaris reached down and pulled him to his feet.

"No," the Roman replied. "But the battle is not over yet."

Together they made their way into the building. All around them, the ranks of Kratons stood motionless. It was bizarre. And a bit terrifying.

4:

On the floating disk, high up above the plaza:
Xaveria Denali spread her long, slender hands wide as she looked up at the massive, powerful form of Erich Krenz's robotic body.

"The Union is concerned with you. And displeased. They are deliberating now and will determine your fate in mere moments." She smiled at him, a grim sparkle in her eye. "And, between us, I do not expect the judgment to be in your favor."

"Why should that be?" he called back to her. *"I am about to secure the greatest triumph the Union has known, in all the time since the day they first conquered this planet."*

"Our masters suspect you are doing none of this for the Union," Denali replied. "They have questions and concerns, and they have ordered me to put them to you."

"Then state them," Krenz barked.

"Our masters are concerned that you have placed your consciousness into a different body without permission."

"Why should this be of any concern? I saw the opportunity to improve my body's resistance to damage. I took it."

"That body was not yours to take."

"Perhaps when our masters have seen the outcomes of the uses I am putting it to, they will think otherwise."

"Perhaps." She gazed up at him archly and continued. "Furthermore, our masters fea–" She might have been about to say "fear," but changed her mind at the last moment. "Our masters are *concerned* that these new nanites you have created and that you propose to send out into the Earth's biosphere from this facility are dangerous."

"Indeed they *are* dangerous, Sub-Administrator," Krenz replied. "As I have previously stated."

"Furthermore, they are concerned that the new nanites could affect their human servants, such as myself. Their *willing* servants. And even other forms of organic life entirely. Not just the humans who labor in the factories and fields and mines."

Behind her, the six on their thrones shifted uncomfortably and babbled among themselves.

At that moment, a wave of vehicles arrived. Some flew, and descended from the sky. Others moved on wheels, and drove up the street. All of them turned out to be the equivalent of troop transports or armored personnel carriers. As each of them came to a landing or a halt in the plaza beneath the floating disk, doors slid open and more Kratons emerged. Soon the entire plaza was crawling with the silvery-gray robots; they stomped about, here and there, some of them stepping carefully over their fallen compatriots from the previous battle, others simply kicking or tossing the damaged metal bodies aside.

This new wave of Kratons lined up in formation behind the ones already there, whereupon they, too, froze in place.

"These Kratons are under my direct control, on behalf of the Union," Denali told Krenz. "They are not under your jurisdiction or your control. And they vastly outnumber what you have left."

Krenz regarded them momentarily and then shrugged, as if they mattered not a whit to him.

"Now," Denali called out, "what is your response to the charges from the Union?"

The big, mechanical body jerked a couple of times and emitted an odd sound. After a moment, Denali realized it was laughter.

"You're mad," she said then. "Of course. Your intellect was damaged in the transferal to this new body. We should have known it could happen."

"To the contrary, Sub-Administrator," Krenz said, his eerie laughter coming to a halt. *"I was merely considering the level of consternation you and your masters are going to feel when I explain the true extent of my plans. And, at this late date, and since they have now resorted to displays of power to force me to obey their wills, I see no reason to hold it back any longer."*

Denali frowned at this. She'd been comfortable lording it over Krenz as long as she had the Union at her back. Each of the aliens on the disk with her represented a massive amount of power over some portion of the Earth and its people and resources—resources they were in their second century of draining dry.

But if Krenz felt secure enough in his own situation to stand up to those aliens… Something no one had dared do since the invasion and conquest of the Earth had ended… It gave Denali reason to pause and reconsider exactly which side she was on, and whom she felt most secure in serving.

"The masters of the Union are right to fear me," he declared, his fiery crimson eyes flaring. *"I have evolved beyond humanity—and beyond mechanical life. I am now an amalgam of the two—and the highest form of either."*

"You *are* mad," Denali whispered, staring at him, aghast.

"And I give them credit, for—in their deep paranoia—they have successfully detected my plan." He swept his black metal arm wide. *"The new nanites I am preparing even now to unleash upon the world will not differentiate between humans and aliens. They will affect* all *organic life, human and alien alike! Those you call your 'masters'--or at least the ones who survive the nanites—will soon bow down to* their *master.* ME!"

Krenz floated down slowly until he was hovering level with Denali, where she stood on the edge of the floating disk.

"In appreciation for your assistance before, I will allow you one opportunity to pledge your loyalty to me. If you do, I will shield you from the nanites. If you refuse, you have a forty percent chance of surviving the nanites. And, if you do, you will be utterly under my domination for the rest of your life.

"Whom will you pledge your loyalty to, Xaveria Denali? *Choose now!"*

CHAPTER 15

ONLOOKERS – XAVERIA DENALI – BECOMING – AN ENDING

1:

Jack Gael and Centurion Lascaris stood alongside John Smith, inside the lab. They watched on the external monitors as the scene unfolded outside. They'd already noted the massive new army of Kratons that had surrounded the building. Now they stared in amazement at the floating disk, upon which sat the six alien overlords.

"There is a possibility this could all end now," Smith told the others.

"Good," Lascaris stated flatly. "Then you can deliver me from this hellish underworld and back to my own." He snorted. "Cherson may be a dung heap, but I find it far superior to this nightmare realm." He paused, then added, "And, truth be told, I miss my dear Lhaza."

Smith pursed his lips at this—and at the thought of how the time machine had exploded and was now gone—but said nothing.

"What do you mean?" Jack asked, confused. "What's happening that could end it?"

Smith pointed at the floating disk. "The supreme leaders of the Union are here. And they're not happy about what Krenz is doing."

"But—can they stop him?" Jack asked.

Smith glanced at him. "I suppose we're about to find out."

While the others talked and watched the events transpiring outside, Torrens stumbled to the far side of the room, clutching at his stomach. The world was spinning around him now, his vision was more blurry than clear, and his hands didn't just tingle—they felt as if they would pass directly through any object he touched.

He fell heavily into his big black chair. A moment later, he fell *through* it, to the floor. It was as if the very molecules that constituted his body had simply *moved aside*, causing them to slide between those of the chair. There he managed to stop himself, before he could possibly continue on down through the floor. But he accomplished it only by sheer force of will.

At this point, he felt as if that described his very existence on this plane of reality: He was lingering here through sheer willpower alone.

How much longer he would be able to remain there, he wasn't sure. And where he would go next, he had no idea at all.

"The overlords and the big Kraton are vying for the loyalty of the woman, Denali," Smith said.

"Does it matter which side she chooses?" Jack asked.

"Maybe," Smith replied.

"It's disgusting to think she–or *any* human–could willingly work for those creatures," Jack said.

"For enough money, or for enough power, human beings are capable of some very surprising things," Smith said.

"Ah," Lascaris said, speaking up for the first time. "Yes. I am familiar with this arrangement. In the old Roman province of Judea, my people would control their king and high priest. They were always willing to betray their own people to us, in exchange for enough inducements."

"Some things never change," Jack said.

2:

"Sub-Administrator Denali," came the voice of one of the Union overlords behind her. "Order the Kraton army to destroy this aberration, Erich Krenz."

Denali looked from Krenz, hovering there before her, to the six aliens on their high-tech thrones behind her, and back. She wavered.

"Do it *now*," the alien said, louder this time. *"Destroy him!"*

"I am afraid you are out of time, Xaveria Denali," the black robotic being stated. *"If you will not declare yourself for me, you have chosen the Union. And death."*

Denali's eyes narrowed and her mouth formed a flat, tight line. She raised one hand high and issued a mental command.

Nothing happened.

Frowning now, she looked over the edge of the disk at the hordes of Kratons congregating below. All of them remained frozen in place, along with the last few that Krenz had brought with him before. The still-living humans had fled the streets; not a creature, man nor machine, stirred down there now.

This time she spoke the command out loud: "Attack!"

None of them moved.

Flabbergasted, she raised her voice still higher. "Kratons! This is Sub-Administrator Denali, speaking with the authority of the Union! You will attack and destroy the black Kraton containing the mind of Dr. Erich Krenz—*now!*"

Still none of them moved.

The sound of mechanically-generated laughter came to her then. She looked up and met the burning crimson eyes of the black robot.

"Did you think I would allow you—or anyone—to come here and attempt to subdue me with my own kind?" He laughed again, then added, *"Behold!"*

Denali opened her mouth to respond, but found she didn't know what to say. Swallowing heavily, she looked down at the Kratons.

They were moving.

Some of them were advancing on the laboratory building again.

Others were congregating in a mass just below the floating disk, looking up at it, and at her.

"The Kratons now obey my will, and my will alone," Krenz declared. *"They exist only to serve me!"*

Denali started to back away from the edge, her cyborg legs carrying her as swiftly as they could.

It was not swiftly enough.

Moving like black lightning, Krenz swooped in and grabbed her by the throat. He lifted her off the disk, spun around, and lofted over the largest mass of Kratons. They were leaping up and down, like robotic sharks or alligators sensing prey.

For a long moment she dangled there, at the end of his mechanical arm. Then he opened his fingers and she fell. Down, down she dropped—right into the mass of Kratons. Instantly she vanished from sight.

In the lab, Smith and Jack and Lascaris looked on in horror.

"I mean, she was an awful, awful person," Jack said, his eyes wide, "but… still...!"

"She was a human being," Smith said. "I don't know what Krenz is—what he's become."

"A demon," Lascaris said. "You described him thusly when first I emerged into this world, and nothing I have seen or experienced since my arrival has changed my mind on that. You were quite right."

"And now we need to send him back to Hell," Smith said.

The six alien overlords of the Union were in utter shock. They'd watched as Krenz dropped one of their primary human servants over the side of the disk and into the clutches of the Kratons—killer robots that Krenz himself now controlled.

Now they shouted at one another in rage and fury and fear and desperation, in a cacophony of voices and clicks and gurgles and barks. For they all now understood one thing, with absolute, crystal clarity:

They would very likely be next.

3:

On the far side of the lab, Dr. Howard Torrens' own lifetime—at least as a human being—had reached its end. What he was now, he was not certain. But "human being" no longer fit the bill. No, not at all.

He raised both hands before his face and looked at them. He didn't see hands. He didn't see flesh and blood. He saw intricate patterns of electromagnetic force, dancing in the air.

He was coming apart at the seams.

He was *becoming* something entirely different; entirely new.

Immense power, he understood, was now his to command.

And his former allies were in desperate straits.

Unfortunately for them, when he thought about those two facts, he couldn't seem to find much of a way to connect them. He was aware that his friends in the room were about to die, along with probably sixty percent of the remainder of the human race. And he was aware that he could probably, maybe do something about that.

But he didn't particularly want to, now.

He was too busy.

Busy *becoming*.

Krenz landed at the center of the floating disk and strode toward the six thrones.

The alien overlords rose as one at his approach. Their servants and bodyguards moved into place in front of them, preparing to give their all to protect their masters.

Krenz blasted all of these lackeys to atoms with the purple bolts of energy emitted by the pulse cannon in his right arm.

The six Union aliens cringed and fell back. Some pleaded for mercy. Some cursed him defiantly. One simply sat back on her throne and closed her eyes, apparently choosing tranquility as the best way to end her existence.

One of the defiant ones—a green, scaled alien with a generally fishlike appearance but massive arms—charged at him. Krenz grasped the being with both hands and hurled it over his head, over the edge of the disk, and down to the concrete plaza some two hundred feet below.

The pulse cannon barked and two more defiant Union leaders were evaporated.

The last three remained seated on their thrones. Two glared at him hatefully; the other appeared almost asleep.

Krenz moved over to the disk's flight controls and put his massive fist through the console.

The disk sputtered, vibrated, shuddered in midair, and then dropped.

Krenz had lofted back into the air before it hit the ground. There it smashed into jagged sections, hurling both its living and dead passengers through the air like rag dolls.

If either of the last three Union overlords somehow survived that fall, the Kratons that swarmed like ants over the wreckage surely finished them off moments later.

All potential rivals for rule of the Earth now eliminated, Krenz returned his attention to the laboratory, and to his purpose for coming there in the first place.

"Inside!" he bellowed. *"And kill them all!"*

4:

Smith at last gave up on Torrens. He'd been calling to the man for over a minute now, but the scientist continued to sit in his big black chair on the far side of the lab, staring at his hands, saying nothing. He also appeared to be… *shining*. It was as if he were generating his own internal light. Smith didn't know what was going on with the man, but clearly he would be no more help to them—certainly not in this state.

So Smith had simply looked around the big facility and begun pointing at different pieces of machinery. "That one," he'd say, and Centurion would blast it with lightning. "This one," he'd point out, and Gladiator would karate-chop it to rubble.

Hopefully, Smith thought, *one of these things we're destroying is the thing Krenz is wanting to use, to finalize his nanites and deploy them all over the world.*

"They're coming," Jack shouted as he looked at one of the exterior display monitors. "Krenz just killed the Union's leaders—

I never imagined I would see *that*—and now he's sending in the Kratons. They'll be here any second."

"We just have to hope we've done enough damage to slow him down a little bit," Smith said. "Beyond that… I'm not really sure." He looked around the room, at Torrens and Lascaris and Jack Gael, and shook his head. "I'd like to tell you that I'm proud of you all, for fighting the good fight and so on," he said. "But, in all honesty, I can't do that. Because this is the worst timeline I've ever followed, and you three have bolloxed it up even worse than I have, and it just can't end soon enough for me."

Jack looked hurt; Lascaris ignored what he surely saw as a mad wizard's ramblings. Torrens was oblivious.

Smith shook his head. What a crap show it had all turned into. The only salvation was that he'd surely be getting another crack at it all, and very soon. At least, he assumed that was the case. Every other time, for as long as he could remember, when a timeline got completely out of control and the Union appeared poised to destroy all remaining opposition, Smith had found himself hurled back in time, there to start the whole process over again.

And it could scarcely go any worse than this attempt had.

Smith vowed to himself to substantially change his approach the next time around. It was probably not a good idea, he decided, to allow Erich Krenz to become a living Kraton, for one thing. He was somewhat satisfied with the performance of Lascaris of Rome this time—the man made for a good and dependable ally, if somewhat single-minded and primitive—and he'd probably seek him out again. But he concluded it was time to choose a different champion than Jack Gael to bear the silver belt.

All of this ran through his mind in a matter of seconds, as he watched the army of robots charging through the front doors of the building and up the stairs, relentlessly closing on their location.

Smith glanced again at the useless Torrens, still not moving on the far side of the room, then looked to Jack and Lascaris.

"The funny thing is, for a while there, I was almost certain this would be the time we won."

They looked back at him, unsure of what he meant—but then the swarm of Kratons smashed through the doors and into the lab.

"Alright, lads," Smith shouted. "It's 'blaze of glory' time!"

The battle was epic and violent and all too brief.

The golden-armored Centurion lofted into the air, able to ascend to about twenty-five feet of altitude given the very high ceiling of the main lab they occupied. From there he blasted away at the enemy with bolts of lightning from each of his fists.

Gladiator met the Kratons' charge, his fists flying. His invisible and indestructible force bubble allowed him to slice through the robots with relative ease.

But Smith, watching all of this from as far away as he could get, understood it was simply delaying the inevitable.

And a moment later, the inevitable entered the room.

Krenz floated in like a grim specter, his feet a yard above the floor. He raised his right arm and fired the pulse cannon located there, and the first blast of purple light speared Centurion and brought him down, smoking. Krenz fired point-blank into his chest twice more, and then the Kratons fell upon him. The Roman's lightning blasts ripped from the scrum a couple of times, tearing into a Kraton here or there, before all signs of resistance ceased.

Krenz's next shots deflected harmlessly off of Gladiator's force field, but then Krenz raised his left arm and pointed at Gael. A deep hum filled the room, and Jack stumbled backwards.

Smith groaned to himself as he recognized the effect. *Krenz has incorporated the harmonic disruptor—the one that was able to weaken and dispel Jack's force field—into his robotic body.*

Lying there on his back, unable to prevent his bubble from dissolving away, Jack was pounced on by an army of Kratons. One of them reached down, seized the belt, and tore it from him. Holding it up, the Kraton crushed it to scrap, then tossed it away. In less than a second Jack was lost from view.

Smith watched all of this in horror. He understood implicitly that both Jack Gael and Lascaris were dead.

He knew as well that he would be next.

And, on top of that, the belt had been destroyed. The one weapon that gave them a fighting chance against the Union—now gone.

He couldn't understand it—he couldn't fathom how all of this could be.

Why hadn't he been yanked back in time yet? Or, failing that-- where was the inevitable opportunity to escape?

It always worked that way for him. At the moment of worst danger, he would be hurled back in time and would be forced to relive it all again—but at least he would be alive, and would have the opportunity to change things. Not that his changes ever seemed to make anything better, of course.

This time, though, nothing was happening. He was forced to look on as his two compatriots were murdered by vicious robotic foot soldiers in the service of a vicious robotic maniac. And no time portal was presenting itself to him, offering some kind of miracle escape.

As the Kratons advanced on him now, he backed away, then dashed over to where Torrens had been sitting.

The chair was empty. Torrens was gone.

A light flickered above his head and he looked up.

High above the chaos of the battle hovered a being of pure, bright white light.

The Kratons caught sight of the presence now, too. They slowed their advance, uncertain of what was happening.

The being gazed down at Smith, and what little of its face he could make out seemed to be looking at him in puzzlement—as if it didn't quite recognize him but felt that it should.

"Torrens," Smith called out. "Is that you? Can you hear me? It's me—Smith. You have to *do* something! You're the only hope left!"

The being that had once been Dr. Howard Torrens looked at him, then at the advancing robots. It appeared to be considering his words. Then it simply vanished.

Smith's heart sank.

Huh, he thought. *Well. I guess it had to end sometime.*

He reached back and drew out a pistol he'd stuffed into his waistband earlier. For an instant he debated whether to shoot at the robots or to shoot himself.

He leveled it at the nearest of the oncoming Kratons.

He never even got to pull the trigger.

CHAPTER 16

WHITE LIGHT – THE FINAL PRICE – THE FINAL ARBITER – A GIFT

1:

The being that was Howard Torrens floated in space, high above planet Earth.

He gazed down at the big blue-white world below, seeing the beauty and the wonder of it as for the first time.

He also saw the immense damage the Union and their slaves had done over the past centuries.

Raw, open pits and strip-mines. Rivers and lakes drained dry. The environment in a shambles.

He considered what the mad Krenz planned to do, by creating a new variety of tiny machines that would contaminate, kill and enslave what remained of humanity.

What remained of humanity. That was a question he asked himself: *What remains of* my *humanity?*

He suspected the answer, in both cases, would soon be: *very little.*

In fact, for me at this moment, does any *humanity remain?*

He decided a tiny fragment of it did still his exist. His soul, perhaps.

Was it enough to spur him to any sort of action?

He continued to gaze down at the Earth. He took it all in, studied it, comprehended it as no normal human ever could.

He thought about what the man who called himself John Smith had said: "You're the only hope left!"

Did he care? Did he care enough, now, in this new and present state, to actually *do* something about it? To *change* it?

No, he decided. Not to *change* it.

But perhaps… just perhaps… he could provide his former colleagues with the opportunity to change it themselves.

One more opportunity.

2:

In the blink of an eye, Torrens was back in the lab. Now, however, he was entirely a being of pure white light and energy. He appeared there in the midst of the Kratons, and turned to see the bigger, black Kraton, Krenz, operating a bank of machinery—one of the few pieces of equipment Smith hadn't directed the other two to destroy earlier. *Poor John Smith,* he thought. The man really had gotten just about everything wrong this time around—and he'd paid the ultimate price for it. The *final* price.

Or—had he? *Was* it the *final* price?

3:

Krenz became aware of the bright light filling the room. He turned away from where he'd been prepping the deadly new nanites and stared at the humanoid that stood there across from him—a figure of pure light.

"What are you?" the robotic voice asked, its tone a combination of anger and wonder and a touch of fear.

"That is actually a very good question, Dr. Krenz," said a hollow, ethereal voice that came at him from everywhere and nowhere. "I am no longer certain precisely *what* I am. Or where my loyalties lie."

"Then begone, apparition," Krenz barked. *"Go and haunt someone else. For I am busy securing my final victory."*

The being of light that had been Howard Torrens turned and strode toward the doors. Krenz, apparently satisfied, returned to his work.

As the bright figure neared the doors, he saw something shiny and silver lying on the floor. It was Jack Gael's belt. He stopped, looked down at it, knelt and picked it up.

It had been crushed. Ruined.

"John Smith thought to send Jack Gael back in time with this belt," he said aloud, understanding some portion of Smith's Machiavellian orchestrations better now. "He failed."

Krenz looked back over his shoulder at the glowing being. *"Smith was a fool. No item like that, with its level of technology, could pass through the time machine Torrens constructed. I could have told him that. It was a miracle they managed to get the Golden Gauntlet to pass back through it."* He laughed a mechanical robotic laugh. *"That turned out to be the great flaw in Smith's plans. The belt could not be sent back in time through that machine. And now the machine is destroyed. There is no more way to go back in time at all. It is finished."*

"Not entirely," the man that had been Howard Torrens said. For a memory had occurred to him.

He strode purposefully across the lab to a collection of metal lockers set into the wall. He thought for a moment, then selected one and opened it.

"Ah, yes. Just where I left it."

Smiling, he reached inside and drew out the only object it contained. Then he turned back to face the big robot.

"And—if I understand my current state properly—there is still *one other way* to go back in time," he said.

Krenz had returned to his work. Now he froze. He craned his skull-like metal head and glanced at the glowing being, and what he held in his hands. Then he looked down at the readouts on the computer consoles before him. He emitted the robotic equivalent of a startled gasp and glared at Torrens.

"Temporal radiation," he squawked. *"That is the predominant force you are emitting."*

The blazing man considered this. "I believe you are correct," he said. "Which would make sense, considering the explosion of the time machine—"

"*—was what made you what you are now,*" Krenz finished for him. *"You are Dr. Howard Torrens!"*

The being nodded. "At least, I was," he said.

"You are *the time machine,"* Krenz added.

"Quite possibly."

Krenz took a menacing step towards him, then another.

"You are far too dangerous to allow to live," the big robot stated.

"I'm afraid you are not the final arbiter of that," Torrens replied.

Krenz shot forward, massive metal hands reaching out to kill.

Still holding the object from the locker, Torrens, like some radiant angel, vanished.

4:

In Cherson, a small city on the Crimean Peninsula, in the year 701 AD, an angel descended from Heaven and manifested itself to the Roman citizens who dwelt there—and to the collection of strange and strangely-clad men that were visiting.

Those that witnessed what transpired at that moment would later swear that the angel approached one of the strangers: a blond man dressed all in red. The angel bestowed upon that man a wondrous gift: a belt made of finest silver.

They would also swear the angel then vanished. As did the strangers, a short time later.

Those strangers were swallowed up, some few souls brave enough to make the audacious claim would say, within the confines of a silver ball.

EPILOGUE:

THE NEW CITY. NORTH AMERICA. THE YEAR 2468 AD.

The robotic monster called Erich Krenz stood alone in the laboratory. He had ordered all the other Kratons out, so that he could work in peace. Now he was nearly finished creating the first wave of deadly new nanites and almost ready to unleash them on the world.

That was when alarms started blaring throughout the lab.

Krenz had been concerned at first that things for him would instantly change if Torrens were allowed to escape back into time. He'd paced back and forth across the laboratory, stepping over the broken bodies of the Kratons and the remains of Jack Gael and John Smith and the time-lost Roman soldier along the way. Massive hands clasped behind his back, he'd resembled nothing so much as an apocalyptic vision of a dark Shakespearean character as seen through the lens of mechanical perdition.

But in the minutes since that had happened, nothing to his perceptions had changed at all. He'd therefore written Torrens off as having lost interest in humanity and perhaps flown away to some other faraway time and place. Consequently, Krenz had gotten back to work.

But now the alarm that was shrieking from a nearby console was attempting to warn him that an unusual energy reading had been detected inside the lab. Inside it—or just adjacent to it.

He checked the readings again, just to be sure. No, he saw, it was not temporal radiation the machine was detecting. A palpable sense of relief flooded through his massive, mechanical body.

That relief was followed instantly by an equal measure of rage, boiling up within his microsystems, at the thought of his being disturbed while endeavoring to put the final touches on his master plan, his great coup that was about to secure him mastery of the world.

He turned and stalked towards the far wall. Beyond it, the computers said, something unusual was happening. Well, it surely wouldn't be the first unusual thing to happen that day. But he was determined it wouldn't disrupt his plans any further. He'd find the cause and neutralize it.

He studied the wall momentarily, then brought his fist back and swung it forward like a massive piledriver. The relatively flimsy material shattered and splintered before his onslaught. Satisfied, he did it again.

After five such blows, he'd cleared out a doorway-sized hole through the laboratory wall. On the other side, he could now see what the sensors in the lab had detected. He stared at it, perplexed.

A large, silver sphere rested on the floor, inside what had to have been a hidden room with no other ways in or out.

"What is this?" he asked himself out loud.

Krenz took a step forward, then another. He reached out and tapped the silver ball; ran his hand along it. Then he punched it.

Nothing. Not a squeak, not a dent.

He leaned in even closer, studying the perfectly smooth surface. Seeing his own hellish skull-face in warped reflection.

He raised his robotic hand and tapped the surface.

"What are you doing here?" he wondered aloud.

And then suddenly he understood. He knew *exactly* what it was.

Frantically he started to back away—to put some distance between himself and the sphere.

He was too late.

POP.

The sphere vanished.

At the same instant, something silvery, shimmering with energy, sliced out of the darkness and cut into his chest.

Bellowing with rage, Krenz scrambled backwards and away from—from whatever that had been.

But he'd only taken two quick steps backwards when he realized he wasn't moving any further. Something—something invisible—was holding him in place. And then the unseen pinions holding him began to squeeze; to crush him where he stood.

Flames gouted out of every seam and fissure of his body. Sparks sprayed out in showers. Smoke poured forth, obscuring his view of the heretofore secret room where the silver sphere had been, before it had vanished.

Out of the smoke stepped one figure, and then another, and then another.

"YOU," Krenz screeched. "ALIVE!"

"I certainly am," Jack said.

"No matter," Krenz bellowed. "My harmonics allowed you to be killed once. They will–"

Jack let the big robot go. Krenz's massive weight caused him to stumble a step forward. He flailed his arms, attempting to stop himself from pitching onto his face.

Regaining his balance, he looked up–just in time to see another figure stepping past Jack and directly in front of him.

"NO!" shrieked the rasping, mechanical voice. "Not *now*—not when I am *so close* to—"

A short, broad blade flashed its deadly arc.

Krenz's head toppled from the black metal body and fell to the floor, where it rolled off to one side. The blazing red eyes sparked, faded, darkened.

Centurion stood over it, looked at Jack and nodded. "Good Roman steel," he said.

The third figure emerged from the smoke then. He was dressed all in blue, and had dark hair and a sharp nose. He looked down at the decapitated robotic body that had briefly contained the mind of Erich Krenz. Then he looked up at Jack and Lascaris.

"I have no idea who or what that being was that brought your belt back to you, Jack," he said. "But I'm awfully glad it did."

"An angel," Lascaris said. "I have heard talk of them, but would not have believed it had I not witnessed it with my own eyes."

Smith surveyed the controls where Krenz had been working.

"The new, deadly nanites were almost ready," he said, "but not quite." He tapped a few controls. "There. They've been purged. Incinerated. And the files showing how to construct them have been permanently erased."

"Excellent," Jack said.

Smith walked over to the nearest surveillance monitor showing the exterior of the building and studied it.

"The Union is dead," he said, "and their vilest bastard child has been destroyed. Now all that remains are the last of the Kratons. They currently surround this building."

"We know what to do with them," Jack said, raising his force field-encased arms.

"Aye," Lascaris agreed, soaring into the air in his golden armored suit and brandishing his glowing sword. "That we do."

With that, Gladiator and Centurion rushed out of the building and into the plaza, there to deal death and destruction to the last of Earth's oppressors.

"After so long—after so very, very long," the immortal warrior called John Smith whispered to himself, "at last I can rest."

He dropped into Howard Torrens' old chair and exhaled slowly, while watching on the monitors as his two companions completed their liberation of the Earth.

"At last."

AUTHOR'S NOTE

This book exists because I've always loved Iron Man.
Wait—*Iron Man?!*
Bear with me:
Being a fan of Iron Man since the 1970s, I naturally checked out *X-O Manowar*, a then-new comic about *another* armored hero, when Valiant Comics came along in the early 1990s. Back then, I never really got into the other Valiant series, such as *Solar* and *Magnus: Robot Fighter* and *Eternal Warrior*, but I did enjoy *X-O*, and I did own the boxed set of trade paperbacks of their big crossover event, *Unity*.

Then the company went away and, years later, I sold most of my old comics. And I mostly forgot about anything to do with Valiant.

In 2017, however, X-O returned to comics when the property was bought by a new company. I read the new version and liked it to a degree, but something was missing; I wasn't sure what. I moved on, but I had been reminded that I had enjoyed *X-O* and wanted more.

Then, in early 2023, I happened across a massive collected edition of the original *X-O Manowar* comics by Jim Shooter and Bob Layton, along with various artists.

After devouring that entire series, I was able to locate copies of the original runs of *Dr. Solar: Man of the Atom*; *Magnus: Robot Fighter*; and *Eternal Warrior*. I blew through all of them in record time, as well as rereading the *Unity* event issues. And suddenly I realized one of the major things that had been missing from the *later* Valiant comics:

Barry Windsor-Smith.

It had been BWS's incredible artwork that had made those early issues stand out for me, I suddenly understood. I loved his work on that stuff.

Then I got to thinking about how Magnus would beat up robots using martial arts. That never made a lot of sense to me, that he could be a normal human being who was trained in martial arts to the point that he could shatter steel. It's a cute idea, but it's the sort of thing that really only works in comics. But, I asked myself—what if a guy were wearing some kind of force field generator, and could therefore punch and kick evil robots and do real damage to them, and without getting hurt in the process?

Separate from all of this, for many years I'd wanted to write a story about a guy with a force field bubble around him. What would be the advantages and the drawbacks? What kinds of cool things could he do, and in what ways would he still be vulnerable? That had always seemed like a fun avenue to explore, but I'd never had the *story* to go along with that gimmick.

Then, as happens so often, the two ideas came together: the force field story, combined with robots to beat up, all done as a tribute to Valiant and BWS! I threw in my version of good old X-O and a sort-of nod to Dr. Solar, in the persons of the Centurion Lascaris and Dr. Torrens. And if I had an armored *Centurion*, then the new robot-fighter must be a *Gladiator!* So he had to start the story as a competitor in some kind of arena, fighting robots and other human gladiators. It all came together instantly. How could I not write the story at that point, I ask you?? The book you've just read flowed from that—almost faster than I could type it! I even decided to call the thing *Union* as an homage to the *Unity* saga, as well as because it made sense for the name of the alien cabal and for what the good guys were trying to accomplish.

The capper on it all was getting my old art partner, Chris Kohler (of *Sentinels* fame) to do a recreation of the BWS cover for *Unity*. And what a spectacular job he (and colorist Daniel Jr.) did! With that glorious illustration in front of me almost the entire time I was writing, I never lost the enthusiasm and drive to complete the story. Never for a second.

So, here we are. I haven't even mentioned how a variation on the Eternal Warrior popped up partway through my plotting the story and basically demanded to take over the lead character role, in the form of John Smith. I hadn't ever read Eternal Warrior when I plotted this book, and I hadn't expected another character to come along and demand so much screen time. But, again, he dropped right into the story as if he'd been meant for it all along. All I could do was try to keep up with where it was taking me.

I hope you liked what resulted from all this unexpected creative alchemy. I openly acknowledge the massive debt this book owes to Valiant, Shooter, Layton, and most especially Barry Windsor-Smith, to whom it's dedicated.

As for my usual line here—I really don't know that these guys will return. This has the feel to me of a single, stand-alone story—a "one-shot," as they say in the comics.

But it wouldn't be the first time I've been wrong about that.
Stay Valiant!

—Van Allen Plexico
Southern Illinois
October 1, 2023 - January 7, 2024

POST-CREDITS SCENE!

Bruised and battered, bleeding in various places, and weary beyond measure, Detectives Hoyt and Rodriguez picked their way over, through and across the aftermath of the battle outside the laboratory building.

"Is it over?" Rodriguez asked aloud as he reached the steps to the lab and stopped, looking back at all the carnage. For as far as the eye could see, in almost every direction, the demonic-looking Kratons lay shattered and sparking on the ground, the evil red lights of their eyes now dark. Mixed in with them were quite a few humans who had fought back as part of the resistance, and had paid the ultimate price in their attempt at freedom.

"I think so," Hoyt replied, making his way up onto the steps and seating himself heavily there.

The two men stared out at the plaza, seeing the wrecked floating platform broken in half on the ground, alien bodies sprawled across part of its surface.

"Did we–did we actually *win*?" Rodriguez asked.

Hoyt glanced over at him, uncertain of how to answer.

"What do you mean by 'we'?" he asked.

"We, as in, we the people," Rodriguez replied. "Humans!"

"Oh," Hoyt said. He shrugged. "I guess so, then."

"*Yes!*" Rodriguez enthused.

Hoyt frowned. He considered it all for a moment, then looked over at his partner. "You do realize, don't you, that we work for Xaveria Denali and the Union? Or, at least, we did."

"Not anymore," Rodriguez said with a grin.

Hoyt seemed about to say something back to him, when suddenly they heard a sound off to their right. They looked and beheld a figure in gleaming golden armor floating towards them. As he drew near, he stopped moving and hovered above them and slightly off to one side, staring down at them, studying them.

Rodriguez waved his right arm enthusiastically and grinned. "Thank you!" he shouted. "Thank you for helping us!"

Hoyt was just staring back up at the man. Rodriguez noticed this and hissed, *"Wave at him! Do you want him to think we're with the Union?"*

Hoyt raised his right hand and waved jerkily a couple of times. "Yeah, thanks," he called up to the guy. Then he looked over at his partner and whispered, "We *do* work for the Union."

"Not anymore," Rodriguez said. "We're free." Then, louder, and directed up at the man in gold, "We're free!"

Still hovering there, the man in gold studied them for a few more seconds, then appeared to lose interest. He floated on into the lab building.

Hoyt let out a sigh of relief, causing Rodriguez to frown and look over at him.

Before either could say anything more, another figure approached, this one on foot—more or less.

The two detectives recognized him immediately.

"Gladiator!" Rodriguez called out, jumping to his feet and waving a greeting at him. "Thank you for taking down the Kratons!"

Jack Gael strode easily over the bodies of the shattered robots, his feet never actually touching the ground as the invisible shield around him fitted itself to the terrain and held him slightly above it. He climbed the laboratory steps until he stood facing the two detectives, and he greeted them with a nod.

"Glad to see some more of our fighters survived," he said. He looked the two men over, in their torn and ragged suits. "Do I know you guys?"

Before Hoyt could answer, Rodriguez said, "You're able to destroy the nanites, aren't you? The ones the Union has been using to influence us all these years."

Gael nodded. "You think you might have gotten re-infected during the battle?" He stepped forward and reached out with both hands, motioning for the detective to approach him. When they were face to face, Gael grasped Rodriguez's hands through the bubble.

"*Diagnostic mode operational,*" came a robotic voice from the silver belt Gael wore.

A moment later, it spoke again: "*Foreign objects detected— potential hazard—initiating purge in three… two… one…*"

Electric sparks flared from around the areas where the two men's hands touched one another. Rodriguez yelped and stumbled back. Hoyt caught him, helping him sit down again.

"Ah, yeah, you did get reinfected," Gael said, once Rodriguez had recovered a bit. "Glad I came along and could help out."

Rodriguez rubbed at his temples. "Ouch," he muttered.

"Yeah," Jack said to him. "The headache is always annoying. But I'm sure you remember that from before."

"Uh–yeah, of course," Rodriguez managed to say. "From before. Well–thank you."

"Yes–thank you," Hoyt suddenly blurted out. "Thanks for defeating those aliens, and that terrible Denali woman, and everything." He looked down at the ground for a second, then back up at Gael, who was regarding him with something akin to suspicion. "I guess you'll want to hurry on in there and catch up with your friend."

Gael didn't move for a second. Then he was suddenly in motion, reaching out, grasping Hoyt's hands firmly in his shield-encased own. For several seconds they stood together, but nothing happened. There were no sparks and the belt said nothing at all.

Hoyt stared back at Gael, fear apparent in his eyes. Fear of discovery. Rodriguez meanwhile watched them both warily from the side, afraid of what might happen next.

Gael, however, simply pursed his lips, frowned, and stepped back. He looked Hoyt over once more, gave a sort of shrug, and said, "Yeah–I guess you didn't get reinfected. You're still good."

Sweat was running down Hoyt's face as he exhaled slowly and said, "That's good to know. I guess I got lucky. Thanks."

Gael continued to look back at him for another long moment. "Sure," he said at last. "Glad to be of help. Thanks to you two for your contributions to the battle–which I'm sure were substantial."

And with that, Jack Gael–the Gladiator–turned away and hurried into the lab building where the man in the armor had gone a few minutes earlier.

Once he had vanished inside, Hoyt slowly dropped to the steps, seated a short distance away from his partner. He breathed a long sigh of relief. Then he looked up at Rodriguez and became aware that the other man was simply staring at him, a strange look on his face.

"Hoyt," Rodriguez said, his voice hesitant, "you didn't have any nanites for him to kill."

"Yeah."

"You didn't *have* any."

"Yeah," Hoyt replied, sweating even more profusely. "Wasn't that lucky!"

Rodriguez continued to stare at him. "But there *was* no earlier time when he killed our nanites," he said. "He just assumed he did. But this was the first time."

"Huh. Yeah," Hoyt replied, looking around nervously. "How about that."

"And he killed mine."

"Yeah. But you don't seem any different," Hoyt said.

"Well, yeah," Rodriguez replied. "Because there's nobody out there sending signals to the nanites anymore. For the last couple of hours, nobody's been pushing me to behave and act a certain way. But–even so–I still *had* them. All along. Until *just now*." He spread his hands wide. "*That's* why I was serving Denali and the Union. Not because I *wanted* to. Because they *made* me."

Hoyt said nothing.

"But *you*. You didn't *have* any. Which means…" Rodriguez was still rubbing at his throbbing head, which was making it hard for him to think straight. "Which means…"

"It means I *never did* have any nanites telling me what to do," Hoyt said. He started to reach for his pistol.

Rodriguez looked up at him slowly.

"It means I served the Union *voluntarily*," Hoyt said. "Because I *wanted* to."

Rodriguez stared back at him, taking this in, processing it. Meanwhile his hand inched towards his own pistol.

Hoyt's hand closed around his as he added, "If that's a problem…"

Rodriguez's hand closed on his. For several seconds he didn't reply and the two of them sat there, motionless, eyes locked on one another.

Then Rodriguez shrugged and said, "I suppose it's a different world now. We all did what we had to, in the old world, to survive. To get by. But the aliens are dead. The Union is gone. Now things will be different for everyone."

Hoyt took this in and nodded slowly. "That's true."

"And old crimes and sins and trespasses will have to be forgiven and forgotten," Rodriguez added philosophically, "if we're to make a go of this new world."

"Very nicely put," Hoyt agreed. "Makes sense to me."

Slowly they relaxed. Their hands moved away from their guns. They quit staring at one another and just sat there in peace and in silence. The sun moved appreciably down toward the horizon.

At last Rodriguez stirred. He stood and looked around.

"It's been quite a day," he said.

"It's been a day," Hoyt agreed.

"I'm getting hungry," Rodriguez said.

"Yeah," Hoyt said nodding. "I could definitely eat."

They both raised a hand to their brows against the glare of the setting sun and searched the distance.

"I think there was a restaurant over there," Hoyt said, pointing down the street. "Maybe there's still some food in it."

"Sounds good," Rodriguez said. "Let's go check it out."

Together, the two detectives set out over the piles of broken Kratons and the occasional human remains, headed down the street. When they reached the old restaurant, Hoyt held the door as Rodriguez entered, then followed him inside.

Approximately five minutes later, from inside the restaurant, a single shot rang out.

ABOUT THE AUTHOR

Van Allen Plexico writes and edits New Pulp, Crime, Science Fiction, Fantasy, and nonfiction for a variety of print and online publishers. He has won five Novel of the Year awards and an Anthology of the Year award from the Pulp Factory and the Imadjinn Awards, and a New Character of the Year award from the New Pulp Awards. He is author of the *Shattering* space opera series, *Lucian, Baranak, Karilyne*, and the groundbreaking and #1 New Pulp Best-Selling *Sentinels* series, as well as the award-winning crime novels *Vegas Heist* and *Miami Heist*, and the award-winning Kaiju novel, *Validus-V*. In his spare time, he serves as a professor of political science and history. He resides in the St. Louis area and is probably working on another book right now.

Harper & Salsa
  Crime caper novels by Van Allen Plexico
  Vegas Heist
  Miami Heist
  Monaco Heist (coming soon)

Van Allen Plexico's *Sentinels*
Super-hero action illustrated by Chris Kohler
  The Grand Design Trilogy
  Alternate Visions (Anthology)
  The Rivals Trilogy
  The Earth - Kur-Bai War Trilogy

The Shattering
  Lucian: Dark God's Homecoming
  Baranak: Storming the Gates
  Karilyne: Heart Cold as Ice
  Hawk: Hand of the Machine
  Legion I: Lords of Fire
  Legion II: Sons of Terra
  Legion III: Kings of Oblivion

Anthologies
  Gideon Cain: Demon Hunter
  Blackthorn: Thunder on Mars

Other Great Novels
  Blackthorn: Dynasty of Mars
  By Ian Watson

**All are available wherever books are sold
or visit
www.whiterocketbooks.com**

www.ingramcontent.com/pod-product-compliance
Lightning Source LLC
Chambersburg PA
CBHW032239310726
48973CB00008B/2218